EXPOSED

CLUB PRIVÉ 2

M. S. PARKER

BELMONTE PUBLISHING, LLC

Copyright © 2016 Belmonte Publishing LLC

Published by Belmonte Publishing LLC

READING ORDER

Thank you so much for reading the Club Privé series. If you'd like to read the complete series, I recommend reading them in this order:

ONE

It took me a moment to realize why my head felt fuzzy.

The light coming in from the curtain was at the wrong angle. I'd overslept. Then I glanced at my alarm clock and saw that it was eleven-thirty.

Shit.

I'd *really* overslept. I must've been more tired than I'd thought. Then again, heat spread through me as I remembered. I'd been quite... *active* yesterday.

That thought reminded me of the person who'd shared my bed, and I rolled over.

Empty.

Before I could freak out about Gavin having taken off while I was still sleeping, I saw a piece of paper on the pillow he'd used. It was folded in half with no name on it. I opened it and read.

Even as I'm writing this, I keep getting distracted by you. How peaceful your face looks when you sleep. The curve of your hip and ass beneath the blanket. The hint of your breasts peeking out from under the covers. I don't want to leave you. Believe me, I would much rather wake you up by kissing every inch of your body, showing you just how thankful I am for your presence last night. I don't think I could have handled talking about my past if your arms hadn't been around me. Unfortunately, I do have to go. Just know that I'd rather be in bed with you than working at the club, but some things have to be done on time. I'll call you later. Know that I'll be thinking about you and all of the things I want to do you. – G

MY ENTIRE BODY was flushing by the time I finished his note. I rolled onto my back and read the note again. I couldn't believe how eloquent he was. There were a lot of men who could charm the pants off a woman with what they said, but very few were equally articulate in the written form. Even after spending more than one night in bed with Gavin Manning, his intelligence and articulation surprised me.

The fact that he was smoking hot, with dark hair and beautiful blue eyes, was just icing on a very delicious cake.

The time that we'd spent together still seemed like a dream, our relationship something out of a fairy tale. Well, an X-rated fairy tale, I amended, blushing.

I'd first met him on a dare from my friends, never expecting to see him again. Fate or destiny or whatever had other plans though. His boss came to the law firm where I worked, and after that, we just kept finding each other, no matter how hard I tried to keep things professional. Except I hadn't really wanted things to stay professional. It'd taken a bit of liquid courage to get me to sleep with him the first time, and a lot of regular courage when I'd seen the kink he was into, but it'd been worth it.

I smiled as I remembered that first night at Club Privé. He'd taken me up to a VIP room, though at the time I hadn't realized that he wasn't just a member. He owned the club, part of it anyway. It'd hurt things between us, him keeping things from me, but it had also given me the opportunity to see how much I meant to him. And how much he meant to me. Whatever this connection was between us, it was stronger than anything I'd ever felt before.

Last night had been more evidence of that, and not only because of the scorching hot sex we'd had. He'd trusted me enough to tell me about his daughter, and about Camille, her mother. The story still made me sick to my stomach. The hit-and-run of a pregnant woman, the emergency C-section to save the baby when the mother didn't survive. The fact that it remained unsolved. It would've been awful even if I hadn't known someone involved. I couldn't imagine losing someone I'd loved for that long. My respect and admiration for Gavin had gone up when he'd explained why Skylar's grandparents were raising her. He'd put his daughter's well-being above what he'd wanted. He truly was a good man.

A knock at the door startled me from my thoughts.

"Wake up, Carrie. Time to eat." The door opened and my roommate, Krissy Jensen, grinned from the doorway.

I glared at her, holding the sheet against my breasts. I hated when she did that. She might not care about wandering around the apartment in the nude, but I wasn't quite so free.

"I saw Gavin sneaking out when I got up." She grinned at me. "I'm guessing your date went well."

"Look, Krissy, it's not–"

She held up a hand. "Talk while we eat. I'm starving."

"All right," I said. I waited and when she didn't leave, I scowled at her. "I'd like to put some clothes on first."

Krissy rolled her eyes. "Prude," she said as she shut the door behind her.

"You're going to have to take that back after I tell you about my night," I called out as I climbed out of bed. I pulled on a pair of shorts and a camisole, then headed for the bathroom. I wasn't going to take the time to shower, but I at least needed to clean up a bit. Again, busy night.

By the time I came out into the kitchen, Krissy was already at the table. She really had made breakfast. Well, I guess, more accurately, it was brunch. There were pancakes, cut-up strawberries, syrup, blueberries, butter, and even whipped cream. She'd also made a small plate of bacon and was currently eyeing it.

"This is amazing," I said as I took my usual seat.

"Well, I figured if you'd had a bad date, this would be comfort food, and if it went well, it could be a celebration." Krissy grinned at me as she popped a blueberry into her mouth. "Besides, you know how bored I get if I wake up before you."

That was true. It was rare, but when it did happen, I generally woke up to Krissy doing something like trying to make new curtains for the apartment or buffing all of her shoes. Unfortunately, her boredom-induced energy rarely channeled itself into cleaning the apartment. I didn't even want to see how much of a mess she'd made cooking. Still, I appreciated the gesture.

"Now that you're here," she continued, "let's dig in." She grabbed half of the bacon before I could even respond.

I laughed and started to fill my own plate.

"Spill," she demanded as she munched on her bacon.

"Where to start?" I mused as I helped myself to a piece of bacon. It was perfect, crunchy without being burnt. I was feeling a bit mischievous as I teased her. "Making out in his town car? Groping him under the table during the gala dinner?"

Krissy's eyes were practically bugging out of her head, and it was all I could do to keep going without breaking out into laughter. It wasn't often I got to be the wild one in the group.

"Almost having sex in the bathroom, or actually *having* sex in an empty conference room? Or should I just skip to when we got back here?"

"I think I heard enough of that." Krissy grinned. "The walls are thin."

"About time you figured that out," I countered despite the heat rising to my face.

"Oh, I definitely understand now," she said. She began to gasp and moan. "'Gavin! Oh, Gavin! Yes! Yes!'"

"Shut up!" I threw a strawberry at her.

She laughed as she deflected it away from her face. "Oh, honey, if he's that good, I want serious details." She winked. "I think it's only fair, since I was treated to the soundtrack."

I rolled my eyes, but I wasn't actually annoyed with her. I wanted to tell her. Krissy had always been the one who'd had the wild sex and the smoking hot boyfriends. Even when I'd had boyfriends before, our sex hadn't really been that exciting. It had been nice, but never anything like what I'd heard coming from Krissy's room.

Not until Gavin.

I supposed being the part-owner of a sex club helped a man know what he was doing.

"All right," I said. "Then I guess I really should start from the beginning."

I began at the point where she'd seen us off to the gala, and then gave her a complete play-by-play, including Howard's flirting with me, and the big-breasted women hitting on Gavin. She made all of the appropriate comments and sounds in all the right places, laughing when I told her how we'd burst in on an old woman in a bathroom stall, and then fanning herself when I described how Gavin had stopped me from touching myself when he'd been taking me on a conference room table, declaring that he wanted to be the one to make me come. When I finally got to our encounter in my bedroom, she'd quit trying to eat and was simply staring at me. The only thing I didn't tell her about was Gavin's daughter and late fiancée. If he'd told only Howard and me, I couldn't break his trust by telling Krissy, even if she was my best friend. It wasn't my place. I'd wait until he told me it was okay before I shared any of that.

When I finished with a vague summary of his note, she let out a low whistle. "Shit, Carrie, where the hell did this guy come from, and are there any more of him?"

I shrugged and took a bite of my pancake. It had cooled during my storytelling, but it was still delicious. Krissy and I spent a few minutes eating in silence before I brought up something that had been hovering in the back of my mind since last night.

"I'm thinking about going on the pill."

Krissy nearly spit out her mouthful of pancake.

I could feel my face burning, but I remembered what Krissy and Gavin had both recently told me. I was an adult. There was nothing wrong with what I was doing, or with what I wanted. And I wanted to know what it would feel like to have him inside me without anything between us. Skin against skin. How it would feel when he finished inside me, filling me up.

I shook my head and cleared my throat. I wasn't going to tell Krissy any of that, of course. I had another explanation, which was part of my reasoning, though not the main part. "When we were going into the bathroom, I remember thinking that I hoped he had a condom because I was going to be pissed if he didn't. Then, when we came back here, I realized that the 'emergency' ones I have wouldn't fit him."

I didn't realize what I'd said until Krissy began coughing and had to take a gulp of her iced tea. I crossed my arms over my chest and tried to look like I hadn't just said something a little more detailed than I'd planned.

"Okay, spill." Krissy's voice was hoarse but demanding. "Are we talking you have mediums and he's a large, or..."

I sighed. I knew she'd never let this go, and if I didn't tell her, she might even consider saying something in front of Gavin, just to satisfy her curiosity. He and I were still figuring out this thing between us, and the last thing we needed was my room-mate trying to catch a glimpse of my man's cock.

"You know those ones that we always joke about in the store? The ones we say have to be there for false advertising?"

Krissy shook her head. "You're fucking with me, right?"

I gave her a slightly embarrassed smile. "Nope."

"Wow." She gave me a once-over. "How are you even walking right now?"

"Krissy!" I practically shrieked her name, completely mortified.

Tears streamed down her face as she laughed, doubling over. I leaned back in my chair and glowered at her as she cackled. I wasn't going to give her the satisfaction of any other type of response. Instead, I decided to call my OB first thing Monday morning and try to get in that same day. The idea of being able to tell Gavin that he didn't have to be prepared, that he could just slide inside me whenever... I shivered.

Finally, Krissy calmed down and wiped her eyes. "I'm sorry," she said. Her voice was sincere. "I just never... I mean..."

I held up my hand and shook my head. "Just stop there. I don't want to talk about it anymore. Let's change the subject."

"Agreed." Krissy took a drink of her tea. "Did you find out anything more about the club?"

I shrugged. "Not much." I sipped on my coffee. Ah, caffeine. "I didn't actually get around to asking him about it, so I just know what he'd said before. Twice a week, the club is closed to the public and only members have access on those days. The same members who can use the room upstairs." I flushed as I remembered my encounter in that room. "I have no idea how many members there are. I didn't ask."

Krissy laughed. "Oh, you mean you were too busy actually having sex to learn more about it."

I rolled my eyes, but I wasn't actually that annoyed. Krissy always teased me about sex. It was just nice that, for once, it wasn't about my lack of it.

"So," she leaned forward, an eager expression on her face. "We got a little distracted before when we were talking about that room. You never did get to tell me much about it."

I picked at a piece of bacon as I answered. "What do you want to know? How there are restraints attached to the orgy-sized bed? Or about the absolutely massive dildo I found in one of the chests?"

Krissy's eyes widened. "So this isn't just a vanilla sex kinda place." It was a statement rather than a question.

I shook my head. "Oh, no. Not even close." I smirked at the look of surprise on Krissy's face. I knew she wasn't exactly vanilla herself, but hearing me talk about a sex club was definitely a new development. Adding something spicier into the mix made this even more fun. "I opened one of the chests and there were ball-gags and nipple clamps." I fought to keep myself from blushing as I listed off the things I'd looked up on the Internet over the past week, just so I could have names to go with what else I'd seen. "There were also cock cages, clamps for... other body parts, and chains to connect the different clamps. All that was on one side of the chest. On the other side were dildos, strap-ons and vibrators in more sizes, shapes, and colors than I knew existed."

"Uh-huh." Krissy was staring at me. "What about in the other chests?"

I shrugged. "I don't know, but if the research I did was any indication, I found the tame stuff."

"Research?" She started shaking her head, like she couldn't believe what she was hearing. "Are you telling me that you...?" Her voice trailed off.

I nodded. "You know me. When I don't know about something, I research it."

"So, what did you think?" She pulled one leg up so that her foot was on the chair and her knee was against her chest.

"I don't know," I answered honestly.

"What – what if Gavin's into the whole S&M stuff?"

I met her eyes. That was one of the things that had been hovering in the back of my thoughts since finding those toys.

"You did say he held your hands above your head," Krissy pointed out. "What if he wants to tie you up? Or something even kinkier?" She munched on the last piece of bacon. "I mean, are you going to go all leather and whips on me?"

I laughed, brushing aside the question as I reached for my coffee. I was going to drink my hot beverage and hope to avoid the question. It wasn't that I had a problem sharing with Krissy, but rather that I didn't know the answer. If someone had asked me a few weeks ago if I'd ever considered anything remotely kinky when it came to sex, I would've laughed at them, but now, I wasn't so sure. Gavin had already made me move beyond anything I'd thought I'd ever do. With the way I felt about him, the way my body responded to him, I wasn't sure how far he could coax me to go.

TWO

I'd been spending pretty much every waking moment working on my paper for school. I hadn't been lying to Gavin's boss when I'd used it as an excuse for why I couldn't join him at his place. I really did need to get it done. Normally, I could just put on headphones and apply laser focus, wading through case law and applying it to my thesis, but I'd been distracted. Sadly, it hadn't even been about anything important, but rather by constant thoughts about when Gavin would call.

I kept trying to focus on my schoolwork, and, for a good deal of the time, I managed to do just that. Unfortunately, I couldn't quite stop the thoughts from popping into my head every now and then, wondering what Gavin was doing, why he hadn't called. The worst part was, I'd never been one of those women who craved attention twenty-four/seven. I told myself it had everything to do with me just wanting to be with him, and nothing to do with me thinking that my boyfriend *had* to be in constant contact, and that brought up a whole other set of crazy thoughts.

Boyfriend? Where had that come from? Granted, Gavin had referred to us as being together, but he hadn't said anything about any type of commitment or label. And though he'd mentioned me meeting his daughter, there was always a chance that he'd just said that because he'd been caught up in the emotion of the moment. For all I knew, his definition of "together" could mean meeting up for sex for a few weeks or months. It didn't necessarily mean the same thing to him that it meant to me. Not that I really even knew what it meant to me.

I glanced at my phone for what seemed like the hundredth time. Even though I'd barely been away from it, and had checked every time I'd returned, I still tapped the button to take off the energy saver. No calls. No texts.

I frowned. Should I call him?

Absolutely no way in hell. I could hear Krissy's voice in my head.

I sighed. Of course not. I stood and picked up my empty glass. I needed more iced tea. I headed into the kitchen, moving through the darkness with ease. When Krissy wasn't here, I rarely turned on lights as I moved around the apartment. As long as I'd cleaned and knew there wasn't anything on the floor to trip me, I could make my way through the entire space without a problem. The refrigerator light was more than enough for me to refill my cup by.

The silence was almost deafening. The people next door had left early that morning and Krissy had gone to the movies with Leslie, so the only sounds I could hear were the noises of traffic below and the muffled voices of those who were above and below. The walls might have been thin, but the ceiling and floor had good insulation. All of this was in the background, the kind of white noise that people get so used to that they barely even think about it.

Then, a sound cut through the air. A clip of music. A ringtone.

Shit.

My phone was ringing. I almost dropped my glass in my

haste to get back to my room. As it was, I splashed ice tea all down my front and across my arm, soaking my t-shirt. When I saw his name on the screen, I forgot about being wet.

"Hi." I sounded out of breath and hoped he wouldn't realize that I'd been racing to get to the phone.

"Hello, there." He sounded amused. "I'm truly sorry I didn't call you earlier. I've been swamped with work."

I sat down and eyed my laptop screen. "That's okay. I really did have to work on my paper." I didn't mention that I hadn't gotten as much done as I'd planned.

"I have to go out of town for a couple of days on business," he said.

A stab of disappointment went through me. I hadn't realized until just then how much I'd been hoping he'd ask me to come by tonight. I reminded myself that I'd just spent a year without a boyfriend and without sex. I didn't need to see Gavin every night.

"I was hoping I could see you Wednesday."

I smiled. "That would be great." My voice came out a lot more nonchalant than I felt.

"Can you come by the club after work, say around five? I'd like to give you the official tour of the place."

"Oh." I suddenly didn't know what to say. I wanted to see him very much. My entire body was thrumming at just the idea. But, I wasn't sure how I felt about going back to the club. Images flashed rapid-fire through my mind.

Gavin showing up pretending to be my boyfriend.

The way he'd looked at me when I was dancing with Krissy.

Kissing him for the first time.

Walking into that room and knowing we would be having sex.

One mind-blowing orgasm after another.

"Carrie?" His voice cut through the memories. "Are you okay?"

"Yes," I answered automatically. Before I could talk myself out of it, I spoke again. "And, yes, I'll come by after work."

"Great!"

I could almost hear him smiling, and I knew how his eyes would be lighting up. Heat unfurled in my stomach.

"Go to the side door and press the buzzer so I can let you in. And I'll have something for you."

I frowned. "No more gifts, please." The necklace he'd given me before the gala was sitting in its box on my dresser, and I was still trying to figure out a way to ask about it tactfully. There was no way he could've meant for me to keep it. Was there?

"It's not a gift. Not exactly," he assured me. "But it will please you."

Heat turned into flames and I shifted in my seat. The way he said the word *please* made me think that he wasn't talking about some little gesture. His tone rather hinted at something deeper and perhaps darker, something that spoke to a primal nature I hadn't realized I'd had until I'd met him. Then again, that could've just been wishful thinking on my part.

"I have to go, but I'll be thinking about you and our next meeting."

He hung up before I could answer.

"Oh, fuck." I put my head down on my desk. "What did I just get myself into?"

I tried working on my paper after that, but I couldn't think about anything other than what Gavin could possibly have in store for me. Finally, at ten o'clock, I gave up. I took a shower and headed for bed, intending to read until I fell asleep. Instead, I stared at the same page for half an hour, my imagination running wild.

Gavin slowly stripping off my clothes, then his own, before jumping into the pool.

Laying me back on the bar and burying his head between my legs until I screamed.

Another trip to the upstairs room where he tied me to the bed and teased me mercilessly.

Exploring the various chests and toys as he taught me the uses for each one.

I was still fantasizing about all of the things he could do to me when I fell asleep, and my desires followed me into my dreams.

THREE

Was it sad that the most exciting part of my week prior to Wednesday was when I was able to get an appointment with my OB on my Monday lunch hour? Not that the appointment itself was exciting, just what it promised. I was able to get my prescription filled that day and start taking the pill right away. Even though the timing meant I was probably covered right away, I was going to wait a week just in case. Still, knowing that I'd be able to tell Gavin that he didn't have to use anything was heady. I thought about calling him, but that seemed a bit too forward, making too much of it when I wasn't really sure where we stood. Then, I thought I'd tell him on Wednesday, but decided against it. Maybe, first, I'd hint around about getting tested so I'd know that there wasn't a reason other than pregnancy that meant we needed to keep using condoms. After that, I'd schedule a night next week for us to meet, and that's when I'd tell him that I wanted him to come inside me, bare. I couldn't wait to see the expression on his face. Imagining it was quite the distraction.

It took a while, but I finally learned how to concentrate when amorous thoughts wanted to take over. Every hour, I'd allow myself five minutes for my fantasies. Once those five minutes were up, I got back to the task at hand.

That task, for the past two days, had been doing more research on Howard Weiss. In anticipation of problems with his divorce case, my boss, Mimi Styles, had instructed me to dig into his life so she could be prepared.

I'd been able to tell when she'd called me into her office first thing Monday morning that things weren't going the way she'd wanted. As soon as she filled me in on what she'd discovered in the prenuptial agreement and Howard's other personal files, I understood why.

Just before the couple married, Howard had been near bankruptcy. His business had been failing and no one would give him a loan to bail him out. Then, a big investor had come along and given him what he needed to get through that rough patch. The investor had been from Howard's wife's family. The day after the wedding, Howard's company had been saved, but to protect the family's investment, the lawyer had written into the prenup that fifty percent of the company would belong to the family. The other fifty percent would be split between Howard and his wife – except in the case of infidelity. If Howard had been unfaithful, his wife would get everything, and Howard would lose his company.

My assignment was to find out if Howard had actually had an affair, which meant I was researching every woman ever seen with him. If any of them were able to testify that they'd had sex with Howard while he'd still been living with his wife, his case would be in serious trouble.

The celebrities were easy. If I didn't know them, a quick reverse image search gave me their names. Once I'd searched for articles linking Howard with each of those women and found nothing, I was satisfied that I didn't need to go any deeper with them. If there'd been any dirt there, the gossip magazines would've found it. No, the ones I had to worry about were the women who weren't celebrities.

They were all pretty – I doubted Howard would ever deign to be seen with anyone less than attractive – but they weren't actresses, models, musicians, or even those celebrities who are famous for nothing but being famous.

By Wednesday morning, I'd exhausted every resource at my disposal. All but two, and I really didn't want to do the last one. After I'd settled in for the morning, I placed the first – and what I hoped would be the last – call. Howard's personal assistant, Annie, answered on the second ring.

"Hello, this is Carrie Summers from Webster and Steinberg." I kept my voice light and professional. It sounded fake to me, but I was working on making it better. "My boss, Ms. Styles, has me working on background information on the women who have attended various events with Mr. Weiss."

I didn't know if Annie understood the implication of what I was asking, but I hoped she didn't. Knowing someone was checking up on your boss's sex life could make things very awkward.

"I'm sorry, Ms. Summers, but I don't have access to that information." Annie sounded almost bored. "Mr. Weiss doesn't provide me with the names of his dates, only instructs me to RSVP either for just him or with a plus one."

"Okay." I was disappointed. "Thank you anyway."

"Have a good day."

I frowned as I hung up. It seemed like the only way I was going to get these women's names would be to ask Howard himself. I didn't want to have that conversation. Aside from the fact that it would be uncomfortable to ask him about his dates when I knew he'd understand exactly why I was asking, it would probably make all future interactions just as awkward, and since I was with Gavin, I had a feeling I'd be seeing plenty of Howard.

Then there was the whole flirting thing. I wasn't sure how he'd take me asking about those women. What if he thought I was asking because I wanted to know for personal reasons? I could see him thinking I was trying to find out about any competition. Gavin might believe that Howard was only a charmer who behaved that way towards all women, but that wasn't the vibe I got off of Howard. I couldn't put my finger on it or provide any type of proof or evidence, which was why I hadn't said anything to Gavin, but something about Howard just didn't sit right with me. I kept getting the feeling that there was something below that veneer surface that was far less attractive.

I decided to put off calling Howard for the time being. There were a handful of other places I could look for information. They weren't exactly reliable, but they did give me an excuse not to make that phone call. Besides, who knew what I could find? If nothing else, maybe they could lead me to another trail.

About two hours later, I was starting to go cross-eyed from all of the tiny print I was reading on my computer, and I almost missed it: an article that mentioned Howard Weiss. It wasn't until I pulled it up and began to read that I realized it wasn't an entertainment piece. Instead, it was a biographical article, one where Howard's family history had been traced. Even though it didn't have anything to do with what I was looking for, I kept reading. If I had to call him, at least I would have a bit more background information.

The more I read, the bigger my eyes got. Howard's New York City roots were deeper than I'd realized. His family had been in the city since before the turn of the century, and I wasn't referring to the recent one. Things were fairly unremarkable until the nineteen twenties, when Howard's great-grandfather, Josiah, rose to power in the Jewish mafia. There were links to Josiah Weiss, so I followed them. He had been ruthless, cold, and calculating. A dozen murders were attributed to him directly, but none were ever brought to trial because witnesses kept disappearing. Some places had the body count as high as fifty or sixty for hits he'd ordered. Three were judges and more than a dozen were cops. Then there were all of the shady industries. Of course, it being Prohibition and all, he'd made a fortune running booze, but he hadn't stopped there. Josiah had his fingers in everything. Police corruption. Blackmail. Shaking down business owners. Prostitution. Gambling. It seemed like the only thing he didn't do was sell drugs.

When I'd finished, I sat back in my seat, trying to absorb everything I'd just read. It shouldn't have made a difference, I knew. The Jewish mafia was all but extinct, and just because Josiah Weiss had been a part of it didn't mean Howard had anything to do with that part of his family history. Then again, a lot of those mafia types had an "it's a family business and blood is thicker than water" mentality. If the business practices had been passed down from generation to generation, there was no telling what Howard had done to acquire his fortune. Or to what lengths he would be willing to go to keep it.

FOUR

When I came back from lunch, a package was sitting on my desk, and on top of it, a single red rose. I smiled as I picked up the flower. I wasn't going to throw this one away. I held it up to my nose and breathed in the unique scent. No matter how close chemistry got to duplicating the smell of roses, there would always be something different about the real thing.

"Is that from Gavin?"

I looked over to see my friend, Leslie Calvin, grinning at me. Flirtatious and drop-dead gorgeous, Leslie had taken Gavin's number when I'd tried to throw it away. She never had told me if she'd tried to call him, but it didn't matter now.

"I'm seeing him tonight." I set aside the flower and picked up the card.

Leslie grinned at me, her bright green eyes sparkling. I knew she wouldn't begrudge me Gavin even though I'd originally said I didn't want him. Leslie never lacked for male attention. Between the lustrous red curls and curvy body, she and Krissy rivaled each other in how many men they'd been with over the years.

"What's in the box?" she asked.

I didn't know, but I had a good idea. The last time I'd gotten a box like this, it had contained the most beautiful Prada dress I'd ever seen. I opened the card and read it silently.

Please wear this when I see you today, and no, this is not your gift. - G

Curiosity piqued, I set the card aside and opened the box. As I peeled back the tissue paper, my jaw dropped. There was clothing in the box all right, but nothing even close to what I'd expected. It was lingerie.

Leslie whistled. "Damn. He's got good taste."

I couldn't nod. My cheeks were burning. It was absolutely beautiful. I'd never worn anything like it, and not just because it had probably cost more than I spent on my entire wardrobe in a month. I like pretty underwear, but I'd always kept it simple. My fanciest pieces were black lace. Nothing sheer or with peek-a-boo panels or anything like that. I'd never thought I was ugly, but I'd also never had the guts to try wearing anything like what was in that box. Tonight, however, I would. For him.

"You've been pretty tight-lipped about the whole Gavin thing," Leslie observed. "Krissy told me last night that you really seem to like this guy. That true?"

Leave it to Leslie to be that direct.

I took a slow, deep breath and raised my head to meet her gaze. "I do."

Leslie grinned. "Good for you." She started back towards her desk, then paused and looked over her shoulder at me. "I hope he's as good in the sack as he looks."

"He's better." The words popped out of my mouth before I could think about them and I almost clapped a hand over my mouth.

I wasn't sure who looked more shocked, me or Leslie. Whichever one it was, she recovered first.

"Looks like he's really loosening you up." She winked at me. "Careful. You'll end up like me if you don't watch out."

She didn't wait for a response, which was good. I wasn't sure how long it was going to take me to get over my mortification enough to speak. As it was, it took me nearly a full minute to be able to move again. I carefully folded the tissue paper back down and put the lid back on the box before setting it aside.

I sank into my chair. I needed to focus. I couldn't think about that or about why Gavin would want me to wear it. I still had half a day's worth of work to do. That turned out to be easier said than done.

It was difficult to sort through all of Howard's women to make a list of all the ones who were known and cleared, then compile pictures of the ones who were, as of yet, still unidentified. Not the work itself, mind you, more like trying to pay attention to the details while my eyes kept being drawn back to that box sitting on the edge of my desk. I kept imagining what it would be like to feel that soft silk on my skin, how it was going to feel riding in a cab knowing what I was wearing beneath my skirt and blouse. Most of all, I tried to picture what Gavin's reaction would be when he saw me in it.

Somehow, despite my distractions, I managed to get my list made with fifteen minutes to spare. I was smiling as I printed out the papers. I was putting them into a folder when I heard my name.

"Carrie."

I looked up to see Mimi standing in front of my desk. She held out a stack of papers. I took them automatically.

"These notes need to be sorted and put into chronological order by first thing tomorrow morning. They're essential to a meeting, so they're your top priority."

She turned and walked away. It was no surprise that she didn't bother to ask if I had plans for the night. No partner would ask a paralegal that, especially not a paralegal who was working her way through law school. We did the scut work because that was how everyone paid their dues. Being Mimi's assistant just meant that it was *her* scut work I did rather than that of random associates. That also meant that when she needed me to stay late, I stayed late.

I spread the notes out on my desk and sighed in frustration. Every one of them had Mimi's barely legible handwriting and not a single one contained a date. The only way I was going to be able to tell chronological order would be to read them and put them together like a puzzle. It was going to take an hour at the very least.

I began to work, using a highlighter to mark relevant portions that I could connect to other pieces. At least, that's what I was trying to do. More than once, however, I found myself reading the same sentence over and over again.

"See you tomorrow," Leslie said as she passed. She grinned at me. "Unless you're too worn out."

I rolled my eyes and managed not to blush. I tried to refocus, hoping I could quickly finish. Instead, my gaze kept sliding over to my phone, wondering if I should just call Gavin and tell him I was going to be late. But what if he decided it'd be too much of a hassle to wait? I had given him my word that I'd be there shortly after five. I was obliged to keep it. Besides, it wasn't like I was getting much work done anyway.

I knew I was trying to talk myself into leaving without finishing the work, but I didn't care. I wanted to see Gavin, and my mind wasn't in the work anyway.

I picked up the stack of papers and put them into my desk drawer so they wouldn't get lost. I'd come in early tomorrow and finish before Mimi even got in. She hadn't specifically told me to stay after, so as long as I had everything done by the time she needed it, there wouldn't be any problem.

The office was mostly empty by the time I picked up the box and headed into the restroom. A couple associates and para-legals were scattered around, and I spotted at least one partner, but none of them paid me any attention as I carried the box into the bathroom. I went into the big stall at the end, a smile playing around my lips as I thought about what had happened the last time I'd entered the large stall in a restroom. Fortunately, this time, it was empty. I quickly undressed and folded the bra and panties I'd worn, putting them in the box. I pulled on the lingerie, my heart pounding as I did so. The color was the same rich red of the dress Gavin had given me for the gala, and as it had done then, it looked amazing against my skin. I wanted to see myself in it before I revealed it to Gavin.

"Hello?" I called softly. My voice echoed off the tile walls, but no one answered. I opened the door a crack and peered out. It was empty. I didn't need to actually walk out. I was across from the mirrors so all I had to do was open the door all the way and I'd be able to see what I looked like.

I took a deep breath and stepped out from behind the door. My eyes widened. Wow. I was used to seeing long golden curls, chocolate brown eyes. Used to my average build and pretty features.

I hadn't, however, known I could look like *that* in something like *this*.

The entire thing was sheer crimson lace and silk. It was strapless, and the bra hugged my breasts, the low cut showing off quite a bit of creamy flesh. The most startling thing, however, was that I could see the slightly darker circles of my nipples through it, but the effect wasn't trashy. From the center of the bra, a thin strip of silk ran down my belly, breaking into two halfway down so that it went on either side of my bellybutton before connecting to the top of my panties. They, too, were see-through. Not completely transparent, they hinted at what was beneath without being crass. They were also tinier than anything I'd ever owned. They sat low on my hips, the waist-band just above the thin layer of hair that covered my more inti-mate parts. The back was barely there, a strip of material that was only a fraction wider than a thong. Add to that the black

thigh-high stockings I always wore and the heels I hadn't both-
ered to take off and, for a moment, I saw myself as sexy. Not
cute, not pretty, not even hot, but honest-to-goodness sexy.

I closed the door and put my skirt and blouse back on. As I
buttoned up my shirt, I was thankful that I'd worn the dark gray
one rather than my usual white. I'd done it because I'd wanted
to wear my black underwear to see Gavin, but now it meant that
I could wear crimson without exposing myself to everyone.

I carried the box back to my desk and discreetly transferred
my panties and bra into my purse before throwing the box away.
I didn't want to have to carry it around. Then, overly conscious
of what I was wearing beneath my business clothes, I left the
building and headed for the club.

No one even gave me a second glance as I flagged a cab, but
I felt like everyone who even glanced at me knew what I was
wearing, what I was doing. I kept my eyes focused straight
ahead as I climbed into the car. I smiled politely as I gave the
cab driver the address and tried not to think about if he knew
what the club was. Krissy and Gavin were both right about not
being ashamed, but it was often easier said than done.

I paid the driver without making eye contact and started up
the sidewalk. Gavin had said to use the side entrance, so I
walked down the alley rather than going to the front door. As
alleys in the city went, this one was better than most. It was rela-
tively clean, with just a few cigarette butts and condoms scattered in with the usual dust and debris that blew around the
streets. It didn't smell pleasant, but there was none of that cat-
pee, garbage, and vomit scent that hung around most alleys.

A few feet down, I spotted a bright red door. Next to it was
a buzzer. I pressed the button and heard the faint sound of its
signaling behind the door. A minute later, the door opened,
filled with the massive bouncer who'd been at the door that first
night. I doubted he'd have recognized me even if I hadn't been
dressed completely differently.

"Yes?" He looked puzzled as he gave me a once-over.

"I'm here to see Mr. Manning," I said. I really hoped I sounded like someone on a professional call rather than the kind of girl who frequented sex clubs. I immediately scolded myself for the thought. It was no wonder I had a hard time not feeling ashamed, thinking things like that.

"Who?" The bouncer crossed his arms over his broad chest. He didn't exactly look friendly, but he also didn't look like someone who was going kill me if I answered his question.

"Mr. Manning. The owner." I supposed it wasn't too strange that a bouncer didn't know the owner.

"You're in the wrong place." He reached for the door. "There's no one here by that name." He gave me another full-body look. "If you're here about the job, auditions are tomorrow."

I didn't need anyone to explain to me what the audition was probably for. He started to close the door and I reached out and grabbed it. I wasn't sure who was more surprised by my action, me or him. I wasn't exactly tiny, but I was far from being close to his size. I doubted most men would've tried to push the issue.

"Miss..." There was a warning in the word.

"Wait, please." I kept my voice calm. "This is Club Privé, right?" He nodded. "And you're saying that no one named Gavin Manning is here?"

"It's okay, Lenny. I asked her to come."

Gavin's voice came from behind the bouncer, his tone saying that he knew the mountain of a man currently looking down at me. My heart started to pound and my mouth went dry, but none of it was from arousal. What was going on here? Why didn't Lenny know who Gavin was if Gavin knew Lenny?

The bouncer stepped out of the way and Gavin was suddenly there. He smiled at me as Lenny walked away, shaking his head and muttering something I couldn't hear. All of my instincts said that something was wrong, that I should leave, but before I could, Gavin reached out and took my hand, pulling me through the doorway into a small corridor.

"I was starting to worry that you'd changed your mind," he said.

I yanked my hand out of his and took a step back. He looked startled, but made no move to touch me again.

"What's wrong?" he asked.

"Who are you?"

"What?"

I wasn't going to fall for that innocent look. Something weird was going on here, and I was going to find out what. If he wasn't Gavin Manning, I was going to find out who he really was.

"Who the hell *are* you?"

FIVE

He stared at me, as if he didn't understand my question. Fine, I'd explain it.

"The bouncer said there wasn't anyone named Gavin Manning here, but there you are, and obviously, he knows who you are, which means he was either lying to me, or you're not who you said you were. And since you've lied to me before, I think I'll err on the side of caution with this one. So, I repeat, who the hell are you?"

Gavin held up a hand, as if sensing that it wouldn't be a good idea to try to touch me at that moment. When he spoke, his voice was calm, not defensive.

"Lenny was just being careful. He's been my driver and bodyguard for over a year. A few months back, this crazy woman came after me with a gun. Lenny wrestled it away from her, but was shot in his hand. He's been a bit more cautious than usual since then."

I gave Gavin a skeptical look. "A woman with a gun?"

He gave me a half-grin. "Her husband was one of my consulting clients. The day before she came after me, she found lipstick on his shirt. She confronted him and he admitted that he'd been having an affair, then told her that I'd set him up with the woman. She got pissed and decided to come after me."

"Did you set her husband up with a woman?" I couldn't believe I had to ask the question, but something about this just wasn't sitting right with me.

"No. I'd never do something like that. I may own a sex club, but I do have certain standards. If married men come here and hook up with someone, that's one thing, but I'd never purposefully set a married man up with a woman for a sexual encounter."

He sounded like he was being honest, but I wasn't so sure I could believe him. I'd never heard him talk about other clients, and that last line had come across almost like he'd rehearsed it.

"Are you ever going to trust me?" His voice was soft.

I looked at him then and saw the hurt in his eyes. I wished I could tell him that I didn't have any doubts, but that would be a lie. Things between us hadn't exactly been 'normal.'

"Look." The corners of his mouth twitched up as he reached into his pocket and pulled out his ID. He held it out to me and I took it. "My license says Gavin Manning. I would show you my birth certificate, but I left it at home."

I handed his ID back and his fingers brushed against mine when he took it. I supposed I was being sort of silly. He'd given me an explanation that had made sense and he hadn't been on the defensive. Why did I still doubt him? From the moment he'd promised me no more lies, he'd kept that promise. I needed to decide if I was going to trust him or if this was going to be a constant thing, me always questioning, him always having to explain. It was no way to have a relationship.

I held out my hand. He smiled and took it, leading me down the short hallway and into the main club area. Aside from the lack of people, something was different. It was still beautiful and opulent, but something was missing. It was so large and obvious that it took me a couple minutes to realize what it was.

"Where's the pool?"

In the space in the center of the room where there'd been a large pool on opening night, there was only floor.

Gavin smiled at me and pointed towards a panel on the wall just a couple feet away from us. He reached into his pocket, took out a key, and inserted it into the slot next to the panel. He twisted the key and pushed one of the buttons.

With a faint hum, the floor began to split. I watched as it parted, slowly revealing the water beneath. I had to admit, I was impressed. I knew there were schools that had pools under their gym floors but I'd never heard of a club doing it. Then again, I'd never heard of a club with an indoor pool next to their dance floor.

"Why was it hidden?" I asked as he returns the floor to its original place.

"We only use it for special events," he said. "Do you have any idea how much it costs to maintain a pool with the health department? This way, we don't have to worry about weekly inspections; only every month, since it's only going to be used for specific events."

"Like what?" I asked as he began to lead me further along the wall.

"Well," he said, thinking. "Like our members-only nights. We open the pool and hire... entertainment."

His hesitation told me what he meant by *entertainment*. I scowled. He was bringing in hookers for his clients.

I started to pull my hand away, but he tightened his fingers around mine.

"Dancers, Carrie." The look on his face said that he knew exactly what I'd been thinking. "Exotic dancers. Strippers, if you like that word better, but all they do is dance. They're paid for the event, not by the men, and it's all high-class stuff." He paused, then added, "Though in the spirit of total honesty, as I've promised, if any of them decide to accept a man's offer to go upstairs, I won't stop them. Consenting adults, and all. I'm not their parent."

I wasn't sure how I felt about that aspect of the business, but I didn't say anything. I followed along in silence, smiling and nodding as Gavin showed me all of the intricate details of the club. It was really quite beautiful and, after a few minutes, it pushed thoughts of members' night to the back of my mind.

SIX

"So, I heard that you were having trouble getting the information you needed about some of the women in Howard's life."

I looked up at him, startled. He appeared to be faintly amused by my reaction and, when I thought about it, I supposed it should have been obvious. It did seem to be part of his job to know everything to do with Howard.

"Let me show you my office."

I thought the change in subject seemed a bit abrupt, but I didn't say anything about it. Obviously, he had something on his mind and I had an idea that it'd be better to just let it play out rather than try to figure it out on my own.

As we stepped onto the elevator, my heart gave a little skip and I rubbed my palms on my skirt. The last time I'd been in this elevator, Gavin's hands had been on me the moment the doors had closed. I watched the door panels slide into place and kept staring straight ahead as we rode up. I wanted to look over at Gavin, to see if he was remembering that night too, but I was afraid that if I did, either I'd see he was staring at me with lust in his eyes or, worse, was completely unaffected. The first would be bad because I didn't have much self-control when it came to the man standing next to me. None, actually. The second would be bad because it would mean that our encounter wasn't enough to spark the memories. So, I stayed a chicken and kept looking directly in front of me.

The elevator dinged and the doors opened. Gavin stepped out first and I followed. We walked side-by-side, not joining hands again. I knew why I didn't reach for him, and I hoped he had the same reasoning for not doing the same. One touch and I wasn't sure what I'd do. We stopped in front of one of the doors marked for employees only, but my gaze kept traveling down to the door at the end of the hall. The door that lead to the room for members only.

The door looked innocuous enough, but I knew what was behind it. The memories of everything Gavin and I had done that night in that room came rushing into my mind. How we'd laughed at the vibrating bed. The first time I'd seen him naked. The expression on his face when he'd seen me...

"Carrie?"

Gavin's voice brought me back and I realized that he'd opened the office door and was waiting for me to go through.

"Sorry," I said, heat rising to my cheeks.

"It's okay." He lowered his voice as I stepped past. "I think about that night every time I see the door too. Makes coming to my office... hard."

I shivered, the double meaning not lost on me. Now I was wondering if that was why he'd brought me here. Did he want us to have sex in his office? Maybe some sort of role-play thing? Immediately, the images popped into my head, one after the other.

Gavin as the boss, me on my knees, working hard for a good review.

Him bending me over his desk.

Me riding him in his chair.

Desire unfurled low inside me. It was just a tendril of heat, but I knew it wouldn't take much to get it stoked to a full flame.

"Here."

It took me a moment to realize that Gavin was holding out a file. I was puzzled, but I took it.

"Have a seat." He motioned around him.

A couch sat against one wall, two plush chairs against the other. A large desk was in front of a window, the chair behind it looking like it cost more than some cars. The entire office was tastefully decorated, the subtlety saying that it cost a lot to look this simple. Nothing was cheap, but nothing was outlandish either. I liked it.

I could have taken one of the two high-backed chairs that sat across from the desk, but I still didn't know why we were there, so I decided to go halfway. Rather than sitting on the couch like I wanted to, I chose the closest chair. Gavin perched on the arm as I opened the file.

"That should have everything you need on the women you couldn't find."

I stared at the papers and pictures in front of me. Where had he gotten these? I began to flip through the files and saw head shots, personality tests, questionnaires. A suspicion started to form. The only types of places I'd ever seen use this kind of information were dating services. I remembered what he'd said earlier this evening about a client's wife thinking he'd set her husband up with a woman. Then I remembered the women from the gala. Were they his doing too?

"I know what you're thinking."

I looked up. I seriously doubted that.

"After Camille died..." His face tightened briefly. "I was lost, but I found my way back by finding something that I was good at. Writing software."

Okay, not what I'd been expecting.

"Howard saw my potential and gave me a loan for my start-up money. The first thing I developed was dating software. That's where all of this," he gestured around him, "came from."

"Dating software." I'd thought that was what the information looked like.

"Yes. It scans the Internet for information about potential dates. It's more thorough than any dating site out there, and I use it to find matches for millionaires, men who have to worry about women's only wanting them for their money."

"Or married bastards who want to cheat on their wives?" The question came out more harshly than I'd intended, but I didn't apologize. I could put up with kinks, or even people who wanted to invite other people into their relationship. That might not have been my thing, but who was I to say anything against consenting adults? What I did have a problem with, however, was adultery. I'd seen what infidelity could do to a marriage. My brother's ex had cheated on him, and it had nearly destroyed him. It was bad enough to have to have people like that as clients, but I could never be with a man who assisted in that deception.

Gavin was studying me intently, as if those deep blue eyes could read my everything, my very soul. "No." He shook his head. "I have two types of matches. Possible romantic dates for single or separated men, and companions for men whose wives don't want to attend events."

"Really?" The word dripped my disbelief.

"You'd be surprised at the women who want to rub elbows with the rich and famous. Being on the arm of someone like Howard can get women into places that they could never get to on their own."

I closed the file and folded my hands. This was sounding more and more like one of those escort services who said they only provided companionship so they wouldn't get in trouble with the law.

"It's not a call girl service, Carrie," he said. "The women

aren't paid and every single client, male and female, agrees to our terms of service, which specifically state that no money is to be exchanged for sex."

"Sure," I said. "I wasn't thinking anything like that."

Gavin laughed and shook his head. "We said no more lies."

I grinned, the mood lightening. "You said that. Not me."

He laughed again, the deep sound rumbling through me and making parts of me throb.

"Thank you," I said. I wasn't sure what I'd find when I looked more deeply into his business, but I appreciated that he was helping me.

"Here." He took the file. "I'll have someone deliver that to your desk tomorrow morning. You shouldn't have to carry it all night."

He stood and held out his hand. I took it and stood.

"Now, for your surprise."

"This wasn't it?" I asked.

He smiled, that slow, sensual smile that made me quiver inside. "That wouldn't be very romantic, would it?" He started towards the door. "Come, let's go eat."

SEVEN

As we headed back downstairs, I kept trying to think about what my surprise could possibly be. Dinner couldn't be it. We'd eaten meals together before.

"Are you cooking for me?" I asked.

He laughed and reached over to take my hand. He threaded his fingers between mine as we walked across the club floor towards the side door I'd used to enter.

I was going to ask for a reason behind his laughter but as soon as we stepped outside, something else caught my attention. A limo was waiting. I suddenly felt very underdressed, even with my sexy lingerie.

A thought occurred to me. This was the second time he'd had a car appear without having called. "Do you have some sort of telepathic connection with the driver?" I joked.

"Better than that." He held up his phone. "It's an app." He grinned and my stomach did a flip. "Whenever I need a limo or town car, I just press this button. The company at the other end uses the GPS in my phone to locate me and then they contact the closest available driver. I called for it when we were on our way up to my office."

"Well, that is a fancy little app," I said as the driver opened the door for me.

"Thank you," he replied as he followed me into the limo. "And it's quite the time saver. I haven't waited for a ride since I helped develop it a few months ago."

My eyes widened. Okay, now I was impressed. I'd thought he'd just been bragging about his ability to have limos and town cars at his beck and call. "Just how much software have you developed?"

He chuckled and shrugged, his eyes flicking away from mine for a moment before coming back again. The thought immediately popped into my head that he was hiding something, but I pushed it away. I'd already decided that I was going to trust him. I wasn't going to let myself go back down that path over something that was probably just an embarrassed little tic.

"Is there anything you don't do?" I made it into a tease.

He laughed again, this time louder. "Actually, yes, and that would be why I laughed when you asked if I was cooking for you. I'm an awful cook."

"Come on, you can't be that bad." I let him veer away from talk of work. He seemed like one of those rare guys who actually didn't want to make everything all about how wonderful he was.

"Trust me," he said. "I am." He raised our linked hands and pressed his lips against the back of mine. "I've screwed up boiled eggs."

"How in the world do you do that?" I laughed.

"The water boiled away and the eggs exploded."

We laughed over that for several minutes before I finally asked, "Where are you taking me, then?"

"Wait and see," he replied cryptically.

I tried to scowl at him, but couldn't manage it. He was giving me that sideways look that made his hair fall across his forehead and made me think about what he must've looked like in high school. I had a feeling he'd been one of those kids who'd never gotten in real trouble in school because he'd just give his teachers that same look and they'd let him off easy. Girls would've fallen all over themselves to get that smile, and guys would've followed him anywhere.

The limo pulled up in front of a magnificent high-rise. I'd seen this building, of course, and knew that it housed some very rich people.

"Does Howard have a place here too?" I asked as he helped me out of the limo. I hadn't seen this listed on his assets. Maybe he was trying to keep it from his wife.

"No." He slid his arm around my waist and kissed my temple. "I do."

Of course Gavin lived here. Why hadn't I thought that? I tried not to look like a gawking schoolgirl as I followed him inside. By the time we reached his top-floor suite, I was feeling overwhelmed. I waited for him to open the door so we could go inside, but instead, he turned towards a different door.

"Let's go up the stairs."

"Okay." Now I really had no clue what was going on. I'd thought he'd brought me to his place to show it to me. We'd order in, and after we'd eaten, we'd head to his bedroom. The roof hadn't factored into my thoughts at all.

A warm breeze caressed my skin as I stepped out onto the roof. I caught my breath. At first, all I could see was the view. The sun was just sinking below the horizon, casting pinks and purples across the Manhattan skyline. I couldn't hear the noises of the city, and the silence took me out of that space, making me feel more like I was looking at a vast painting. It looked almost too beautiful to be real.

"Just wait until it gets dark. It's even more amazing." Gavin pressed his lips against my ear.

I nodded mutely. I could only imagine what that would be like.

Gavin's hand on the small of my back nudged me forward,

and that's when I saw the rest. Just a few feet away was a small, intimate table. Surrounding it were candles, some on the ground, some in tall holders. Once the sun was gone completely, they and the lights of the city would be the only things to see by.

"Welcome." A tall, thin man in a sharp black tux gave a little bow, and it was all I could do not to laugh. Not because it was funny, but because I was suddenly nervous.

Gavin pulled out my chair and I sat. Once he settled across from me, he leaned across the table and took my hand. "I hope you don't mind eating here instead of in a restaurant."

"Are you kidding me?" I gestured around us. "This is perfect."

The waiter returned with wine and poured us both a glass. I took a sip and made a sound of approval. I was far from a wine snob, but I could tell this was quality stuff.

"I wanted to take you to Le Petit," Gavin said.

I almost choked on my wine. Le Petit was one of the priciest and most elegant restaurants in the city. That was where the old money of the city liked to dine because it cost far too much for even high-paid lawyers to afford.

The waiter came back with two small bowls of soup, placing one in front of each of us before vanishing into the rapidly falling shadows.

"Did you know that the waiting list for a table is six months?" he asked as he took a taste of the soup. "And that was with me using some of my biggest connections."

I wasn't sure where he was going with this, but I had no problem listening while I ate. The soup was amazing.

"But they do have some of the best food in the world," he continued. "So I figured out a way to get what I wanted."

I remembered how he'd told me that when he wanted something, he obsessed over it until he got it.

"I talked to the chef and convinced him to make us a three-course dinner of his speciality entrée."

Wow. I set my spoon down in my bowl. That was impressive. I didn't know of anyone else who would dare ask a top chef at a world-famous restaurant to make a three-course meal for a date. Butterflies fluttered in my stomach. I was starting to be a bit overwhelmed by the lengths to which Gavin was going for me.

"What's next?" I joked. "Three guys with violins to serenade us while we eat?"

A combination of horror and astonishment came over Gavin's face. "You don't want that?"

I laughed as he played along with my joke. The amusement only lasted a few seconds as I realized he wasn't joking.

He called over his shoulder. "Hold the trio." His cheeks were red and he couldn't meet my gaze.

Now I felt awful. He'd gone to all this trouble and I'd made it into a joke. "No," I said. I reached out and put my hand over his. He looked at me then. I smiled. "Music would be nice. Thank you."

He gave me that shy smile, the one that didn't have any of his charm or swagger, the one that I hoped was only for me. He waved a hand back towards the door we'd come through. A moment later, three men in tuxedos appeared, carrying violins. They began to play a soft piece of classical music. It was vaguely familiar but I didn't know the name.

"I know it's tacky," he said. He still looked a bit sheepish and I knew that was my fault. "But I just thought, what if you expected it and I didn't have it? I didn't want to disappoint you."

I swallowed hard. I released his hand and leaned forward enough so that I could place my hand on his cheek. I made sure he could see how serious I was before I spoke. I needed him to believe me, because I needed that insecure look to leave his face. I hated that I put it there, and I wanted my words to take it away.

"You can never disappoint me."

He smiled then, all shadows gone.

EIGHT

I'd never eaten anything quite like that meal. For the most part, I found fancy restaurants to be overpriced and the food not worth the effort. This, however, would've been worth a six-month wait and whatever exorbitant price La Petit charged. I didn't consider myself a foodie, but I did appreciate a good meal. The soup was just enough to whet the appetite, and then came the chicken in some fancy sauce I didn't even have a name for. It was spiced just right, flavored but not overwhelming. The portions were perfect, enough to be filling, but still leaving room for dessert. And what a dessert it was. A thin slice of the richest chocolate cheesecake I'd ever eaten. Gavin and I split it, and even though half was barely three bites, it was perfect. Any more would've been too much.

"I need to remember to send a thank you to the chef," Gavin said as he set his fork down on the empty plate. "That was magnificent."

I nodded in agreement.

He turned to the trio of musicians. "Thank you, gentlemen. You have truly been wonderful." He reached into his jacket and pulled out several folded-up bills. Judging by the way the lead musician's eyes widened, I was willing to bet Gavin hadn't handed over twenties. The men each gave a little bow and disappeared into the shadows.

"I'd like to show you my place, if you're interested." Gavin stood and held out a hand to me.

Was he kidding? Of course I wanted to see his place. I had so many questions about him, who he was, what he did. Any opportunity to see behind the man, I'd take. I slid my hand into his, shivering as his fingers closed around mine.

There was that too.

I didn't doubt for a moment that part of seeing Gavin's apartment would involve sex, and I wanted that almost as much as I wanted to know more about him.

He led me back downstairs, leaving our table for the waiter to clean up, or at least that's what I assumed would happen. I wasn't going to dwell on that, though. He'd arranged the date. It wasn't my responsibility.

"I bought this place a year ago," he said as he pressed his palm against the electronic pad next to the door. "But it took me a couple of months to get everything just the way I liked it."

The red light next to the door turned green and I heard the lock click.

"Biometric locks." He threw a grin over his shoulder. "The most secure ones in the business." He opened the door and we stepped inside. "Lights."

The room was immediately illuminated with the soft, warm glow of lights made to resemble candlelight. Finding out that Gavin had made his money developing software, and then seeing his security system, I fully expected the apartment to reflect an electronic, technological type of style, very much metal, and cold colors. Instead, I found a modern but cozy place decorated in warm earth tones. It was all very open, the main area containing the kitchen, dining room, and living room without walls to separate them. The main area alone was as big as my entire apartment, all rooms included, and I knew this wasn't all there was. I saw one hallway to the right and one to the left, but couldn't tell what either one led to.

Something about the uniformity of the colors and furnishings told me that he hadn't done the designing himself, but I could see where his personality had influenced the choices. Whoever had done the decorating had done well in reflecting the type of person Gavin was.

"Do you like it?" Gavin's question was almost shy, as if my opinion of his home truly mattered to him.

I suddenly wondered how many women he'd brought here. It seemed like something more intimate than he'd show to someone he was just fucking. I smiled. "It's beautiful."

He beamed as he kicked off his shoes. I followed suit, letting my stockinged feet sink into the plush carpet. The feel was sensual, and I suddenly remembered what I was wearing beneath my work clothes.

"Shall we enjoy an after-dinner drink?" He led me over to the couch. "If it was cooler, I'd light a fire, but I think it's too warm for that." He looked down at me as I sat. "Unless you're cold?"

I shook my head. I had heat running all over my skin. I was far from cold, but it had little to do with the weather. I looked around as Gavin headed for the kitchen. It wasn't until I'd studied three of the pictures on top of the mantel above the fireplace that I realized something strange. There weren't any personal pictures. None of him, of his daughter, or his fiancée. All the pictures were impersonal photographs or portraits. Still lifes, landscapes, that sort of thing. I could tell they were of things that he liked, but they still weren't of people who meant anything to him. At least not as far as I'd looked. Not that I intended to go snooping. Maybe it was too painful for him to have the pictures always there, staring him in the face.

"Champagne?" Gavin held out a glass of bubbly golden

liquid.

I took it and sipped. It was light and delicious, very similar to what we'd had at the club that first night together.

Gavin set down his drink on the glass coffee table in front of the couch, and slipped off his jacket. He draped it over the back of a nearby chair. When he untied his tie, I shifted in my seat, wondering how far he was going to go. He left the tie hanging, undone, and pulled his shirt from his pants.

"That's better," he said with a smile. He sat down next to me, not quite close enough for us to be touching, but at little enough distance that I could feel the heat from his skin. Though that might have just been my imagination.

I took a drink of champagne, letting it join the wine I'd already consumed. I was far from drunk, or even close to as tipsy as I'd been the first night Gavin and I had spent together, but the alcohol had taken enough of the edge off that my bold side felt like it could come out and play.

"I never did say thank you for your gift, did I?" My voice was low.

Gavin looked surprised. "You did."

I set down my half-finished drink and stood. "Not the files." I put my fingers on the top button of my blouse, and Gavin's eyes followed. "Your other present." I smiled. "Though I think it was just as much for you as it was for me."

Gavin's breathing quickened as I began to slowly unbutton my blouse. I made my movements deliberate, taking my time with each and every one. I didn't pull the material aside, instead letting it hang open, exposing just a thin strip of pale flesh and crimson lace. When I reached the last button above my skirt, I untucked my blouse, enjoying the way Gavin's eyes darkened at the quick flash of lingerie.

When I finished unbuttoning my shirt, I turned, then shrugged off the garment, letting it drop to the floor. I glanced over my shoulder at Gavin as I reached up and pulled out the clip that had been holding my hair up. The curls tumbled, hot and soft, over my shoulders. I shook them out, letting them fan across my bare skin until they hid most of my back from Gavin.

"Carrie," he breathed my name.

I didn't respond other than unsnapping my skirt and slowly lowering the zipper. I heard him make a sound as I let the skirt fall to the floor as well. The air was cool against my ass, reminding me that this was far skimpier than any panties I owned. I refused to be embarrassed. I'd seen what I looked like in this, and I let that image give me the courage to turn.

"Fuck." The word came out strained.

I smiled. "I'll take that as a compliment."

Gavin nodded. "You should." He leaned forward. "I knew it would look good on you, but this is more than I'd imagined."

I walked towards him, letting the lust in his eyes fuel the fire in my belly. When I was directly in front of his knees, he reached for me, but I shook my head. He looked puzzled, but dropped his hands. The moment I'd started undressing, I'd known what I wanted and I was going to have it.

I put my hands on his thighs, pushing them apart as I lowered myself to my knees. I could practically hear his pulse racing. I slid my hands up and down his thighs, loving the feel of his solid muscles beneath my palms.

There were two things I needed to know before I started, because they would determine just how far I got to go. I really hoped his answers would allow me to finish the way I wanted. I rarely had the guts to get this bold, and I wasn't sure if I would again.

"Were you planning on this being a long night?" I asked as my fingers flexed on the upper part of his leg. "Or once you've gone, are we done?"

He blinked, surprised by my question. I didn't think he'd quite figured out why I was asking, but that was okay. "Are you asking if I can go more than once tonight?"

I nodded.

He grinned. "I may need a little time to recover, but I plan on us spending a very long night together before we pass out."

That was good. I reached for the waist of his pants. Here was the awkward question. There really wasn't a good way to ask it, but I'd thought of something that would be at least tactful. It would also let me know if my fantasy about next week would be feasible.

I looked up at Gavin as I lowered his zipper. His eyes locked with mine as I tugged his pants lower on his hips, but I broke it to drop my gaze to the tight, black boxer-briefs he was wearing. The bulge told me that he'd been enjoying the show I'd put on, and that made me smile. I hooked my fingers under the elastic of the waistband and slowly pulled down his underwear.

My stomach and things even lower tightened as I revealed him. Black curls that were softer than they had any right to be. A base so thick that when he was fully aroused, I wouldn't be able to wrap my hand around it completely. The impossible combination of hard and soft, like silk-covered iron.

He was only half-hard now, his shaft resting against his hip, and already he was nearly as big as my largest previous lover had been. When he was fully erect, he rode the border between holy-fuck-that's-huge and there's-no-way-that'll-fit. Even after preparation, he was a tight fit. Without foreplay, he was too much, but I knew from experience just how good he could make even too much feel.

I ran my fingers over the hot flesh, smiling as it twitched beneath my touch. I wrapped my hand around him, and he was still soft enough that my fingers touched my thumb. My other hand moved between his legs to cup his balls, and he moaned. I worked him with my hands for a minute, feeling him swell and grow. Before he could get too big for me to be able to take much, I lowered my head.

He swore as my mouth engulfed him, taking almost all of

him in that wet heat. My tongue swirled around him, the flavor of him bursting across my taste buds, mingling with the leftover chocolate and the more recent champagne. Gavin's hand rested on my head, not pushing or even guiding, just brushing over my curls, his fingers twisting in them.

He was heavy on my tongue as I raised my head. My hand continued to stroke him, the motion nice and slow, keeping him at his full, impressive size. I looked up at Gavin and found his face flushed, his pupils blown wide. Now it was time to ask.

"Are there any reasons," I started, "that I can't finish this," I flicked out my tongue across the tip of him, "bare?"

He stared at me, as if he wasn't sure he understood what I was asking.

Okay, I was going to have to be blunt. "I want you to go in my mouth."

"Shit."

I continued, making my voice rhythmic, almost matching the pace my hand was using. "I want to feel you spurt across my tongue. Taste you. Swallow every last drop."

Gavin shuddered, as if my words were working him up.

"Is there any reason why I can't?" I hoped he was thinking clearly enough to understand that question at least.

He shook his head. "I'm clean." His voice was hoarse. "Carrie, you'd don't have to–"

"I know." I smiled. "I want to."

I lowered my head again, determined not to come up again until he was done. I released his balls and put my hand on his hip, a reminder for him not to thrust. My other hand remained wrapped around his base, working in a circular motion. I bobbed my head, hollowing out my cheeks every time I went up, the suction making Gavin writhe beneath me. His fingers twisted in my curls, sending little pinpricks of pain through my scalp, but I didn't care. I wanted to feel him come apart beneath me, wanted to know that I'd done this to him with just my mouth and hands.

The muscles beneath my palm twitched and his hips jerked, telling me he was close. I inhaled slowly through my nose and lowered my head further than before. The tip of him bumped against the back of my throat, and I fought my gag reflex. A moment later, the end of him slipped down my throat and my nose brushed against his curls. I swallowed once, twice, then began to raise my head, knowing I couldn't stay long. I didn't need to. Even as the head of his cock began to slide over my tongue, Gavin came. The thick muscle pulsed in my mouth, spilling his seed, and I swallowed. I could hear Gavin swearing and calling my name as I used my mouth and tongue to draw out every last drop, but it all seemed so far away. I was focusing everything in me on the taste and feel of him.

Finally, when I allowed him to slip from between my lips, spent and soft once more, I looked up at him. We were both breathing heavily, our skin flushed. Gavin reached for my face and brushed his thumb across my bottom lip. I smiled at him and he cupped my chin, drawing me towards him. His lips brushed against mine, and I assumed that would be it, but he surprised me. His tongue pushed for entrance and I opened my mouth to him. His arms wrapped around me, pulling me against him as his tongue plundered my mouth, exploring every crevice as if it were new. He didn't release me until my lungs were burning, and even then, he kept his arms around me, turning me so that he was cradling me on his lap.

"Wow," he said, his voice shaky. "That was... wow."

I smiled. "Glad you liked it."

"'Liked it'?" He echoed my words. He tipped my chin so that I was looking up at him. "Give me a minute to get the strength back in my legs and I'll show you just how much I liked it."

"So the night's not over?" I asked.

"Hell, no," he answered. The heat in his eyes felt like it could burn me if I wasn't careful. "We're just getting started."

NINE

When Gavin had taken me back to his room with the promise of reciprocation for what I'd done, this hadn't been what I'd had in mind. Not that I was complaining, just surprised.

The bed in Gavin's room wasn't nearly as big as the one at the club, but it was still king-sized, so that made it big enough for us both to be on it comfortably. The only light came from a lamp next to the bed. I had a feeling there was an overhead light that would be used for more mundane things like changing clothes and reading, but the lamp was perfect for sex. Just enough light to see by without being harsh and unforgiving.

Not that I'd know, because right now I couldn't see anything other than a faint red glow.

When we'd gotten to the room, Gavin had stripped out of his clothes while I watched – all right, while I'd ogled – but he'd shaken his head when I'd moved to take off what little I was still wearing. Instead, he'd had me climb to the center of the bed, stretch out on my back, and put my hands above my head.

He'd leaned over me with two red scarves in his hands. While he was tying my wrists with the first one, he'd spoken in a low, gentle voice. "I promise you that this will be amazing, but you have to trust me."

I'd nodded mutely. I was starting to get there with my heart, but I'd already decided that it was well worth the sexual trust. He'd never done anything that I hadn't loved, even when I'd been reluctant to admit it to myself.

"If you want me to stop, just say so," he'd continued. "I will, and I won't start again until you ask me to. I won't do anything that you don't want."

I'd nodded again, and that had been when he'd tied the other scarf over my eyes. It was thin enough that I wasn't in complete darkness, but I also couldn't truly see either.

When Gavin began to speak, his voice was like warm water caressing my skin. "One of the easiest ways to heighten sensation when having sex is by denying one or more of the other senses. Taking away sight makes your other senses sharper. Taking sound too would make it even more intense." I felt the heat from his body as he leaned closer to me. "But I wanted you to be able to hear me."

I shivered. I was glad I could hear him. I loved listening to him talk. He had one of those voices that I could listen to all day, the kind that could make me wet even if he was reading a grocery list.

"I'm going to teach you some of the ways you can react to touch," Gavin said. "And you're going to come harder than you've ever imagined possible. Only then will I fuck you."

I swore, my voice trembling almost as much as my body was. If this was going to be as intense as it sounded, I wasn't sure I was going to survive.

Something light and airy, just this side of tickling, made its way over the undersides of my arms. I giggled as it reached my armpits and then danced over the tops of my breasts. When it moved down my stomach and over my ribcage, I started to squirm. I wasn't very ticklish, but whatever Gavin was using was light enough to do it. Then he nudged my legs apart and I caught my breath. Whatever he had trailed over my inner thighs and I caught my breath. Little tendrils of pleasure crept up my legs straight to my core. I felt Gavin's finger brush against my leg as it hooked under the elastic of my panties, then there was cool air as he pulled the crotch of the panties aside.

"Dammit." My body twitched as those light tendrils brushed against my wet lower lips. It was too light for any real friction, but my skin was sensitive enough that it garnered a reaction. It played over me for a moment longer, then disappeared. I felt my underwear put back into place. The bed moved and I knew that Gavin had gotten up for something. A minute later, I felt it dip again under his weight.

"Have you ever heard of ice play?" Gavin asked, his tone almost conversational.

I shook my head. I hadn't heard of it, but I wasn't naïve enough to not be able to figure out the gist of it.

A moment later, I gasped as something hard and cold ran over the bare flesh of my breast. Gavin chuckled, that deep, purely male sound. My fingers curled into fists as I fought to keep my hands above my head. It wasn't easy. Gavin slid the ice cube over every exposed inch of my chest before dropping to circle one of my nipples. It hardened instantly, the combination of the cold and the friction from the now-wet material making my sensitive flesh into a hard little bullet point. I whimpered as he moved to the other one.

"Fuck!" I shouted as something wet and hot covered my nipple.

Gavin began to suck on the wrinkled flesh, sending jolts of pleasure straight through me. He worried at my nipple through the bra even as he circled the other one with the ice cube. A moment later, I was thankful that he'd thought to buy strapless lingerie. He pulled down the top of the bra, spilling my breasts from the confining material.

When the ice touched me again, I shivered, but it was more from anticipation than the cold. Every cell in my body felt the intensity of the cold moving through me, and when Gavin's tongue began to lick up the water, burning across my skin, I cried out. He alternated ice and mouth until I wasn't sure if I was hot or cold. My body was freezing and burning at the same time, ready to combust only to be brought back from the edge by the chill. I writhed against him, wondering what I looked like, my skin shining with liquid, my nipples hard and distended. Had he marked me with his mouth? Not being able to see him was more erotic than I'd imagined.

I gasped as the ice ventured into new territory. It slid over my belly, moving across the thin strip of silk that connected the top to the bottom. Droplets of water slid down my sides and were absorbed by the bedspread. I laughed as the ice circled my belly button, the sound catching in my throat when Gavin's tongue dipped into the water.

Gavin's fingers brushed over the places where the silk attached to the panties. I felt him do something, then there was give. Apparently, there'd been a hook connecting them. I didn't dwell on the thought, however, because Gavin was slowly peeling my panties off. When they were gone, he slid his hands up my legs, moving from my stockings to my bare thighs.

"I'm going to leave these on this time," he said. "I've been dreaming about feeling them against my skin when your legs are wrapped around me."

I swallowed hard as the now-exposed space between my legs throbbed. I wanted very much to wrap my legs around him now, draw him into me, but I knew it wasn't time yet.

Nearly painful cold shot through me and I cried out, my back arching, my hips twisting in an attempt to get away. Gavin's hands held me firm as he ran the ice cube up and down my slit. When he slipped it between my folds and it brushed against the top of my clit, my body convulsed. It was sharp and just this side of painful, almost like a bite, but with an edge of pleasure to it that took my breath away.

My hands tugged at their restraints as Gavin's mouth chased the ice, shocking my body with the sudden change in temperature. I couldn't take it. It was too much. I was just about to tell him that, to beg him to stop, when his lips wrapped around my clit and he pushed the rapidly melting ice cube inside me.

I wailed as an orgasm smashed into me. It wasn't the roll of a wave or even the sudden crescendo after a build. This was hard and fast, and I couldn't process it. Heat melted away the cold, but left in its wake a molten lava that coated every inch of my skin, leaving me raw. I could feel everything touching me. The fine hairs on Gavin's arms. The dips and whorls of his fingerprints where his hands held me down. Every fiber of the bra just under my breasts. The soft silk beneath me. Even the air had weight.

Gavin pressed his lips almost chastely against the top of my sex and that one extra sensation was enough to send me outside myself, rocketing towards that white-light bliss that would hold me until I could function again.

I was still shuddering when I came back to myself. The blindfold was still on, but my hands were untied. Gavin's arms were around me and I could feel him hard and ready against my hip. I reached down with one shaking hand and ran my fingertips over him.

"Carrie?" He made it a question.

I nodded. There was no way I'd be able to speak any time soon. I heard a rip, then latex moving over flesh. I rolled onto my back, spreading my legs as I went. He slid inside me slowly, the heat of his body burning away the last of the chill. I knew I could take off the blindfold now and see him as he moved above me, but I didn't. Instead, I gave myself over to it, letting my body absorb the sensations in a new way.

His breath puffed against my ear for a moment, then his lips were there, tugging at my earlobe. His stomach slapped against mine as I raised my hips to meet him, finding our rhythm. I hooked my legs on either side of his waist, rubbing my calves against his ass. The movement rocked me against him in a different way and little sounds began to fall from my lips.

My hands explored his body, my fingers seeing what my eyes didn't. The ridges of his muscles. The flat, wrinkled flesh of his nipples. The soft, fine hairs at the base of his neck. The way the muscles in his back and shoulders rippled beneath his skin as he thrust into me.

And then there was that. The in and out motion that pushed against parts of me never reached by anyone else. The way my body adapted to accept him, molded around him. I could feel places inside me I'd never felt before reacting to his touch. It wasn't just the friction, either; there was something else I couldn't name. All I knew was that it was greater than the nerves connected to the surfaces of that sensitive flesh. It ran somewhere deep, somewhere I'd never known existed until this moment.

Even as I thought it, Gavin was groaning against my neck and his hand was sliding between us to touch that place that would bring me with him. I clung to him as I joined him, and felt our bodies merge into one as we rode our pleasure together, each wave taking us higher than the last until I couldn't take any more. I let myself go even as I heard him saying my name.

TEN

At some point during the night, Gavin and I had moved under the covers and the blindfold had come off. I wasn't sure when it had happened, but it didn't matter. I was waking, warm and content.

And I could smell cinnamon and coffee.

I rolled over onto my back, my hand automatically sliding across the sheets next to me. I was alone in bed. I frowned even as I opened my eyes, and that's when I saw why Gavin wasn't in bed with me. He was standing next to the bed, wearing blue and green plaid boxers and nothing else. In his hands was a tray with food that I couldn't recognize from this angle.

When he set it down in front of me, I saw a plate with two of the gooiest, stickiest cinnamon rolls I'd ever seen. They were both lathered in thick, buttercream frosting and still steaming. A small bowl of fresh fruit, neatly sliced, sat to one side of the plate, and next to it was a small plate with two eggs, sunny side up. My stomach growled loud enough for me to blush, but Gavin didn't say a word. I shifted my gaze across the tray to the mug of coffee, and right next to it was a single rose. It was the most exquisite flower I'd ever seen. Pure, snow white with just the tips a deep, crimson red.

"Thank you." The words came out in a whisper. I reached out and brushed my fingers over the rose petals. They were as soft as they looked.

"You're very welcome." Gavin sat on the bed next to me. "Shall we share this amazing-looking food?"

"I thought you said you couldn't cook?" I teased.

"I can't." He grinned at me as he picked up one of the two forks. "It's room service."

"Room service?" I asked. "This isn't a hotel."

His grin widened. "No, but next door is."

I gave him a puzzled look, but didn't waste any more time asking questions. The food smelled far too good. The first bite of the cinnamon roll was just as good as I'd imagined.

"I send my out-of-town clients to the hotel and they give me... perks." Gavin took a bite of the roll, chewing as slowly as I was to savor the flavor. After he'd swallowed, he clarified, "I order their room service from time to time."

I leaned forward to take another bite and Gavin's gaze dropped. It was only then that I realized the sheet had fallen, exposing my breasts. I flushed and pulled it back up to cover myself.

Gavin reached for me, his eyes blazing in that way that made my mouth go dry. He slid a finger between the sheet and my skin.

"You have nothing to be embarrassed about." His voice was a soft caress. With a gentle tug, he pulled the sheet from beneath my hand, baring my flesh to the cool air. "I could stare at you for hours."

I shivered as he lightly traced across the top of my breast and down to my rapidly hardening nipple. He circled the dusky rose-colored flesh with his fingertip, then pulled his hand back. Without another word, he resumed eating. After a moment, I did the same, not bothering to cover myself again. I was still feeling a bit self-conscious, but the admiration I saw on Gavin's face was enough to keep it at bay.

We were halfway through our meal when Gavin broke the silence. "We should go away next weekend."

I stopped with my fork halfway in my mouth. I had to have misheard him. There was no way he'd just asked me to go on a trip with him.

Gavin either didn't seem to notice my silence or he was intentionally ignoring it. "A nice, romantic weekend in the Hamptons. What do you think?"

I was grateful that I had a mouth full of food. It gave me the opportunity to think as I chewed and swallowed. I loved the idea of spending an entire weekend with Gavin, and the fact that he wanted it to be someplace romantic made it all the more special. If he'd just wanted sex, all he would've have to do would be to ask me to come here. Taking me to the Hamptons, that meant something more. That was the kind of thing couples did.

"I'd love to," I said as soon as I could manage the words.

Gavin beamed. He leaned over and brushed his lips across my forehead. It was a chaste gesture, almost out of place, but I loved that he'd done it. While I enjoyed the passion and the sex, it was nice to know that he would do something nearly platonic. It made me feel like there was more to our relationship than just fucking.

"It's getting late," Gavin said. I could hear the reluctance in his voice. "I need to get ready for work."

I sighed. He was right. Our little bubble was nice, but it couldn't last. The real world was out there and we'd both have to face it sooner or later. "Me too." I didn't even want to think about the work I was going to have to do when I got in to the office. It had been worth it to put off doing those files last night, but that didn't mean I was looking forward to having to do them this morning.

Gavin stood and started towards the bathroom. I watched him go, my eyes drawn to his trim waist and firm ass. It may have been covered now, but I knew what lay beneath.

"You know." He paused in the doorway. "We could save some time if we showered together."

I froze for a moment, images of naked, wet Gavin dancing across my vision, and then I was moving. I tried not to look too eager, but the grin on Gavin's face told me that I might not have succeeded. When his hand closed around mine, I no longer cared if I'd looked like I was desperate for him. The truth of the matter was that I did want him, and the feeling was so intense that desperation was a fairly accurate description.

The bathroom was bigger than my bedroom. It followed the same warm tones that decorated the rest of the condo, and the brass fixtures matched that style. The shower itself was encased in glass, a separate entity from the tub that sat just a few feet away. For a moment, I wished Gavin and I had the time to indulge in a long, slow bubble bath. I could see it in my mind's eye, the soapsuds sliding across our skin...

The sound of water being turned on brought my attention back to the present. Gavin left the door open a crack as he removed his boxers. I wasn't sure when the rest of the lingerie Gavin had bought me had come off, but it had. The only thing I was wearing were my stockings and I had a feeling those weren't going to be good for much after this, not after having slept in them all night.

"Allow me," Gavin said as he knelt in front of me. He lifted one of my feet and I put my hand on his bare shoulder to balance. As he rolled the stocking down my leg, I realized that his position put him very close to other things, and my pussy throbbed. Two of my previous four lovers had gone down on me, but none of them had been even close to as skilled with their mouths as Gavin was.

Almost as if he could read my mind, Gavin turned his face

as he put one leg down and lifted the other. His breath was hot against my inner thigh, but he didn't close the distance. By the time he returned my foot to the cool tile floor, my skin was humming with anticipation.

"I think the water's warm enough." Gavin stood.

I let my gaze wander down his body as he turned. He wasn't fully erect, but knowing that just being near me had brought him to half-mast was enough to make me smile. I don't think it would matter how often we made love, I would always love that his body responded to me like that.

Gavin stepped into the shower and held his hand out. I followed him under the warm spray, letting the water rinse away the sweat and sex of the night before. I closed my eyes as the water soaked into my hair, keeping them closed when I heard the snap of a plastic lid and the fresh, clean scent of shampoo filled the steamy air.

A moment later, I felt Gavin's hands in my hair. I made a sound in the back of my throat as he began to massage the shampoo into my thick curls. I'd always loved having my hair washed, but I'd never had it done like this. As his fingers worked against my scalp, my hands began to slide across my skin. From one side of my stomach to the other. Over my belly button and just above the pale curls between my legs. Up to my breasts, cupping them, feeling their weight on my palms.

"All rinsed," Gavin spoke low in my ear, his voice merging with the sound of the water falling.

I turned towards him, opening my eyes at last. Every drop of water was a new sensation on my skin. I blinked through wet eyelashes and tilted my head to look up at him.

"My turn."

I held out my hand and he squirted some shampoo into it. I pressed gently on his shoulder and he went to his knees. His eyes closed as I began to work the shampoo into his hair. The strands were silky soft as they slipped between my fingers. I worked it into a lather and then began to rinse his hair clean. I smiled as I realized that we would smell alike today, and I was glad that he hadn't used something spicy. That would be a bit too obvious.

As the last of the suds swirled down the drain, Gavin's hands began to move up and down my legs, running from knees to hips. His head tilted back and he opened his eyes. With our gazes locked, he lifted my left leg and hooked it over his shoulder. Still looking at me, he leaned forward, opening his mouth so that I had no doubt about what was coming.

"Ah..." I sighed as he licked me. One long stripe, before settling to tease around my opening. All the while, his eyes were open and fixed on me. His hands held my hips as he kissed me, his tongue exploring my pussy as thoroughly as it ever had my mouth. It danced up to circle that little bundle of nerves and I cried out.

I fell back against the wall, barely registering the cool tile against my back. All I could feel was Gavin's mouth, his tongue and lips passing over sensitive flesh until I was a quivering mess, held in place only by the man between my legs. He sucked and licked until I was calling his name, begging him for release. The moment he slid a finger inside me, I began to come. Then he crooked it, brushing against that spot that made the world go white.

I wailed, not caring if anyone could hear me. My nails dug into his shoulders, deeper and deeper, until I knew he'd be bruised, but I couldn't let go. It was too much pleasure, too much sensation. I needed to get it out somehow.

Then, after what felt like an eternity, Gavin's hand and mouth were gone, my body empty and craving to be filled by something larger and thicker. My eyelids fluttered open as Gavin reached for the door.

"Where are you going?" I managed to ask the question. I

didn't care how late we'd be, I wasn't about to let him leave just yet.

He grinned at me. "I don't actually store condoms in the shower."

My body gave a long, low pulse. "Is that all?" I turned so that my back was to Gavin. "Don't."

I could almost hear him going completely still. This would be my choice, I knew. It hadn't been a full week, but I didn't want to wait anymore. I turned my head so I was looking over my shoulder at his startled face.

"I went on the pill."

His eyes widened and his breath caught in his throat. He wanted this too, but I could tell he was torn. He wouldn't want me to feel like I'd been forced into anything, so I had to make him believe that this was all me.

"I want you inside me, Gavin," I said. I slid my feet further apart. "I want to feel you, nothing else, nothing between us."

"Fuck," he groaned.

The door slid shut behind him and he crossed to me in two long strides. He pressed his body against the length of mine, his cock hot and heavy against the swell of my ass. His hands ran along the front of me, cupping my breasts, fingers tugging at my nipples until I was pushing back against him.

"Take me." The words came out almost involuntarily and I felt his body shudder against mine. I repeated them, "Take me."

His lips found the soft skin of my throat and began to work it even as I felt him nudge against my entrance. My fingers curled against the tiles as he buried himself inside me with one swift thrust.

I cried out at the sudden fullness, my body going rigid as it made room for the intrusion. He didn't pause, but rather began to withdraw right away, his thick shaft rubbing against me, the sensation new and welcomed. Skin against skin, our cells calling to each other, searching for the perfect match that existed only in another's body. His thrusts were hard and deep, each one nearly lifting me off of my feet.

I squeezed my eyes closed, wanting this memory forever imprinted in my brain. The way the water felt against my skin. How the heat wrapped us in a cocoon. The feeling of him sliding back and forth between my legs. His mouth on my neck, sucking on the skin there until I knew I'd have a mark. His arms holding me in place as he thrust up into me. The way the pressure was building inside me until tears streamed down my face, mingling with the rest of the water.

"Please, please," I begged without knowing what I was begging for. I could barely hear my own voice as I drowned in pleasure.

"Do you want me to come inside you?" Gavin whispered in my ear.

He pressed my body flat against the wall, trapping me between the heat of him and the cool of ceramic. He laid his arms across mine, his hands covering mine. I could feel the flex of his stomach against my back, the powerful thrusts of his hips.

"Do you?" he asked the question again and only then did I realize he wanted an answer. "Do you want me to come inside you?"

"Yes," I gasped out the word. My body tried to shudder, to shiver, but I couldn't move.

"Tell me." Gavin's voice was fierce, the kind of harshness that made me wet. "Tell me what you want."

I whimpered as his teeth scraped over the shell of my ear. I knew I should be embarrassed to say the words aloud, but I wasn't. I just knew what my body was craving and I couldn't lie about it.

"I want to feel you come inside me."

The words brought a primal near-growl from Gavin and my eyes rolled back in my head as the vibration traveled through me.

"I want to feel you pulse inside me, filling me." I was barely able to breath, but I forced the words out. I needed him to know the truth. "I want my thighs wet with your cum."

"Fuck." Gavin's fingers tightened around mine as his hips jerked against my ass.

I felt it then, what I'd been waiting for. The warmth of his seed spilling inside me. His cock emptying, not into some impersonal latex, but into me. It was amazing, everything I'd imagined, but it wasn't enough. I made a sound of pure frustration, desperate for that last little bit of friction I needed to finish. I started to drop my hand, to slide it between us. It wouldn't take much, I knew. One or two little touches to bring it to a head.

"No." Gavin's fingers closed around my wrist, shoving my hand back where it had been before. "I told you before."

Then his hand was there, right where I needed it, his fingers rubbing just right so that my climax finally arrived, ripping through me with hurricane force. As wave after wave of pleasure crashed over me, I heard Gavin's voice again.

"Mine."

He lowered us until we were sitting directly under the spray, my body cradled against his. I put my cheek against his chest, listening to his heart pounding in my ear. I could feel his cum trickling out of me, mingled with my own juices. As I finally caught my breath, I asked the question I'd meant to ask before when the subject had come up.

"You said 'mine.'" Okay, that wasn't a question, but I was pretty sure he'd know what I wanted to know.

I was right.

Gavin pushed wet hair back from my face. "When I'm with you, I want every part of you." His expression was somber, serious. "I don't mean it in some macho, caveman kind of way, but I want you to be mine. Every inch of your body to belong to me in that moment. To know that I'm the only one you're thinking of, that you're not fantasizing about some other man's hands on you."

I shook my head. "Never."

He smiled, but there was still a darkness in his eyes. "I want to possess you, but not control you, or make you into something you're not." He shook his head. "I'm not explaining it right."

I reached up and put my finger against his lips. "It's okay. I know what you mean."

And I did. I understood what he was trying to say, even if he couldn't express it himself. Saying "mine" and claiming me as his had nothing to do with bossing me around or degrading me. It wasn't about me belonging to him. It was about us belonging together. If I was his, then he was mine, and I liked that.

I put my hand around the back of his neck and pulled him down for a kiss. Just before our lips met, I whispered, "Mine." His eyes lit up and his mouth covered mine.

ELEVEN

It was tempting to stay in the shower until Gavin was ready for round two and then spend the rest of the day in bed, talking and making love. Neither one of us had used the "l" word or even truly made a declaration of what we were to each other, but I was feeling more on solid ground now than I had before. That feeling of trust grew when Gavin finished dressing first and told me to lock up when I left.

I stood, wrapped in a large brown towel, drying my hair and trying to wrap my head around what had happened. Not only had Gavin brought me back to his place, but he'd also felt comfortable enough to leave me here while he went to work. I think the quickest I'd ever left a boyfriend alone in my apartment had been after five months together. It wasn't like I'd thought they'd go through my journal or something, but there was something too personal about leaving someone in my space. And I'd never liked it when they'd left me at theirs. Until now.

When my hair was finally dry enough to manage, I wrapped it up, pinning it behind my head. I wished I'd brought clothes with me, but I hadn't thought I'd be spending the night. My stockings were a total wash, but at least my bra and panties were cleaner than the rest of my clothes. Before I put them on, however, I was going to work on the other essential. Make-up. Fortunately, I had brought some of that with me. Not much, but enough cover-up to mask the pair of hickeys Gavin had left on my neck. The one on my left breast was low enough that nothing I owned would reveal it.

"Next time," I muttered to myself. "We'll see how he likes having to wear make-up on his neck."

I wasn't really angry though. I liked the reminder of what we'd done, though the throbbing ache between my legs wasn't going to let me forget any time soon. He hadn't hurt me, but I was definitely going to be tender for a day or two. I'd had vigorous sex with a more than well-endowed partner too often over the past few weeks. Krissy was right. It was amazing I could walk right.

I laughed at that, then clamped a hand over my mouth at the sound. It was strange, knowing Gavin wouldn't be coming in to ask what was so funny.

I checked the mirror one last time and tossed my lip balm into my purse. Now to find my clothes. The search didn't take long, but what happened when I picked up my skirt from under the end table distracted me.

Last night, I hadn't been paying much attention to what was around the couch. I remembered thinking that he hadn't had anything personal around. Apparently I'd been preoccupied enough to miss these. Two simple silver frames. One held a picture of a much younger Gavin, dressed in a tux, standing with his arms around a beautiful blond girl. Judging by her dress and the corsage on her wrist, it was their senior prom. They were smiling and very much in love.

I smiled sadly as I put the picture back on the table. I wasn't jealous. How could I be? I knew what happened after that picture was taken, how many years they had together, the life they'd never have. Being jealous of a memory was petty and foolish.

I picked up the second frame. I didn't need anyone to tell me who this was either. She may have had her mother's fine, model-like features and straight pale blond hair, but those dark blue eyes were all Gavin.

I gently set the frame back down. My finger traced along the top of it. "You have a beautiful family." I whispered the words, unsure if I was speaking to Camille or to Gavin until I added, "I promise, I'll take care of them."

TWELVE

Have I mentioned before how much I hated being late? Today was even worse because, not only was I late, I was wearing the same thing I'd been wearing the day before, sans stockings. Fortunately, I kept a fresh change of clothes at the office – most interns, associates, and paralegals did – but that didn't mean I wasn't feeling the walk of shame on my way to my desk.

Leslie, Krissy, and Dena all stared at me as I hurried past them, and I refused to make eye contact. I could feel my cheeks burning as I grabbed my back-up pack from my bottom desk drawer and started towards the bathroom.

"Carrie!"

I froze. Shit. It was Mimi. I slowly turned, hoping she wouldn't be able to read my recent activities on my face.

"You're late."

"Yes, I am." I knew lying would just make things worse. "I'm so sorry–"

She waved a hand. "I don't want excuses. I want those reports."

"Right. The reports." Something very close to panic was threatening to take over.

"Where are they?" Mimi put her hands on her hips, the expression on her face more unfriendly than anything I'd ever had her direct at me.

I didn't know what to say. How could I tell her that I didn't do my work because I was too busy fucking her client's consultant? I stammered, "I–"

"Delivery for Carrie Summers."

I nearly squeaked in surprise, but managed to keep it to myself. "I'm Carrie Summers."

I turned towards the voice as I answered. A middle-aged delivery man walked towards me, two thick envelopes in his hands. I quickly signed for them, peeking at the sender information. Gavin. Praying that these were the files he'd shown me yesterday, I turned back to Mimi.

"I had to send for some files about some of the women Howard had been seen with," I said. "Express delivery of course."

"And the information I asked you to note chronologically for the meeting?" she asked.

"I'll have that for you in less than an hour," I promised. I wasn't sure how feasible that really was, but I was going to try.

"Since you were working late on the case, I'll cut you some slack this one time." Mimi pursed her lips and gave me a once-over. "Please tell me you at least have a change of clothes so you're not looking all rumpled in the meeting."

I held up the little black bag in my hand. "I was just heading to the bathroom to change."

Mimi nodded. "Good. The meeting's in ninety minutes. Have those notes with you when you come to the big conference room. And I'll expect the reports on Howard's women by the end of business today."

I nodded, eager to get started. When she turned, I hurried away.

New clothes and a little over an hour later, I was on my way to the conference room with the information Mimi had wanted in my hand. It had been crazy to get it together that quickly, but it was surprising sometimes just how much a person can do when they're motivated enough.

The meeting ended up running all the way to lunch, thanks to the opposing counsel, who appeared to be older than the law profession. He moved more slowly than anyone I'd ever seen before and before we were halfway done, I found myself wondering if he'd taken the fable of the tortoise and the hare to heart as a child. By the time everyone left and I finished tidying up the documents we'd spread across the table, I was starving. I'd eaten a good breakfast, but I'd also been very... active.

A small smile played across my lips as I allowed myself to remember what a great morning I'd had. It had been difficult not to let my mind wander during the meeting, so it was a little reward to myself to give in and enjoy a few moments before joining my friends for lunch. We made small talk as we ate, but it was clear that my relationship with Gavin was the real point of interest. I answered what I could without giving away what I thought Gavin wouldn't be comfortable sharing. Fortunately, they were more than willing to be distracted by me talking about my sex life.

It wasn't until we were riding the elevator back up to our floor that Dena asked the question I knew they'd all been wanting to ask. I had to admit, I was a bit surprised that she was the one who said it. She was the quiet one of my friends, the one who most easily faded into the background. Not because she wasn't beautiful enough to be noticed, but because she didn't have Leslie's or Krissy's flash. She never drew attention to herself and seemed to enjoy it that way.

"I have to ask, is this all about sex or is this something more?" Her pale eyes were serious, her expression one of concern. "I don't want to see you get hurt."

I smiled down at her. I wasn't tall, but Dena was the definition of petite. "Gavin and I haven't really had 'the talk,' but it's definitely more than sex." I gave her a sideways hug. "There's a connection between him and me that I've never had with anyone else."

"Just be careful," she cautioned.

"I will," I promised.

The doors opened and the moment was broken. It was time to get back to work. I headed back to my desk, working on refocusing on what I had to do next. I'd glanced at the files Gavin had given me, but hadn't really examined them. It was time to do that now.

It took me about five minutes to realize a similarity that had escaped me yesterday. All of the pictures in the files were professional. The poses, the quality, the lighting, it all spoke of someone who knew what they were doing. All of these women were taking model shots.

And that was the second thing I noticed. Even though every document I found stated that the women were at least eighteen years of age, a good third of them looked younger. Not just maybe a couple of months shy of being legal, but some looked like they were barely fifteen or sixteen.

Now, I knew there were some women who looked younger than their actual age. Dena was a perfect example. She was actually the oldest out of the four of us, having turned twenty-five nearly six months ago, but she still got carded when she tried to buy alcohol. If she'd dressed younger, I could've seen her passing for eighteen, maybe even sixteen.

That was when it hit me why the pictures of those younger women were making me so uncomfortable. If they were, in fact, eighteen or older, they'd intentionally been dressed to look younger. They didn't look like children, but whoever'd taken the photos hadn't done anything to give them the appearance of an adult. They looked like girls, not women.

It seemed as if the more I found out about Howard, the less

I liked him. I wasn't sure what that was going to mean for me and Gavin, but I did know that it didn't bode well for Mimi's case...or her crush. I needed to talk to some of these girls and find out how much damage control we needed to do.

I began to scour the documents for contact information, but there were no phone numbers, no addresses, no emergency contacts. No Social Security numbers were listed, and the birth dates alone would never give me what I needed, especially not if half of them were false, as I was beginning to suspect they would be. The names weren't going to be any help either. I'd done enough Internet research over the years to know how many hits would come up with a name that was anything less than unique. These girls were Jessica and Jennifer, Sarah and Allison. Even the ones with the more original names of Monique, Callie, and Tricia had last names that would give me hundreds of hits, and that was if they were from New York. If any of these girls had come in from another state, I'd never find them.

I'd just about given up when a name caught my eye. Patricia Vinarisky. The first name wasn't completely unique, but with that last name, it just might be enough.

I pulled up my web browser and typed in the name. Over three hundred results nationwide. Okay, that wasn't too bad. I just needed to narrow the search. It was possible that she wasn't from New York, but I was going to start here anyway. A moment later, three matches popped up. Much better. One link led me to a Patty Vinarisky who most definitely not the girl in the picture, since she'd been born closer to the turn of the last century rather than this current one. The second took me to a phone number listed for a Frank Vinarisky. The third hit a dead end. Since I couldn't do anything about the last one, the second one was the only chance I had.

I picked up my phone and dialed the number. After two rings, an automated message told met that Frank Vinarisky wasn't available and that I should leave my name, number, and a brief message.

"Mr. Vinarisky." I kept my voice brisk and business-like. "My name is Carrie Summers and I'm trying to reach a Patricia Vinarisky. If you know Ms. Vinarisky, could you please call me?" I left my number, saying it slow enough that I didn't need to repeat it.

I sighed as I hung up. Now all I could do was wait.

THIRTEEN

While I was waiting, I began compiling the other information Gavin had given me. Mimi was going to pitch a fit about this. Aside from the personal ramifications, she was going to be pissed when she saw what these were going to do to our case. If Howard's wife's attorney had even a fraction of this, we were through.

Before I could get too immersed in my work, my cell phone vibrated. I glanced at the screen, and my stomach did a flip when I saw Gavin's name. I figured the call was personal in nature, but since he did consult for a client, I felt only the slightest twinge of guilt when I answered.

"Hi."

That single word shouldn't have been able to thrill me as much as it did. "Hello." It was difficult not to lower my voice and make the conversation more intimate.

"I'm so sorry, Carrie," he began. "Howard just called me and told me that I have to go to Miami next weekend. There's a business meeting of some kind at his mansion on Star Island."

"Oh." I tried not to let my disappointment color the word too much, but he heard it anyway.

"I am so sorry," he repeated. "I really wanted to go away with you."

"Me, too." I hoped he didn't think I was pouting. There was no way I could tell him the truth, not here, and if I got up, I'd attract attention.

There was a moment of silence, then he asked, "You're at your desk, aren't you?"

"Yes." I glanced around, but no one was looking at me.

"So you can't really react or respond to anything I say, can you?"

I made a noncommittal noise. He chuckled, and the sound made me forget that I'd be spending next weekend alone rather than snuggled up with him in some romantic getaway.

"Then I guess you can't react when I say that I can't stand the thought of being away from you for that long, and I want you to come with me."

My heart did a funny little skipping dance.

"And you can't respond when I tell you that I'll only be working for a couple of hours and I want to spend the rest of our time split between the private beach and a very lavish guest room."

I searched for something innocent I could say. "That, uh, sounds good."

He laughed again. "Trust me, Carrie, what I want to do with you, to you, is so far beyond good."

My breath caught and it was all I could do not to make an embarrassing sound.

"I can't wait to stretch you out on the beach, rub lotion over every inch of that creamy skin of yours."

I closed my eyes, pressing my lips together.

"Maybe I'll even slide my hands underneath your top, make sure those beautiful breasts of yours don't get burned."

Okay, closing my eyes was making it worse because now I could visualize what he was saying.

"Would you let me kiss you, cover your body with mine?" His voice had taken on that husky sound that it got when we were in bed together. "What if I pushed aside that thin strip of fabric that covered you, slid my finger into that tight, wet heat?"

Fuck. What was he doing? What was I doing? I could feel my entire body heating up.

"Would you let me take you, right then, right there on the beach? Fuck you out in the open—"

I jumped when my office phone rang. A wave of relief mingled with disappointment washed over me. "I have to go, Gavin. I need to take that call."

"Okay." He sounded amused. "But I'll want answers to those questions."

I grabbed for the receiver even as I ended the call. My mind was so muddled that I completely forgot to say the business line in greeting.

"Hello?"

"Carrie Summers?"

It was an unfamiliar man's voice.

"Yes?" I desperately tried to clear the hormone-induced fog in my brain.

"This is Frank Vinarisky."

"Oh, hello, Mr. Vinarisky."

Before I could say anything else, he cut in. It was only then that I recognized the tension in his voice.

"How do you know Patricia? Have you seen her?"

"Seen her?" I echoed his words, not understanding.

"I don't know what kind of game you're playing, Ms. Summers, but I don't have the time or patience for it. What do you know about Patricia?"

"I'm not following, Mr. Vinarisky. I'm sorry. I was calling to speak with her."

He gave a laugh so bitter than I winced. "That might be

difficult, Ms. Summers, since Patricia's been missing for more than two years."

FOURTEEN

I sat at my desk, frozen, my phone against my ear. I had to have misheard, right? There was no way I'd just stumbled on a former companion to Howard Weiss being missing for two years. It was like something out of a made-for-TV movie.

"I'm sorry, Mr. Vinarisky. Did you say that Patricia was missing?" I hoped my voice sounded more natural to him than it did to me.

"Two years ago last month," Frank Vinarisky said. "Are you seriously trying to tell me that you didn't know? Why would you be calling unless, you knew something about her kidnapping?"

"She was kidnapped." I made it a statement rather than a question because I had a feeling Frank would think I was patronizing him, but he still took it poorly.

"Of course she was kidnapped! My daughter is a sweet, innocent girl. She wouldn't have run away, no matter what anyone says." His voice was getting louder and more intense.

"I truly am sorry, sir. I didn't know."

"Bullshit!" Frank practically shouted the word, and I

winced. "You have to know something! How did you find out about my daughter? How did you know to call me?"

"I'm sorry." I repeated the only thing I could say. I couldn't tell him that I'd been led to his daughter's name through a client. I might not have been Howard's actual attorney, but I was still a part of the law firm that represented him and I couldn't violate attorney-client privilege, especially when it was just based on speculation.

"If you know something, you have to tell me!"

I didn't say anything. What could I say? Sorry, sir, I found your daughter's picture when I was researching the possibility of affairs for a rich, womanizing client. I didn't think that would go over well.

"You tell whoever you work for that I will find out what happened to my daughter, and they're going to pay."

The line went dead as Mr. Vinarisky ended the call. I set down my receiver and stared at the phone for nearly a full minute. That hadn't gone like I'd thought it would at all. A missing daughter and an angry father. Files on ordinary women who were seen in pictures with Howard, but didn't seem to have any other sort of media presence. In this day and age, that alone was suspicious.

I closed my eyes and inhaled slowly, calming myself. I hadn't been afraid – no point to that on a phone call, since it wasn't like he could've hurt me – but my heart was racing nonetheless and my hands were trembling. I counted to twenty, then opened my eyes. Better. I still felt a bit shaky, but I was in control.

I needed to figure out what was going on.

I went back to the stack of magazines and began to look for Patricia's picture. I needed to know when she'd been photographed with Howard. The picture or pictures were probably in Gavin's file, but I wanted to find my own copy. I needed a file that I knew hadn't been tampered with. Not that I was accusing Gavin of doctoring photos. He wouldn't do that, but I wasn't sure I could put it past Howard to hire someone to plant false information if he'd had anything to do with Patricia's disappearance.

It took me a few minutes, but I finally found the magazine I'd been looking for. The picture was huge, taking up half a page. The caption didn't mention Patricia by name, but it was her. And the date of the event she'd attended had been two and a half years ago, months before she'd disappeared, according to her father.

I breathed a sigh of relief. None of these no-name women had appeared with Howard for more than a month. He'd moved on by the time she'd vanished. Maybe that was why she'd disappeared. Maybe she'd left the city because she'd been heartbroken. Her father had said she was sweet and innocent. I could only imagine what Howard's indifference would've done to a girl like her. It could have been enough to make her behave contrary to her usual manner.

My eyes fell on another picture of Howard with an unnamed woman. She, too, was in the files Gavin had given me. A horrible thought struck me. What if she'd disappeared too? What if all of these no-name women had vanished after their encounters with Howard? They weren't celebrities. Only their families would miss them – if they even had families – and who would take a distraught father seriously? I could hear the police telling parent after parent that their twenty-something daughters were just out having fun, that there was no reason to suspect foul play. With so many obviously violent crimes to solve, these missing girls would just get shoved aside.

What did it mean if more of these women were missing? I leaned back in my chair. Did that lead directly to Howard, or could it be a bizarre coincidence? And what about Gavin? What was his role in all of this?

As always, when I thought of him, the image of his face

floated through my mind. The way his eyes darkened when he was aroused. The smile that wasn't slick and charming, but boyish and sweet.

No. I shook my head. No, he wouldn't be involved in anything so shady. I was speculating rather than letting actual evidence lead me to a conclusion. I wasn't a detective. I was a lawyer. I had to go where the facts led me, and the fact was, Gavin wasn't stupid. Why would he give me a file on Patricia if he knew anything about her disappearance? That wouldn't make any sense. If I was going to accuse anyone of anything, I would need a hell of a lot more proof than what I had here.

I closed the files and put everything into a nice, neat stack. I had a report to type and I had to include only facts, not speculation. I pulled up my program, sat with my fingers on the keyboard for a moment, and then began to type. As uneasy as I felt about Howard, I had to be honest and conclude that there was no evidence of infidelity. If I hadn't found receipts or records about any of these women, celebrities or otherwise, I doubted Howard's soon-to-be-ex-wife would be able to find anything either. I wrote out all of my findings and conclusions, sent a copy to the printer, and emailed the file to Mimi. I really hoped this case closed quickly. I was tired of researching Howard Weiss.

My head was starting to hurt. I closed my eyes and rubbed my temples. I had far too much going on in my head at the moment. The initial disappointment when Gavin had to cancel our plans, then the excitement of him asking me to come with him to Miami. Then his titillating conversation, which had been interrupted by Frank Vinarisky. That had thrown a whole other set of emotions and thoughts into play. And now a missing girl.

I was starting to miss my boring old life.

I opened my eyes again. I may have finished my report for Mimi, but I wasn't done with those files of Gavin's. I needed to find out more about Patricia's disappearance. It could lead nowhere, or it could lead back to Howard, but it didn't matter. I just needed to know what had happened to her. Part of it was because I couldn't stop thinking about Mr. Vinarisky and how much pain had been in his voice, but another part was just who I was. One of the reasons I'd wanted to become a lawyer was because, eventually, I wanted to be able to take on cases for victims and families of missing and exploited women. The cause had always been close to my heart, and Patricia's disappearance was striking a chord with me. I might not be a lawyer yet, but I could still investigate and see if I could find something.

I just needed a better place to start than Frank Vinarisky's phone rant, or even Gavin's file. I needed to know about the actual disappearance, and that meant police records. If the case was still open, there was no way I could get to them short of a subpoena, but I didn't have anything close to enough evidence to make that kind of request, even if I had been a lawyer. I frowned. How could I get those files?

Suddenly, an idea popped into my head. It was crazy, but it just might work. I picked up my phone and crossed my fingers.

FIFTEEN

It was getting late, and I knew Gavin had to get up early to leave for Miami first thing tomorrow morning, so when my phone rang, I wasn't expecting it to be him. My heart did a funny little skipping thing when I saw his name and I wasn't able to keep the eagerness out of my voice when I answered.

"Hi."

"Hi yourself." Gavin sounded amused. "I just wanted to call to give you the details about tomorrow."

"Details?" I'd just assumed he'd have a ticket waiting for me for the evening flight to Miami. That was how Mimi usually did her business flights for clients.

"You didn't think I was going to have you fly commercial, did you?" His tone was teasing.

"I-I," I stammered, unsure how to answer the question.

"I figured as much." He was enjoying this far too much. "No, Carrie, that's not how I do things."

"Okay then," I countered. "How do you do things?"

"Well, the first thing you need to know is that you'll be taking a private jet."

It wasn't like I didn't think he could afford it, but that wasn't cheap. I shifted uncomfortably on the couch. I wasn't sure if he was trying to impress me or bragging. I didn't really like either one.

"And you'll be coming directly from work. I have a limo scheduled to pick you up after work and take you to the plane."

"Gavin, you don't have to—"

"I know," he cut off my protest. "I want to do this. The earliest commercial flight available after work wouldn't be until nine o'clock, and I don't want to miss any more time with you than I have to."

What was I supposed to say to that?

"Now, I've also arranged for you to take an extra hour on your lunch break tomorrow for you to go shopping."

"Excuse me?" The private jet was one thing, but I hadn't expected something out of a Hollywood-hooker montage.

"Saturday evening is a very exclusive party, even more exclusive than the gala, and I want you to outshine every person there." His voice lowered. "Not that I don't think you'd be the most beautiful woman there no matter what you were wearing."

"I can wear the same dress I wore to the gala," I protested.

"Many of the same people will be there, and you can't wear the same dress twice to events like these. This is my gift to you, Carrie," he said. "Don't pack anything. I want you to buy everything new. Bathing suit. Casual clothes. A dress for Saturday night. Lingerie."

The last word made my stomach twist. I'd never been much of a fancy lingerie kind of girl, but what he'd bought me before had whetted my appetite for it. Still, I couldn't accept. "I can't let you buy me clothes for an entire weekend."

"If you won't let me do it for you, then will you do it for me?" he asked. "I love seeing you in beautiful, expensive things. And I love taking them off of you even more."

I closed my eyes. Shit. He knew how to say the right things to get my thoughts going in a lower direction.

"I'll be sending a driver – just a car, not a limo – at noon. He'll take you to a boutique where I have an account. They've already been told you're coming and that you can have anything you want."

I was getting flashes of a certain long-legged red-headed prostitute making her way through high-priced Beverly Hills stores. It didn't help with my recurring feelings of having my "services" bought and paid for.

"These are gifts, Carrie, not payment." Gavin displayed his uncanny knack for knowing what I was thinking. "If I had less money, maybe I'd only be able to buy you a pretty dress, but I have the money. Let me buy you these things."

"Okay." I let out the word in a breath, hoping I wouldn't regret my decision.

"You should take Krissy with you. Make it a fun little excursion. I cleared that with Mimi too, just in case. And make sure Krissy gets something for herself, too."

I wasn't sure if that made me feel more or less like a hooker.

"Speaking of clothes." Gavin's voice changed into something deeper, more authoritative, the kind of voice that made me instantly wet. "What are you wearing right now?"

"Pajamas," I answered automatically, not really thinking about what I was saying or why.

"Describe them to me."

A thrill went through me. I knew where this was going. "Give me a minute," I said, getting to my feet. "I'm in the living room. Let me get to my room."

"No."

I froze mid-step. He couldn't be serious.

"Is Krissy in the living room with you?"

"No," I squeaked. My face flamed at the sound. "She pulled an all-nighter last night. She's already asleep."

"Good. Put on your Bluetooth and sit down on the couch, feet on the floor."

I had a choice here. I could either pretend I was doing what he wanted and head back to my room to continue what I was sure would be a fantastic conversation, or I could follow his instructions to the letter.

I went back to the couch and positioned myself accordingly. I put my headset in my ear and set my phone down on the seat next to me. My heart was thudding so loudly that I was sure Gavin would be able to hear it.

"Now, describe what you're wearing."

I looked down at my very unsexy outfit. Again, I chose the truth rather than a lie. "Gray sweatpants, and an oversized, light pink t-shirt."

"Bra and panties?"

My face grew hotter even though I knew he couldn't see me. "No."

He chuckled and I shivered as the sound caressed my skin. "I want you to do exactly what I say."

"Okay." I closed my eyes, shutting out the living room around me. If I was going to be able to get through this, I needed to stay in my head, and I couldn't do that staring at the blank television screen.

"Slide your hands under your shirt and play with your tits."

I bit my bottom lip as I did what he said. My hands moved under my shirt, fingers squeezing and teasing.

"Pull and twist your nipples until they're standing up."

I heard the unmistakable sound of a zipper. I began to roll my nipples between my thumbs and forefingers. Each time I tugged on them, little jolts of pleasure went through me and I could feel myself growing wetter with each passing moment.

"The thought of you playing with those beautiful breasts turns me on." Gavin's voice had an edge to it that I recognized. That was the sound he made when I touched him. "Are your nipples hard?"

"Yes," I whispered. I could picture him in my mind's eye.

He'd be completely clothed, sitting in a chair. His pants would be open, his thick, swollen cock in his hand. It was too big for me to get my hand around it, but his hands were bigger. He'd move his fist up and down over the silky flesh, each stroke making him harder than before.

"Good. Keep one hand working your nipples and slide the other one into your pants. Down between your legs."

I spread my legs further apart as my fingers skimmed over my sensitive flesh.

"Touch yourself," he said. "Rub your clit. Plunge your fingers into your wet pussy."

I moaned when my index finger brushed over my clit. I'd touched myself before, of course, but never with someone telling me what to do. It was different.

"I want you to think about me when you're fucking yourself." His breathing was growing ragged. "Imagine that it's me touching you, fucking you. My fingers inside you."

I slid my middle two fingers into my pussy and whimpered. I was tight.

"Stretching you, getting you ready for my cock."

The heel of my hand rubbed against my clit as my fingers moved in and out.

"I'm thinking about you," he said. "Imagining that I'm thrusting into that tight heat, feeling you grip me like a glove."

"Yes," I moaned the word. The pressure was building inside me, growing with each stroke of my fingers, each twist and tug to my nipples.

"There are so many ways I want to take you."

I could hear the strain in his voice and knew he was getting closer. I moved the hand between my legs faster. I wanted to come with him.

"Up against the wall in an elevator so that when the doors open, everyone will see your clothes disheveled and know what we were doing."

My teeth fastened on my bottom lip. If he kept going, I didn't know if I'd be able to stay quiet.

"In a hot bubble bath. In the backseat of a car at a drive-in like a couple of horny teenagers."

Each phrase flashed an image behind my eyelids and pushed me that much closer to my release.

"Bent over the back of a chair. Stretched out on a Persian rug in front of a roaring fire. On a blanket in a forest clearing." He groaned. "So many places and ways I want to fuck you."

"Yes," I gasped. "Please. Please." I didn't know if I was begging for him to follow through or for him to keep talking so I could climax.

"I want to kiss every inch of you. Taste you on my tongue. Mark your body with my mouth."

I moaned. I wanted that too. I wanted him to do that to me and I wanted to do it in return to him. I could almost taste him, feel the weight of his cock in my mouth.

"How many fingers?"

I almost didn't register his question. As it was, it took me a moment to answer. "Two."

"Add another."

I didn't even hesitate, and the moment my index finger squeezed in next to the other two, that last little bit of stimulation was enough to tip me over the edge. I yanked my shirt up to my mouth and bit down on it, the material stifling my cries as my body shook. I heard Gavin cry out my name and knew that he'd come too. The picture of him holding himself, cum spilling over his fingers, was enough to send another ripple of pleasure over me.

We sat in relative silence, the only sound our heavy breathing as we began to come down. After a moment, Gavin broke it.

"The next time we do that, I want to see you."

I didn't argue. That sounded like a pretty good idea to me.

SIXTEEN

"Carrie. Earth to Carrie!"

I jumped, startled. Krissy stood in front of me, an amused expression on her face.

"Where in the world did you go just now and can I join you?"

I flushed. I'd been having a difficult time concentrating all day. If I wasn't being distracted by thoughts of what Gavin and I were going to be doing all weekend, it was the memory of my "conversation" with him the night before. Before I'd left for lunch, I'd had to borrow panties from my recently replenished back-up pack and change in the bathroom, because the underwear I'd put on this morning was thoroughly soaked.

"Never mind," Krissy said with an eye roll. "You were thinking about Gavin. It was dumb of me to ask."

I let the comment stand. No need to let her know the details. She'd never let me live it down if she found out I'd had phone sex in the living room while she'd been asleep in her bedroom.

"I have dresses for you to try on." She held out an armful of dresses that ranged from simple to glamorous. The bathing suits she'd already selected were hanging up on the rack the boutique owner had given me when I'd arrived. And, yes, that was *suits*, plural. While I was still uncomfortable spending Gavin's money, Krissy didn't seem to have a problem with it. She'd insisted that I get three different suits so I'd have one for Saturday, one for Sunday, and a back-up, just in case. I wondered if Gavin had known what he'd gotten himself into by letting Krissy come with me.

I took the dresses into the back room and Krissy followed. This wasn't a typical dressing room where there were half a dozen tiny rooms with doors. This boutique was the kind that had just two large rooms, both split in half so that one person could change, then come out into the other half of the room and model for whoever was out there. I'd never seen anything like it. Then again, I'd never been in a clothing store that had to buzz you in, and sold everything from lingerie and bathing suits to sundresses and evening gowns.

"So, how many women do you think Gavin sends here?" Krissy's tone was conversational, but I could hear the negative undercurrent.

"How long have you wanted to ask that question?" I pulled on the first dress and immediately frowned. Definitely not. I took it off and hung it on the "discard" hanger.

"Since you told me he has an account here," she admitted. "He probably sends his escorts from the club here before they meet their billionaire dates. Makes sure they have the slinkiest dresses and sexiest lingerie."

"It's not like that," I said. I zipped up the side of the dress. Not bad. The color was good and it fit well without being too tight. I stepped out to let Krissy see how it looked.

"If you say so." Krissy shrugged. She nodded as she gave me a once-over. "That's a keeper."

"I thought you liked Gavin," I said as I went back into the room to try on the next one.

"I do," Krissy said. "But I don't like that he has an account at a boutique. Just seems a bit shady to me."

"He said you can get something too." I'd forgotten to tell her that.

"Oh, well, in that case..."

I could imagine her grinning and laughed softly. Maybe Gavin had known what he was doing with her. I went out in the next dress, a cute pale blue sundress.

"Maybe," she said.

I went back to switch it out for a dark green mini-dress. "Hey, I almost forgot, you know how Mimi had me looking through those pictures of Howard with the different women?"

"Yeah?"

"I did a follow-up on one of them, Patricia Vinarisky." I scowled as I tried to reach the zipper and failed. I stepped out and turned around. Krissy didn't need me to ask, so I continued with my story as she zipped me up. "Turns out, she came to the city three years ago when she was just eighteen, and ended up getting signed to some modeling agency a few months later. The pictures with Howard show up about six months after that."

"Okay, so Howard likes them barely legal." Krissy eyed me critically as I turned in front of her. "Makes him a bit sleazy, but that doesn't really shock me."

"Here's the thing," I said. "Two years ago, only a couple months after those photos were taken, Patricia disappeared."

"What do you mean, 'disappeared'?"

"I mean she completely vanished. No one's seen or heard from her since. No credit card activity. Her apartment was untouched until her prepaid rent ran out. No calls on her cell or the landline in the apartment. No bus, plane, or train tickets, and she didn't have a car. She disappeared."

Krissy gave me a suspicious look. "That's an awful lot of information to have gotten with just an Internet search."

I grinned. "I didn't say that's how I got it."

She sighed. "That's a maybe dress. Go try on the next one."

As I walked back into the other room, she continued, "Now tell me where you got all that information."

I was glad I wasn't out there with her. She wasn't going to be happy about this. "It was in the police file."

"And how did you get access to that?"

I put on the next dress. "You remember Pete Connors? That detective you dated a couple years ago?"

"Yes." The word was clipped.

"Well, I kind of told him you'd have a drink with him tomorrow."

"You did what?" Krissy barely managed to keep her voice down.

I stepped out into the other room. "Come on, Krissy, he's a sweet guy. And not bad-looking either."

She glared at me.

"That golden blond hair." I tried doing to her what she always did to me when I was mad at her for something like this. "Those pretty green eyes. And he's really fit."

"He goes to comic book conventions," she countered as she crossed her arms.

"I seem to remember you telling me that he was... well-endowed." For once, I didn't blush. "And he certainly made you scream."

"He lives with his mother, Carrie. He's twenty-nine and lives with his mother."

"He's a good guy, Krissy." I dropped the teasing tone and went with serious. "When we talked before, you asked why you couldn't find a guy like Gavin. I said maybe the problem was that you were looking for the wrong type of guy. Well, Pete's the right kind of guy."

Krissy sighed. "Whatever. I'll get a drink with him, since he obviously already gave you the information."

"Thank you." I held out my arms and twirled. "Keep?"

"Yeah." Krissy didn't sound quite so enthused.

"I want to look for this girl, Krissy." I didn't need to explain my reasoning to her. She knew how I felt about cases like this.

"You're a paralegal, Carrie, not a cop." Her words could've been harsh if her tone hadn't been gentle.

"I know," I said as I went back in for the last dress. "But if I can find something new, maybe it'll help the cops find her." I paused as I switched dresses, then I asked, "Do you think it's possible Gavin or Howard could be involved?"

"Gavin?" Krissy sounded surprised by the question. "No. I've seen how he is with you. I don't think he'd ever hurt a woman."

"And Howard?" I stepped back out.

"Howard?" she repeated, a thoughtful expression on her face. "Maybe."

My eyes widened. I'd expected her to tell me I was reaching or imagining things. I hadn't expected any form of agreement.

"There's just something about him," she said.

I nodded. I knew what she meant. I couldn't put my finger on it, but I didn't trust him. And it wasn't like with Gavin, where my head told me to use common sense and my body wanted to give myself over to him completely. Every fiber of my being told me that I shouldn't believe a word Howard said.

We continued clothing selection in a much more somber mood than we'd begun, but by the time we'd finished and Krissy had her own expensive new dress, some of the previous levity had returned. As we took the rack to the front of the store, I wondered out loud where I was going to keep all of the bags at work.

"Oh, Ms. Summers, didn't Mr. Manning tell you?" The

saleswoman appeared so suddenly that I jumped. She either didn't notice or was too polite to say anything.

"Tell me what?" I was almost afraid to ask.

"He asked us to have your purchases taken directly to the plane so you wouldn't have to worry."

I saw Krissy grin and had to shake my head in near exasperation. "Of course he did."

SEVENTEEN

If I'd thought it was difficult working that morning, it was nothing compared to the agony that followed my two-hour lunch-slash-shopping spree. To make matters worse, it seemed like everyone knew about my trip. Obviously Mimi had known because Gavin had called her about letting Krissy and me take the extra hour, but when we headed for our desks, we were on the receiving end of some very interesting looks.

Leslie and Dena made no effort to hide their jealousy, but it was the same kind of jealousy we shared when one of us ended up with a great guy or an awesome pair of new shoes. We wished it was us, but we didn't resent the other's good fortune. They, of course, knew the details because I'd filled in all three of my friends about the entire trip. Some of our other coworkers, however, weren't being quite so generous. And based on some of the mutterings I was hearing, the rumors were flying.

Mimi was pimping me out to clients.

I had some sort of blackmail on Mimi or a client.

Some rich old client was now my sugar daddy.

My personal favorite was one I overheard when I walked into the restroom and two other paralegals were talking between stalls. They'd heard that Krissy and I were running a brothel out of the law office and Mimi was covering for us for a cut of the profits. That rumor was my favorite, because I just stood outside the stalls and waited for the women to come out. I wasn't sure whose reaction was funnier, Jerrica who squeaked and ran back into the stall, or Meghan who tried to walk defiantly past me and tripped over her own two feet, almost face-planting right there on the tile floor. When I told Krissy the story, she laughed until she cried.

As entertaining as I found the entire thing, it was wearing, and I was only too glad when the day was done. Still, I hung back for a couple of minutes, waiting for the majority of people to clear out. Gavin had said he was sending a limo for me. If the people I worked with saw me get into a limo after everything else, there'd be no end to the rumors. While they might suspect it was for me if they saw it outside, there was still room for reasonable doubt – a defense attorney's bread and butter – and I could deflect any questions.

My friends waited for me, taking their time tidying up their desks and double-checking that they'd finished all of their work. When only a handful of people remained, the four of us headed for the elevators together. I almost laughed as they formed a little knot around me, keeping up a constant stream of chatter so that no one else had the chance to ask me any questions. Well, Krissy and Leslie did most of the talking, but Dena's presence was just as important, keeping yet another body between me and my would-be interrogators. That was one of the downsides of working at a law firm, particularly one that specialized in divorce. Everyone loved a good scandal, and they were good at ferreting them out.

While we stepped outside, the limo was indeed waiting, as were half a dozen of the biggest office gossips. I sighed. I could keep walking, pretend that it wasn't for me, and just take a taxi to the airport. I knew Gavin would hear about it, and it would be a slap in the face to treat such a kind gesture with what would look like disdain, but I really didn't want to give my coworkers more fodder.

"Don't you dare," Krissy hissed.

I looked over at her, startled.

"I can read you like a book, Carrie," she said. "And don't you dare walk away from that limo because you're worried about what some blabbermouths are going to say about you."

"She's right," Leslie said. "You care about Gavin, and he obviously cares about you. You didn't ask for any of this."

"Who cares about them?" Dena spoke up. "You know yourself, and you know how you feel about Gavin. Don't let anyone taint that."

As usual, my quiet friend had hit the nail on the head. I'd been telling myself that I didn't want people to think Gavin was buying me, but that wasn't the real reason his gifts made me uncomfortable. Every woman has that little voice inside her that's made up of every vicious attack she's had in her whole life. Mine was constantly telling me that I was lying to myself, that I didn't really care about Gavin, that I was only after him for the things he could give me. Of course, that meant I had to prove that voice wrong and refuse as much as I could. I couldn't accept anything without wondering if my motives were pure, or if I was turning into Samantha.

Samantha had been my best friend in junior high, and she'd loved manipulating men into doing things for her. She'd tried to convince me that men deserved to be used and that any woman who said they didn't want gifts from a man was lying. She said it so often that by the time we parted ways sophomore year, I was constantly second-guessing myself, wondering if I was just using the men in my life.

Krissy snapped her fingers in front of my face. Apparently I'd been overthinking things. Not exactly a surprise.

"Get in the limo," she said firmly. "Get on that private jet, wear those fabulous clothes, soak up the Florida sun, and have wild, kinky sex with your man."

I rolled my eyes, feeling only the slightest hint of a blush. Maybe I was getting more comfortable in my skin after all. I nodded. "All right. I'm going."

As I approached the limo, the driver climbed out and came around the car to the back door. He opened it, giving me a little bow of his head. "Ms. Summers."

I stopped before getting inside, a question occurring to me. "How did you know who I am? Or did you just assume whoever walked up would be me?"

One side of his mouth tipped up in a half-smile. "Mr. Manning sent a photograph to my employer so that I would know what you looked like." He paused, then added, "And Mr. Manning warned me that you might have a bit of an... attitude."

I grinned. "I suppose I do." I climbed into the back seat. I hoped Gavin had sent my photograph from the company's website, because the only other photograph I could think he'd have would be one he'd taken himself. I didn't remember him taking any pictures.

I stared out the window, pondering pictures, as we drove toward the airport. It wasn't until we started turning away from the main entrance to the airport that I noticed we'd arrived.

"Where are we going?" I asked. "Don't we have to go through that way?"

"No, Ms. Summers," the driver said. "That entrance is for commercial flights. Since Mr. Manning's jet has its own runway we can drive straight to it. And because it's not an international flight, you can bypass customs and all of that completely."

I hadn't thought of that. There really were advantages to having money. We pulled up next to a huge plane. Okay, it wasn't as big as any of the commercial airliners I could see on the other runways, but it was definitely big enough to make me feel small. Back home in Alabama, there were men who bragged that they had planes, but those were little two-seaters, barely anything more than a hang glider. This, however, was a real jet.

The driver opened my door and held out a hand to assist me. I took it and let him help me from the car. I couldn't take my eyes off the plane. The door to the jet was open and stairs had already been pushed up against it. A man in a pilot's uniform was standing at the top of the stairs.

I thanked the driver and headed for the stairs. I was starting to feel like Cinderella must've felt when she was on her way to the ball. The new wardrobe. The unexpected transportation. And, of course, the handsome prince waiting for me.

"Ms. Summers," the pilot nodded at me as I walked past him and into the plane.

I stopped just a few steps inside and stared around me in awe. This wasn't like any other airplane I'd ever been on; it was like something out of a movie. There were no rows of seats, or other passengers for that matter. A pleasant-looking woman in a navy blue pantsuit stood nearby, and on the other side of the cabin was a handsome man wearing khakis and a blue dress shirt the same color as the woman's outfit. The entire space was done in beige with that blue trim. The furnishings were more lavish than what I had in my apartment. Half a dozen plush chairs flanked by little side tables, a bigger table with four high-backed chairs around it, and a full bar. A couch sat across from a flat screen television, and a shelving unit beneath the TV held what looked like a hundred DVDs. At the front of the cabin was a door clearly labeled "Cockpit. Authorized Personnel Only," while the door at the back clearly led some-where else.

The pilot was speaking to me. "I'm Captain Anders and I'll be flying you to Miami. My copilot is finishing up the preflight checks, so we should be ready to go shortly. Please make your-self comfortable." He headed for the cockpit door.

I looked towards all of my seating options. I wasn't usually so indecisive, but my already strange day was turning even more surreal with each passing moment.

"Would you like a drink?" The woman spoke up.

"Yes, please," I said as a rush of relief went through me. I needed something to help me relax before we took off.

She moved towards the bar. "I'm Robin and he's Malcolm." She gestured towards the man, who gave me a nod but didn't speak. "If there's anything you need, please let one of us know."

She poured me a drink and I drained it in one gulp. The liquid burned on the way down and I wasn't sure if I liked the taste, but it did ease my nerves a bit. I wandered around the cabin, opening doors and cabinets, waiting to be told I needed to stop. The cease and desist never came, however, so I kept looking. I found that the door at the back led to a short corridor with three doors. One went to a bathroom, the next a closet where I found the bags of all of the clothes I'd purchased earlier. The dresses were even hanging up in their clear bags. The final door opened into what could only be described as a small bedroom. The bed was only a single and barely fit. The sheets, however, were high quality. That'd be one way to join the Mile-High Club, I thought as I closed the door.

The captain's voice came over the intercom, telling me I needed to go back to my seat and strap in. I did as I was told, thinking that when we were almost to Miami I'd freshen up and put on one of my new dresses just in case Gavin and I would be eating out. Butterflies fluttered in my stomach. This was really happening.

I had a feeling that whatever happened this week, whether good or bad, would be a turning point in my life. And I was ready for a change.

EIGHTEEN

I wasn't sure what Gavin had planned for when I arrived in Miami, so I picked out the outfit I'd liked the best. A sheer pale green bra with matching panties went on first. Next was the mint green maxidress I'd found just before Krissy and I had finished shopping. It wasn't fancy, but it hugged my curves and the hemline hit me mid-thigh. I felt comfortable moving in it, but a little edgy since I still had to be a bit careful sitting so I didn't flash my underwear. I considered wearing heels, but decided I'd wear a pair of casual sandals. I wasn't sure I could manage the steep stairs from the plane in any of these heels, and my work shoes didn't match my outfit. If Gavin wanted to take me somewhere fancy, I could always change.

My heart was racing in anticipation as the plane taxied to a stop. I waited for the go-ahead and stood. I hoped I didn't look as eager as I felt. I was halfway to the door when I realized I'd forgotten all of the clothes in the back. I turned and started to go back to the room.

"Ms. Summers, we'll bring your luggage out to the car for you," Robin said with a smile.

I nodded and turned back towards the exit, wondering if I'd

ever get used to having people do things for me. Malcolm opened the door for me and stepped back so I could go through. I wasn't sure if I should even be thinking about getting used to any of this. I didn't doubt that Gavin cared about me, but I had this nagging fear that if I tried to think too far ahead, everything would collapse.

I was so caught up in my own thoughts that I was halfway down the stairs before I noticed that a limo was waiting. Of course. I took two more steps and realized that the man standing at the back door wasn't a driver. It was Gavin.

It said something about how he looked in his tailored charcoal gray pants and fitted dark blue short-sleeved shirt that I didn't even feel how warm and muggy it was. New York was still cool in the evenings, but Florida was already heading towards hot. Not that I cared. At the moment, all I could think about was how wonderfully Gavin's clothes clung to his body and what he looked like without them.

"Ms. Summers." Gavin gave me a grin, the heat in his eyes saying that he was thinking similar things about me.

"Mr. Manning." I returned the smile. "You're looking very nice this evening."

His smile widened. "I think you stole my line." He opened the door. "Though I was going to say beautiful rather than just 'nice.'"

I looked up at him as I slid into the backseat. "Do you want me to tell you you're beautiful?" There was a teasing note to my voice, but I saw something cross Gavin's face that wasn't humorous. He closed the door, leaving me wondering. He was so confident that it had never occurred to me that he might not fully appreciate just how gorgeous he was.

He opened the other door and slid in beside me, his expression back to the almost-cocky charm to which I was accustomed.

"You are, you know," I said. When he raised an eyebrow in question, I leaned forward and let my fingertips lightly trace his jawline, then move up to his lips. "Beautiful," I finished my thought.

He stared at me for a brief moment, then closed the rest of the distance, capturing my mouth with his. I made a sound that was a cross between a moan and a whimper as his tongue parted my lips. I leaned into him, my hands running over the soft fabric of his shirt, up over his broad shoulders to rest at the base of his neck. His hands slid down my back, then back up my sides, his thumbs brushing the sides of my breasts.

After a moment, he pulled back, his eyes bright. "I missed you."

Warmth spread through my body. Three simple words.

The limo started to move and Gavin settled into a more traditional position in his seat. He reached for my hand as he spoke, "I have reservations for us at this amazing new restaurant. It's not too fancy, but it's got this great view of the ocean and the chef is supposed to be superb."

I hadn't been able to eat much for lunch, so I knew I should've been ready for a big meal, but I wasn't hungry for food, no matter how well-prepared it was. I heard my friends in the back of my head, telling me to stop being a wimp and let Gavin know what I wanted. It didn't take as much convincing as I'd thought it would for me to act on the advice.

"That sounds great," I started as I disentangled my hand from his. A flash of hurt crossed his face and I realized that he thought I was angry about his plans. That look strengthened my resolve. I put my hand on his thigh and locked eyes. "But I'm not interested in a meal at the moment."

"Oh really?" His voice was husky.

I slid my hand higher until my fingers brushed against the bulge in his pants. "I don't know if I can keep my hands to myself through an entire dinner." I moved my hand until I was cupping him. "You remember what happened at the gala when I tried?"

Gavin reached up behind my head and took out my clip, sending my hair falling over my shoulders. "I remember having to find somewhere to fuck you because I couldn't control myself either."

I lightly squeezed him and felt him swell under my touch. He made a small sound and grabbed my wrist, gently but firmly removing my hand from his crotch. Without releasing my wrist, he leaned forward and pressed a small white button.

"Change of plans," he said. "Take us back to the hotel."

"Yes, sir," a man's voice responded.

He leaned back again, then lifted my hand and kissed the palm before releasing it. I started to reach for him again, but he smiled and shook his head. "Patience."

I stared at him. The man who'd been all over me on the way to the gala was telling me to be patient? Then I saw the twinkle in his eyes and realized he knew how much I wanted him and was enjoying making me wait. I tried glaring at him, but he just looked more amused. If I hadn't been so annoyed, I would've thought it was cute. But I didn't think it was cute. Not at all.

I kept telling myself that, until we pulled up in front of one of Miami's most expensive luxury hotels. It was like something out of a movie, one of those places that look almost too beautiful to be real. The driver opened my door and held out a hand. I let him help me out as I stared up at the front of the building. Gavin climbed out and stood next to me for a moment before taking my arm.

"Shall we?" His voice revealed none of the sexual tension that had been so thick in the backseat of the limo.

We walked into the lobby and went straight for the elevators. I half-expected him to kiss me then, but he didn't. He barely even looked my way. If I hadn't been able to feel how tense his body was from where my arm was entwined with his, I'd have thought he was bored.

Of course we went to the penthouse suite. Part of me

wondered if Gavin would've stayed here if I wasn't with him, and that thought was quickly followed by my traitor brain thinking that perhaps this was where he brought all of the women he was trying to impress. As soon as we stepped inside, however, those thoughts were pushed to the back of my mind.

The suite was absolutely stunning. I wasn't always the best judge of how many square feet a space had, but even I could tell that this was at least twice the size of my apartment. Floor-to-ceiling windows lined the two outside walls, giving us an uninterrupted view of bright blue sky and the Miami skyline. The color scheme was black and white, with shades between, but it didn't come across as cold. Everything matched, even the huge hot tub that sat in the corner where the two glass walls met.

"Wow," I said.

Gavin chuckled. "I'm glad you like it."

I glanced over at him and saw in his eyes what his voice didn't say. He was relieved that I liked it, and that meant more to me than the suite itself. He wanted me to like it. If this was just some sort of routine he did with other women, he wouldn't have cared so much. I reached for him, but he shook his head and took a step back, a smile playing on his lips.

"What now?" I sighed.

He made a tsking noise. "Didn't anyone ever tell you that patience is a virtue?"

I raised an eyebrow. "The man who owns a sex club and fucked me six ways from Sunday in an empty conference room is going to lecture me on virtue?"

He laughed, an open, freeing sound that automatically made me smile. "Touché," he admitted. "But you still need to learn to wait."

He walked over to what I now realized was a wet bar and pulled out a glass decanter of amber liquid. He poured himself half a glass, took a sip, and then turned back towards me. I felt the atmosphere shift and knew that something good was coming.

"I want to do something different tonight," he said. "But you have to trust me."

Familiar butterflies fluttered in my stomach, but I didn't hesitate. "Okay."

"For the rest of the night, I'm going to give you instructions, and I want you to follow them, no matter what." He paused, as if waiting for me to protest. When I didn't, he continued, "If you're truly uncomfortable, just tell me and we'll go back to something more... traditional. But, I believe if you let yourself go, you'll find the experience to be quite... pleasant." He took another sip of his drink.

I swallowed hard and tried not to let him see how nervous this idea made me. "Okay." I answered with a single word because I wasn't sure I could handle anything else.

He didn't smile, but his eyes shone, telling me how pleased he was at my decision. "Go turn on the spa while I order room service."

Okay, that wasn't the first instruction I'd expected when I'd agreed to do whatever he asked of me. Still, I did it. By the time I'd figured out how the thing worked, he was off the phone and watching me. The water started heating up as I wondered what was coming next.

"I've noticed," he said, "that you seem a bit self-conscious about your body."

I blinked. That was blunt. Correct, but blunt.

"You have no need to be." He sipped his drink and settled in one of the plush chairs that faced the spa. "And I want you to be comfortable in your own skin, not just when you're alone, but when you're with me."

My hands were clasped behind my back, my fingers twisting together. Where was he going with this?

"Undress."

I glanced towards the glass walls.

"We're on the top floor, Carrie and the glass is tinted so no one could see you unless you were pressed right up against it, and maybe not even then."

His tone took on the same authoritative note it'd had when he'd stopped me from touching myself when we had sex. It made me shiver in a good way.

"I want you to take off your clothes, slowly. This isn't a strip-tease. I just want you to feel me watching you reveal yourself to me, inch by inch."

My mouth was suddenly dry. That seemed more intimate than a lot of the other things we'd done. Still, I'd promised to do what he said. I reached up to the zipper and lowered it. Keeping my eyes down, I started to let the straps from the dress slide down my shoulders.

"Look at me," he commanded.

I looked up, my eyes locking with his.

"Watch my face while I watch you."

I nodded, not trusting my voice. I kept my eyes on his face as my dress began to fall. I controlled it, keeping it from dropping all at once. Slowly, it revealed the strapless bra I was wearing underneath. My nipples were visible through the sheer material, and Gavin's eyes darkened as he looked at them. When the dress finally pooled around my feet, I stepped out of it and waited.

"Everything," he said. His voice was hoarse and I could see the front of his pants tenting. Everything about him said that he was enjoying the show.

I reached behind me and unhooked the bra. I let the material slide rather than fall, dropping down the mounds of my breasts and then over my hardening nipples. The bra joined the dress on the floor.

"Turn around to take off the panties," he instructed.

I turned and bent over, feeling my face flush. For some

reason, this was more embarrassing than if I'd been facing him, but I didn't stop. I hooked my thumbs under the elastic and lowered the panties. I turned back as I stepped out of them. My hands automatically moved to cover myself.

"No," he said, the word almost sharp. "Hands at your sides."

I stood there, watching him watch me, and finally realized that he was right. I had no reason to be ashamed of my body. Other women might have had a flatter stomach or bigger breasts, but it wasn't about that. It was about being me and accepting who I was, inside and out. Coming to the realization didn't mean I automatically wanted to go skipping around on a nude beach, but it did mean that I was no longer struggling to find something to hide behind.

"Into the spa," he said finally.

I gave him a doubtful look. I was all for using a hot tub, but not naked. Who knew how many people had been in there?

One side of his mouth quirked up as if he could read my thoughts. When he spoke, I knew he'd read my expression correctly. "Don't worry. They empty, sanitize, and refill it every time new guests check in. I asked when I booked the suite. No one's been in it since."

I smiled and walked towards the hot tub. I liked that he knew me well enough to anticipate what I'd want. I went up the stairs, feeling his eyes on me, and then walked down into the warm water. I sighed. It wasn't completely hot yet but between the temperature and the jets, it was heavenly. I sat down, my hair trailing in the water. I'd forgotten it was down.

"Here." Gavin was at the side of the tub holding out my hair clip. "Don't want you walking around with wet hair, now do we?"

I took the clip and put up my curls. I looked up at him expectantly, wondering why he hadn't gotten undressed yet. Hot tub sex should be amazing, but it wouldn't work very well if he wasn't in the tub with me.

"Close your eyes."

Ah, there it was. I did as he said. He was going to make me wait until he was in to open my eyes so I wouldn't get to see him. A tease. Then I felt his hands on my shoulders. His thumbs pressed into the muscles there and I moaned. That was a wonderful pressure point.

"You're way too tense."

His voice was soft as his hands worked over muscles I hadn't even realized were knotted. His fingers found each place they were needed, and I leaned forward to give him better access to the lower part of my back. He didn't touch anything sexual, but my body was throbbing with desire by the time he finished. My back and arms felt like jelly and it was a good feeling.

"You may open your eyes now."

I did, expecting to see him sitting in the water, but he wasn't there. I turned and saw that he was still outside the tub and still fully dressed. His shirt had a few water spots on it, but he hadn't gotten wet.

There was a knock at the door. He stood and my eyes were automatically drawn to what I wanted. He was still enjoying himself, but hadn't made a move to do anything about it. I hadn't known he had that kind of control. Hell, I hadn't known any man could have that kind of control.

"Stay there," he said. "I'll be right back."

I watched him walk away. That was probably room service. I started to lean back when I realized that Gavin would be opening the door, and someone would be bringing the food inside. The living room was an open area. I could see the door from where I was sitting, which meant whoever was coming in would be able to see me. Panic started to flood me, telling me to grab the towel on the edge of the tub and cover myself, but I set my jaw and stayed.

A young man pushed a cart into the room and I saw his eyes flick towards me. He smiled, nodded, then turned to Gavin.

Of course, I realized he couldn't see anything more than the tops of my shoulders. For all he knew, I was wearing a bikini under the water. I relaxed. Gavin tipped the young man – quite well, judging by the look of surprise – then showed him out. He opened the bottle of champagne that was on the cart and poured a single glass. That was good. I could use a bit of a drink. He also picked up a bowl, but I couldn't see what was in it until he came back to the tub. Strawberries.

He sat on the edge of the tub and held out the glass of champagne. I took it and took a sip.

"You stayed," he said.

I nodded. "You told me too."

"You did well."

A surge of pride went through me and I smiled.

"You deserve a reward." He picked up a deep red berry and held it out.

Instinctively, I knew he didn't want me to take it from him. Instead, I opened my mouth and leaned forward, letting him feed me. The flavor of the strawberry burst across my taste buds, enhanced by the champagne. I closed my eyes and savored the taste. The rest of the berry was waiting when I opened my eyes.

"This is just the beginning, Carrie," Gavin said. "I promise you, tonight is going to be unforgettable."

NINETEEN

As Gavin fed me more strawberries, I realized that I was actually hungry. I didn't think I could stomach anything heavy – I was still a little nervous about what was coming next – but the strawberries were settling well, and I knew that if I was going to drink any more than a few sips of alcohol, I would need something to balance it. I didn't mind a bit of the edge taken off, but I wanted to be clear-headed tonight.

"Let's get you out of that tub before you start to wrinkle." Gavin smiled as he set aside the food and my half-empty glass. He stood and held out a hand.

I took his hand and stood, watching his face as his eyes immediately dropped to my body. Despite the cool air, warmth flooded me as I took in the look in his eyes. I started down the steps, halting on the last one when he held up his hand. He reached down and picked up a towel. I held out my hand but he shook his head. Puzzled, I dropped it back to my side. It wasn't until he used a corner to wipe off a few drops that had gotten on my face that I realized what he was going to do.

Without a word, he began to dry me off. Each movement was slow and deliberate. He didn't linger in any one particular place more than another, but it didn't matter. The entire process was sensual. Even his drying my feet quickened my breathing. As he straightened, I wondered if he was going to take me on the couch or if we were going to his room. A thought popped into my head. Was it his room or our room? Had he gotten a two-bedroom suite so that we'd have separate places to sleep or had he wanted us to share?

"Arms up."

I blinked, pulling my thoughts back. I lifted my arms and he wrapped the towel around me. When he tucked the edge under to keep it snug around me, his fingers brushed against my skin, but he didn't take advantage of the touch. I was thoroughly confused now. He'd had me undress and stand in front of him, so why did he want me to cover up if we were just heading for a bed?

"I ordered light. I hope you don't mind."

Food? He was seriously talking about food? I didn't question him, though. Something more than strawberries sounded good. I started to bend over to pick up my dress.

"Leave it," he said. I gave him a puzzled look and he added, "That should be sufficient for our meal."

The towel covered more of my breasts than some of the dresses I'd brought, and it did reach almost to the middle of my thighs, but I still felt oddly exposed. Still, I remember that I was supposed to be following orders, so I just nodded and followed him to the table. He paused to take hold of the cart and motioned for me to sit. I did so, conscious about every movement despite the fact that Gavin had already seen all of me. It was different in this context.

He first poured us both a glass of wine. I started to ask why he'd gotten wine and champagne, but then he set out a plate of cheese and I understood. I wasn't used to meals that cost more than my rent, but even I knew that wine went with cheese. He also took out crackers, bread, and apple slices.

"Eat." He gestured towards the spread. "Whatever we don't finish will keep."

We ate in silence for several minutes, savoring each morsel. Not for the first time, I thought how sometimes it's the simple things that are the best. I wasn't stupid. I knew these cheeses were expensive and the rest probably was too, but there was no caviar or smoked meats or any of the pretentious stuff that some other men might have used if they were trying to impress. I was beginning to see that Gavin wasn't trying to show off. He used his money to enjoy life, but he did it on his terms. I could accept that.

Gavin took a drink of his wine and broke the silence. "In the limo, you said that you didn't think you could keep your hands to yourself and reminded me about our time at the gala. You were bold then, as you were bold at the party."

I took a sip of wine, more for something to do than actual thirst.

"I wish for you to be bold now."

I made a move as if I was going to stand, but he shook his head.

"Not with actions. I want you to be bold with your words." He picked up a small slice of cheese. "Tell me what you wanted to do to me in the limo."

My face burned. I'd done a little dirty talk before, saying things I wanted him to do to me, but it had been either as part of foreplay right before intercourse or in the middle of sex. This was just odd. I was in a towel and Gavin was fully clothed. We were eating, sitting several feet apart. There wasn't anything sexual going on at the moment.

"Get up," he said.

I stood and so did he.

"Pull your chair out from behind the table so I can see you."

I did as I was told and he moved his chair so that we were

facing each other with nothing between us. He sat and gestured for me to do the same.

"Now, Carrie, tell me what you wanted to do to me." His tone was firm.

I took a deep breath and refused to try to talk my way out of it. I'd said I'd obey and, while this was embarrassing, there was something exciting about it too.

"I wanted to touch you."

He made a gesture with his hand that clearly meant he wanted me to say more.

I could feel my face growing hot, but I continued, "I wanted to unzip your pants, reach inside and take you in my hand. Stroke you until you were hard."

"And then what would you do?"

My embarrassment was disappearing, burned away by the arousal that was starting to grow in my belly. "Take you in my mouth. Lick and suck until you came. Swallow every drop and keep licking you until you had to beg me to stop."

I heard his breathing hitch.

"Without exposing yourself, put your hand under the towel and touch yourself."

I spread my legs just enough to get my hand between them. I already knew I was wet, and my fingers slid easily between my folds. I swallowed a moan as I moved across my sensitive flesh.

"Are your fingers inside you?" he asked.

I shook my head.

"Slide one into your pussy."

I whimpered as I obeyed, slowly moving my middle finger, my body responding by loosening with each stroke. I knew how big Gavin was and I'd need more than a single finger to be ready for him without its being too much. If we were going to have as much sex as I thought we would be having this week, I would definitely want to be more prepared.

"Back to your clit."

I did as I was told. A shiver of pleasure ran through me as Gavin's hands moved to his pants. He kept his eyes on me as he unzipped and slid his hand inside. At the moment, all I could see was the movement beneath the fabric, but I knew that it wouldn't be long before he was too big to hide and I'd finally see that thick, beautiful shaft.

"Don't take the towel off. Open the bottom of it so I can see what you're doing."

I swallowed hard. Slowly, I peeled back the sides of the towel until Gavin could see my hand between my legs.

"Wider."

I spread my legs further apart, my stomach twisting and turning. It wasn't like Gavin hadn't seen me naked, and up close. He'd gone down on me, so he was intimately acquainted with that particular part of my body, but he'd never seen me like this. My arousal overpowered any embarrassment I thought I should be feeling.

"Two fingers. You'll need it."

I shuddered as I slid my middle two fingers into my core. They didn't come close to filling me as much as Gavin did, but they were stretching me now. Gavin's eyes were fixed on me, watching my fingers moving in and out. I kept my gaze on his face for several minutes, then, unable to resist any longer, dropped it.

His cock was fully erect now, jutting up from his pants, thick and swollen. His hand moved over it slowly, his fingers barely able to wrap completely around it. I knew it felt like the smoothest silk wrapped around the hardest steel, and that it would make me scream.

"Come here," his voice was rough, conveying a strain that his motions had not.

I stood, feeling the loss as my fingers left me. My pussy throbbed, aching to be filled again, to have finished what I'd started. I walked towards Gavin until I was within arm's reach, and he put his hands on my hips, leaving his cock completely exposed. He guided me forward until I was straddling his lap.

"Down."

I reached for him, holding him in place as I slowly lowered myself. His hands stayed on me, keeping me at the pace he wanted. Bit by agonizing bit, he filled me. The nearly painful stretching was familiar and welcomed. I could never have enough of this, him inside me, reaching places untouched by any other lover. As I came to rest on his lap, every impressive inch sheathed inside me, the tip of him bumped against the end of me. It was like we were two puzzle pieces, interlocking with no spaces between us.

Gavin's hands moved my hips, rocking me back and forth as I adjusted to the intrusion. I began to move with him, using my legs to add a rise and fall that let part of him withdraw before I took the full length again. Each movement caused little tingles of pleasure to ripple across my nerves.

His hands slid up my sides and then around to the front of the towel. "I want to see your body while you ride me."

I shuddered at his words, tossing my head back even as he pulled the towel off of me. His hands and mouth found my breasts as I arched my back. Teeth, tongue, and lips worked at the sensitive flesh even as I moved faster. I could feel my body chasing my orgasm, desperate for release. I ran my hands over his chest, wanting to tear his shirt off so I could feel his skin beneath my fingers, but I didn't even ask him to take it off. There was something erotic about me being totally naked and him clothed, the only exposed part of him sliding in and out of sight as I rode him.

His teeth scraped across my nipple and I cried out, my body shaking as I came. I squeezed him tight as I ground down against his lap, the head of his cock hitting the end of me and sending a shockwave through me. I fell forward, wrapping my arms around his neck as my body quaked around his. He groaned in my ear and I felt him come inside me. His arms wrapped around my waist and he held me as our bodies ground against each other, dragging out every last drop of pleasure they could hold.

His hands moved across my back, leaving trails of heat across my cooling skin. He turned his head and pressed his lips against the side of my neck and I shivered. Part was from the touch, but part was because I was starting to feel the chill of the air conditioning. Gavin's hands shifted so that he was helping me stand. My knees were a bit shaky but I stepped back so that he could stand. While he tucked himself back into his pants, I retrieved the towel from the floor. I loved having him bare inside me, but it made clean-up a bit more necessary.

"Here."

I looked up and saw Gavin holding out his shirt. I took it gratefully. It said something about how chilled I was that I pulled on the shirt before ogling Gavin's bare chest. It was well worth a stare or two. He was lean and strong, his muscles defined under golden skin. He was the perfect balance of muscled, but not too big. I knew his back was equally as nice, complemented by the tattoo across the top. Angel wings, a date and initials. The initials of his daughter as well as the date of her birth. It also happened to be the same date that his fiancée had been killed in a hit-and-run.

TWENTY

"Would you like to see the rest of the suite?" Gavin asked, holding out his hand.

I took it and nodded, shaking off the shadow of his past. If he wasn't going to dwell on it, then neither would I.

Since the main area was open and the kitchen separated only by a half wall, he didn't bother with it. Instead, we headed towards one of the two hallways. It was short, with just a single door.

"This is the smaller bedroom," he said as he flipped on the light.

If this was the smaller one, I couldn't wait to see the master bedroom. It was bigger than my room in my apartment and held a queen-sized bed, a dresser, and a table on either side of the bed. An open door near the closet showed what I assumed was a full bathroom.

Gavin led me out of the room and back into the living room. I hadn't seen my luggage in the smaller bedroom and he hadn't said anything about that being where I was sleeping. I was hoping that meant what I thought it meant. I really wanted to spend the weekend waking up next to Gavin.

He stopped just before the hallway and turned towards me, his expression serious. "Now that you've had a couple minutes to process, I need to know, did you like me telling you what to do?"

I could sense an undercurrent of tension and realized that he was nervous as to how I was going to respond to what we'd done. I took a moment to consider the question, wanting to give him a totally honest answer. It had been a bit embarrassing and nerve-wracking, following his orders, but it had been exciting too. I was enough of a control freak that I'd never thought giving up that control would be a turn-on, but I had to admit that it was. I looked up at him and nodded. "I did." I turned the question around. "Did you like telling me what to do?"

He took a step towards me, his eyes darkening. His voice was almost hoarse when he answered, "I enjoyed it very much." He lowered his head, taking my mouth in one of those full, deep kisses that I could feel all the way down to my toes.

I reached between us, my fingers skimming over his chest and down the flat plane of his stomach. My tongue twined with his as I started to slide my hand beneath his waistband.

He chuckled and pulled my hand away. He broke the kiss, but didn't step away. "I didn't say you could touch me." His tone was half humor, half serious.

I grinned, feeling a bit mischievous. I took a step back, freeing my hand from his grip. I ran the tip of my tongue across my bottom lip and slid my hand under his shirt I was wearing. It hit only about an inch or two below my thighs, so I had easy access.

"If I can't touch you, I suppose I'll just have to touch myself."

He moved so fast that my fingers had barely brushed the light smattering of curls that covered my pussy. His hands closed around my arms, jerking my hand out from under the shirt, and he pushed me back against the wall. There was no violence to it, but it still took my breath away. He leaned close until every breath I took made my breasts brush against his chest.

"I didn't say you could touch yourself either."

He released my left arm and shoved his hand between my legs, forcing them further apart. He pushed two fingers into my pussy and I whimpered.

"Haven't I said that this is mine? I'm the one who decides if and when you're allowed to come." His hand was rough, sending new and exciting sensations across my nerves. "Open your eyes."

I hadn't even realized I'd closed them. I forced them open as my body began to writhe against the wall. He worked a third finger inside me, stretching me almost as wide as his cock. I met his eyes and saw that while he was into the moment, there was a part of him waiting for me to stop it, wondering if I was going to think this was too far. Instead, I pushed against his hand, wanting more friction.

His other hand moved up to pull out my hair clip and bury his fingers in my hair. "I think maybe you need a lesson in obedience."

His thumb rubbed my clit, almost too rough but not quite, and my legs began to tremble. I was there, balancing on the edge of that precipice, waiting for him to send me over.

And then, suddenly, his hand was gone. He was gone. He'd moved back so that he wasn't touching me at all. I stared at him, gasping for air, my body screaming in protest. My hands were shaking, my mind whirling. What was he doing?

He wiped his hand on his leg of his pants. "Until you learn to behave yourself, you won't be allowed to come."

My jaw dropped. He couldn't be serious. Could he? He took a step towards me and I couldn't stop myself from catching my breath. I wanted him so badly that my entire body ached.

"Shall we finish the tour?" He held out his hand.

He wasn't joking. He really wasn't going to finish what he'd started. My pussy gave a throb that was nearly painful. Men complain about what it feels like when they get worked up but don't get a release. Trust me, it wasn't exactly pleasant for a woman either.

I looked up into his eyes and saw what he wasn't saying. My response was going to tell him if he'd gone too far. He would let this go if I said I'd had enough. The question was, had I? My body was screaming for release, but I remembered all of our previous encounters. He'd never left me wanting. I remembered the first time he'd stopped me from touching myself to get off. He'd told me that he wanted to be responsible for my pleasure. I could see that same desire in his eyes now. I had a choice to make.

I scowled at him, but I took his hand and let him lead me down the second short hallway. This one had two doors. The one was obviously a closet and the other led to the master bedroom. Despite my annoyance, I was impressed. A king-sized bed with silk sheets. A massive dark walnut dresser and wardrobe. A chair in the corner with an elegant lamp behind it. We walked through the bedroom to the bathroom. It was almost as big as my bedroom back home. There was a tub, a large shower surrounded by beveled glass, and three sinks set into a counter that took up an entire wall. Like the room at Gavin's club, there was a separate small stall for the toilet.

"What do you think?" he asked.

"It's amazing." I had to be honest.

As we stepped back into the bedroom, I saw something that made my frustration with him fade a bit. My luggage was sitting at the end of the bed. He did want me in here with him. I glanced up at him and saw that he was watching me carefully, his eyes vulnerable and unguarded.

"If you want to move to the other room, I'll understand," he said softly. He moved our joined hands up to brush the back of his against my cheek. "If I was too much..."

I smiled and shook my head. "I'm supposed to do what you tell me, remember?"

A smile flashed across his face and then I saw his authoritative expression return. "Yes, you are."

TWENTY-ONE

He led me back to the living room, taking me over to the nearest glass wall. He turned me so that I was facing it and moved to stand behind me. The sun had set while Gavin and I had been busy with other things, and that deep blue twilight sky was settling over the city. I couldn't help but think that it was the same shade as Gavin's eyes when he was aroused. I loved that color.

His hands slid under his shirt, moving up to cup my breasts. I made a noise in the back of my throat. As he began to roll my nipples between his fingers, he spoke in my ear, sending a rush of wet to my already soaking pussy.

"So eager for my touch," he said. "Would you let me do this to you on a balcony where anyone could see us?"

I shivered, the thought turning me on more than it should have.

"The things I would do to you," he continued. "You'd want to scream my name, but you couldn't, not unless you wanted everyone to see us. I'd make you come so hard that you wouldn't be able to walk. You'd have to just stand there, trusting me to hold you up until you could stand."

I made a sound in the back of my throat. Oh, I wanted that very much.

He removed his hands. "Take off the shirt."

I don't know what made me say it, but the words popped out of my mouth before I could stop them. "I think you should take off your pants first."

He took a step forward until the length of his body was pressed against my back. I could feel the heat from his skin through his shirt. His voice was nearly a growl in my ear and the sound made me shiver.

"I should spank you for refusing to do what I said."

My mouth went dry.

"Turn that ass cherry red." He bent his head and scraped his teeth over the side of my neck. "But I won't. Not today, anyway."

A wave of relief went through me, but I was shocked to feel a hint of regret. Did I want that too? I didn't know.

Before I could spend too much time reflecting on my reaction, Gavin was turning me around and yanking the shirt over my head. He dropped it on the ground, his eyes locking with mine.

"Lean back against the glass."

I wanted to ask why, but I didn't. Instead, I did as he said. The glass was cool against my back, whatever heat it had garnered from the sunlight leeched away by the dark. It felt good against my flushed skin.

Gavin knelt in front of me, never taking his eyes away from mine, not even when he leaned forward to press his mouth against that most intimate part of me. I broke the connection first, unable to keep my eyelids from fluttering when he ran out his tongue, dipping it between my folds.

His hand moved behind my thigh, maneuvering my leg until it was hooked over one shoulder, opening me wider. His tongue moved over me, the flat of it laving over my sensitive skin, then the tip dancing through, circling my core, then up to my clit. I put my hands on his shoulders, needing his help to balance; I'd find no purchase on the glass. When he took that swollen bundle of nerves between his lips, I gasped. Yes, this was it. The pressure inside me spiked, pushing me towards climax.

The loss of his mouth was sudden and I cried out in frustration. My eyes opened and I looked down to see him watching me. I flexed my fingers, digging my nails into his flesh. I had been so close. My body was humming with unreleased tension.

"Me telling you what to do isn't about power, or about pleasuring me," he said softly. "I get pleasure from it, but it's all about you trusting me enough to let go of your control."

I blinked. I hadn't expected an explanation in the middle of this, and that certainly hadn't been one I would've expected at all, no matter when it came. I wasn't sure if what he said made sense logically, but it fit with what I knew about him, how we'd been together.

He moved forward again, burying his head between my legs. I cried out at the sudden heat of his mouth on my pussy. His tongue darted inside me, deeper than a tongue should have been able to go. He kissed that part of me as he'd kissed my mouth, thoroughly and with a passion I'd never felt with anyone else.

I could feel my orgasm approaching rapidly and began to beg, "Please, let me finish. Please, please."

When Gavin pulled away a second time, I swore in frustration. My entire body was one giant knot.

"Do you want to come?"

The question was so absurd that I almost laughed. Of course I wanted to come! I needed to come. I nodded, not trusting myself to speak.

He ran the tip of his index finger along my slit, using just enough pressure to send a shudder through me, but not enough to give me what I wanted. He stood.

"And what would you be willing to do if I let you climax?"

"Anything." The word tore out of me. "Please, just let me come."

He smiled slowly. His hands slid up my sides to cup my breasts. His thumbs brushed against the hard points of my nipples and I moaned. Every touch was like fire.

"Do you mean just now, or whenever I want?"

I hesitated. I didn't think he'd ever force me to do something I truly didn't want to do, but the idea of telling him that I'd do what he wanted all the time gave me pause.

He wrapped his arms around me and pulled me towards him. I expected him to press my body against his, but he didn't. Instead, he positioned me so that I was straddling his leg, my overly sensitive pussy and clit flush against his thigh. He wrapped one arm around my waist, keeping me in place, then moved his leg ever so slightly. I cried out. Even that little bit of friction made my body tremble.

"You know I'd never do anything to hurt you," he said. His voice was gentle, but the hand on my breast was a little rougher, tugging on my nipple and sending little jolts of edged pleasure through me.

I nodded. I did know that.

He moved his leg again and my knees shook. He was giving me just enough to ride that edge, but not enough to push me over or let me come down completely.

"I promise you, Carrie, I can make your body sing, give you pleasure in ways you can't imagine. True ecstasy."

His words flowed over me. He meant them, I knew. He wanted that for me, wanted me to feel those things.

"Please, baby," he whispered. He ground me down against his leg, drawing a whimper from me. "Say the words and you'll come harder than you've ever come before."

"Yes!" The word was nearly a sob. "Anything. Anytime." I needed relief.

He released me and took a step back. I stared at him in horror. Why had he stopped? He'd promised. I squeezed my eyes shut, tears burning against my eyelids.

"Hey, Carrie." His touch was gentle on my cheek. "Look at me."

I opened my eyes.

"We're not done." He smiled. "I keep my promises. I wasn't going to bring you like that." He leaned down and brushed his lips across mine. "Trust me?"

I nodded, fighting back the doubt.

"Then kneel." It was a command, but a gentle one.

I knelt down, keeping my eyes on his face. I trusted him. He would take care of me just as he had before.

"Undress me."

I smiled as I reached for the waistband of his pants. I made short work of the button and zipper, then took both his pants and his underwear down at the same time. He didn't chide me for being impatient this time, but once I saw how hard he was, it wasn't a surprise. His cock was so swollen I knew it had to be almost painful. Now I understood that he had to mean what he'd said about doing this for me. It was the only explanation as to why he hadn't just given in and fucked me ages ago.

"Open your mouth."

I did as he told me. He put his hand on the back of my head, burying his fingers in my curls. He guided me forward until his thick shaft slid between my lips. He didn't go far, letting just a few inches move back and forth across my tongue. I let him set the pace, trusting he wouldn't give me more than I could handle. My tongue swirled around his tip, tasting the salt of his skin. I sucked on him gently, knowing that if I applied too much suction, he'd finish in my mouth, and that wasn't where I wanted him. I just hoped he was thinking along the same lines.

When he pulled me back completely and looked down at

me, his pupils were so wide that only a thin sliver of blue could be seen. I shivered. The end was near.

"On all fours." His voice was rough and a thrill went through me.

I immediately bent forward. I'd been bent over a table before, but I'd never done it like this. My previous lovers had all been missionary or me on top. Not much variety.

Gavin moved behind me. His hands ran down my back and over my ass. I looked over my shoulder at him. He was hovering just as close to the edge as I was. This wasn't going to go long, and that was good. If I didn't come soon, I was going to explode. I saw the question in his eyes and nodded.

"Please."

The word turned into a wail as he buried himself inside me with one thrust. I was stretched enough that it didn't hurt at all. It was pure pleasure. He didn't pause at all but immediately began to slam into me, each thrust forcing the air from my lungs so that my cries were little more than breaths. The carpet burned my knees and hands, but it just added to the sensations I was feeling. He went deeper with each stroke, hitting the end of me until I cried out. He slid a hand around my hip and dipped between my legs. The moment he touched my clit, my world went white.

I was only vaguely aware of what was happening. Every cell in my body was pulsing with the intensity of the pleasure coursing through me. My arms buckled and he caught me, holding me as he kept thrusting, his cock forcing its way between my quivering walls. Each time he moved inside me, another wave of ecstasy rolled over me. This was no gentle wave, but rather the crashing of the ocean, the undertow dragging me beneath until I couldn't breathe and my lungs burned.

His hand tightened around my breast as he drove himself into me one final time. He came with a shout, his body shuddering as it wrapped around me, dropping me to the carpet with him. The motion pushed his pulsing cock against that spot inside me and my body went rigid. I opened my mouth, but nothing came out. Rather, the darkness came up to swallow me. Before it did, I had one thought.

If this was what obedience meant, I'd do whatever he asked.

TWENTY-TWO

Waking up next to Gavin and knowing that neither one of us was going to be rushing off was like something out of a dream. When I was in that place halfway between sleep and waking, I became aware of his body behind mine, his arm around my waist, the scent of the expensive soap the hotel had given us. We'd showered after our explosive orgasms – well, once we'd been able to walk – and spent the rest of the evening curled up on the couch together, watching movies on the massive flat-screen television that hung above the fireplace. When we'd finally gone to bed, we'd changed out of the fluffy robes we'd been wearing, Gavin into a pair of black boxer briefs that hugged him perfectly, and me into a dark red teddy that Krissy had helped me pick out. I knew if we hadn't both been so tired, another round of sex would've followed, but instead, we snuggled together and fell asleep.

Now, I could feel his hard length pressing against my ass and a bolt of desire went through me. I wanted nothing more than to push back against him, ask him to take me right then and there. I could feel the dull ache between my legs that came after a night of intense sex with someone incredibly well-endowed, and knew that going again probably wasn't a good idea, especially without any prep work, but it didn't stop me from wanting it. I'd never craved anything like I craved him.

"Mmm." Gavin made a soft sound and nuzzled under my ear.

He shifted behind me and I couldn't resist giving him a little backwards nudge. He chuckled, a lazy, sleepy sound that made a familiar heat coil in my stomach.

"Do you know how badly I want to just bury myself in that tight pussy of yours?" Gavin murmured against my ear. "Fuck you nice and slow, feel you gripping me as I move in and out."

"Yes, please," I whispered the words as I closed my eyes.

Gavin sighed and his arm loosened around my waist. "Dammit, Carrie. What you do to me..."

I rolled over as he moved onto his back. He put his arm across his forehead and closed his eyes. I propped myself up on my elbow and watched him, curious as to what had prompted that reaction.

He opened a single eye and looked over at me. "Seriously, do you know what you do to me?"

I started to say that after last night, I had a pretty good idea, but something on his face stopped me. Instead, I shook my head.

Gavin rolled onto his side so that we were facing each other. His expression was serious as he reached out a hand and cupped the side of my face. "You asked me once how many lovers I'd had and I told you that it was fewer than you'd expect."

I was confused. What did this have to do with anything? I really didn't want to hear about his sexual history at the moment. Still, I stayed quiet and let him continue.

"That was true, but what I didn't say was that, since Camille died, none of them were anything more than sex. I made sure they knew up front that's all I wanted. We'd occasionally spend time doing other things, but it always ended the same way. I never wanted to know what they were thinking, what they were feeling, outside the physical. I never wanted to show them beautiful things to see their faces light up." He twisted a curl around his finger. "I never wanted to wake up next to them, content to have them in my arms."

My heart was pounding so loudly I was sure he could hear it.

"That's what you do to me, Carrie," he continued. "You make me want things I haven't wanted in a very long time."

What was I supposed to say to that? I turned my face towards his hand and pressed my lips against his palm. I couldn't look at him as I whispered, "You make me want things I never knew I wanted."

He slid his hand around the back of my neck and pulled me towards him, rolling us so that I was on top of him. He was hard beneath me.

"If it was up to me, we'd stay here all day, making love until we were both spent." His lips curved up in a wistful smile. "But, unfortunately, I have a meeting with Howard's financial officer in ninety minutes and I can't be late."

I gave him a pout that made him laugh and then I rolled off of him. My libido would apparently have to wait. I stared up at the ceiling as the bed dipped, telling me he'd gotten up. "What time do you think you'll be back?"

"Come with me," Gavin said.

I sat up, surprised. "What?"

"Come with me," he repeated. "It's supposed to be a short meeting and, afterwards, I want to take you out on Howard's boat."

"His boat?" I echoed.

Gavin grinned. "All right, it's a yacht. Doesn't change the fact that I want to take you out on it." He held his hand out to me. "What do you say? We'll order room service, get dressed, then head out to Star Island. You can look around the mansion while I'm in the meeting, and then we'll go out on the water."

I took his hand and let him pull me to my feet. He didn't release my hand, but rather used it to pull me into his arms. I tilted my head back. "I say, it sounds like fun."

An hour later, Gavin and I stood on the sidewalk in front of the hotel as a Bentley pulled up. All right, that was impressive. It was sleek, black, and in perfect condition.

"Howard loves his Bentleys," Gavin said. He opened the door for me and I climbed in. "I prefer Italian cars."

He slid into the seat next to me and took my hand. That surprised me. I hadn't been expecting much physical contact while he was in business mode. Then again, he wasn't exactly dressed like he was on his way to a business meeting. He was in shorts. Nice shorts and a collared shirt, but still more casual than anything I'd thought Gavin would wear for work. He'd told me that this particular associate of Howard's tended to wear loud Hawaiian shirts and neon shorts with flip-flops to meetings, so he was dressed up by comparison. The guy was apparently eccentric but absolutely brilliant. He just didn't get invited to many of the formal gatherings Howard hosted.

I'd followed Gavin's example and picked one of the simpler sundresses to wear. The rest of our clothes were packed up, currently being loaded into the trunk of the car. We'd be staying at Howard's mansion for the rest of our trip. I still wasn't entirely sure how I felt about that, but as long as Gavin was with me, I wasn't going to complain.

The drive to Star Island was pleasant, the scenery beautiful. When we pulled up to the gate surrounding Howard's property, I leaned forward slightly. I'd seen pictures of the mansion when working on Howard's case, and had been wondering if they'd done the property justice. As we drove up the driveway, I saw it was even more beautiful than the pictures had shown. Brilliant landscaping, elegant architecture. I had to admit, no matter what else I thought about Howard, he had great taste.

He was waiting for us, a smile plastered on his face. I

couldn't give an exact reason, but I didn't trust that smile. I plastered an equally fake one on my face and followed Gavin out of the car.

"Carrie! Darling!" Howard held out his hands as his eyes ran over my body.

I resisted the urge to squirm uncomfortably under that gaze and took his hands. He pulled me towards him and kissed both of my cheeks. As soon as he released me, I stepped back to Gavin's side and reached for his hand. I needed something to get rid of the feel of Howard's hands on mine. Gavin gave me a puzzled look, but didn't ask what was wrong. That was good. I didn't want to have to lie.

"Leroy's already here," Howard said to Gavin. "He's in my office." He turned towards me. "I'll take care of your lovely lady while you're busy. I think a tour of the mansion is in order."

Gavin looked down at me. "I won't be long," he said. He took a step forward, stopped, then turned back to me. He took my chin in his hand, tipped my face up, and gave me a slow, thorough kiss.

When he stepped back, I was breathless and my heart was racing. Had he done that for my benefit or Howard's? If he was staking a claim, I definitely didn't mind. I didn't want Howard thinking I was anything close to available.

"Shall we?" Howard said to me as Gavin headed inside. "I have some wonderful historical pieces that I'm sure you'll love."

I started towards the house without giving Howard the opportunity to offer me a hand or arm. He fell in step beside me, already extolling the wonderful qualities of his mansion. I let the words roll over me, nodding and making approving noises. I took in everything, appreciating the beauty of some of the paintings and sculptures, but didn't let myself get too absorbed in my surroundings. The more time I spent with Howard, the less I wanted to be alone with him.

"And this is the library," Howard said as he pushed open a door.

I stepped inside first. The bookshelves reached nearly to the ceiling, but it was a table against the wall to my right that caught my attention. I walked over to it.

"These items date back to the turn of the century," Howard said. "The twentieth century, of course."

"Around the time your great-grandfather was alive," I said. I recognized some of the people in the pictures that hung above the table. I'd seen them in pictures of known Mafia members.

"That's right," he seemed pleased by my response.

"I read about him." I kept my voice carefully blank. I wasn't sure how Howard felt about his ancestor's criminal activities.

"He was a great man," Howard said.

I wished I'd been surprised by his words, but I couldn't, not really. Howard seemed like the type to think organized crime was a noble family enterprise.

"I didn't know him, unfortunately," Howard said. "And most of his possessions have been lost over the years, but I do have one item of his." He pointed at a glass case.

Inside was an ancient-looking book. I leaned closer to try to read the gold-leaf letters.

"*The Art of War* by Sun Tzu." Howard saved me the trouble. "It was my great-grandfather's favorite book."

Of course it was.

"This is an original copy of the first English translation, printed in 1910." Howard took a step closer to me, as if he wanted a better look at the book.

I instinctively took a step back, turning so that I was looking at a pistol from the nineteen twenties. I hoped he thought I'd moved to look at it, but I wasn't going to risk a look up to see if he bought it.

"Carrie, Howard." Gavin's voice came from the doorway.

I nearly sighed in relief. I turned towards him, unable to

keep myself from smiling. He crossed to my side and leaned down to kiss my cheek as he took my hand.

"Is everything in place?" Howard asked, his tone strictly business.

Gavin nodded. "Leroy has the accounts set up the way you requested."

"Excellent," Howard said.

"So, are you two ready to get out on the water?" Gavin asked.

Howard smiled and shook his head. "I have a great many things to do before tonight. Why don't you and Carrie go out on your own?"

"Are you sure?" Gavin asked.

I bit my bottom lip to keep from telling him not to question our good luck. I didn't like the idea of being stuck in a confined space with Howard, even if Gavin was there.

"I'm sure," Howard said. His eyes slid over to me, running down my body again in that way that made me want to take a shower. "I look forward to seeing what stunning attire you'll be wearing tonight."

"So do I," Gavin said. He raised our hands and kissed the back of mine. "I trust Krissy found something amazing."

I nodded and forced a smile. "She did."

"Great!" Howard said, flashing that smile I hated. "You two kids run along now and I'll see you both tonight."

As Gavin and I left the library, I found myself hoping that I'd find Howard easier to take once there were hundreds of other people around. If not, this was going to be a very long night.

TWENTY-THREE

I'd never been on a yacht before. I'd seen pictures of this one in Howard's asset file but, as with the house, pictures didn't do it justice. It was large and gleaming white, nicer than a lot of houses. I couldn't imagine being able to own something like this. When we went aboard, Gavin introduced me to the two-man crew – Franz and Carlos – and then led me to the spacious deck. The men, Gavin said, would stick with piloting the yacht while he and I enjoyed ourselves.

I was still trying to decide what he meant as he showed me around, and then we were in a bedroom. I'd seen pictures of this, too, since the interior of the yacht had been documented, but what the pictures had failed to reveal were the leather restraints hanging from the headboard and base of the bed. I didn't need to ask this time what those were for. I remembered Gavin's explanation back at the club. What I did want to ask was if he was going to ask me to use them.

To my surprise, however, Gavin led me back out of the bedroom and up to the deck. We walked over to a pair of deck chairs and I saw two plastic coolers sitting on either side of them. Leaning against the railing were a pair of fishing poles.

Now I was truly confused. Was this some bizarre kink I didn't understand?

"Have you ever been fishing?" Gavin asked.

I raised an eyebrow. "Are you serious? Fishing?"

He gave me that boyish grin I loved so much. "It's relaxing."

I started to shake my head. "I don't know, Gavin."

"We'll throw back anything we catch," he said. "And I promise that I know how to do it right."

I looked up at him, squinting against the sun, then sighed. The things I was willing to do for this man. "All right. What do I do first?"

Fifteen minutes later, I was sitting in the deck chair, my fishing rod lightly grasped in my hands, the line in the water. Gavin sat in the chair next to me, looking rather pleased with himself. I wasn't sure if it was because he'd actually talked me into fishing or because he was truly enjoying it. I didn't think this was going to become a hobby of mine, but there was something soothing about watching the waves behind us, the wind blowing across the deck, the gentle tug of the pole in my hands.

Thing was, neither that nor the bottle of sparkling water I'd gotten from the cooler next to my seat was able to completely clear my mind. My thoughts kept returning to those leather restraints on the bed below and the comments Gavin had made last night about spanking me. After I'd first discovered what kind of club Gavin owned, Krissy and I had talked about what I would do if Gavin was into the whole S&M scene. I hadn't been able to give her an answer because I hadn't known what my response would be. He'd shown dominant tendencies before, but last night had been intense enough to make my previous questions return.

"Your body's here but your mind's a thousand miles away," Gavin said. "Is something wrong?"

I turned towards him and saw the concern on his face. If I couldn't talk to him about this, how could I ever have a relationship with him? I needed to know, and this was as good a time as any to ask.

"I was wondering," I began. "In the bedroom, there were those straps on the bed, like the ones at the club."

Gavin nodded, but didn't interrupt.

"And, last night." I could feel the flush threatening to creep up but didn't let it stop me. "You said you wanted to spank me."

He went very still, and I knew that if he hadn't been wearing sunglasses, I'd see worry in his eyes.

"I guess what I'm trying to ask, and doing a bad job of it, is how much into the whole S&M thing are you?" The words came out in a rush. "And I need to know why."

Gavin leaned forward, a thoughtful expression on his face. "I suppose it is time we talked about this." He clasped his hands in front of him. "Let me answer the why first. The other is a bit more detailed." One corner of his mouth twitched like he wanted to smile.

I nodded and tried to make my face as expressionless as possible. I wasn't sure what Gavin was going to say or how I was going to feel about it. The last thing I wanted to do was have a knee-jerk reaction and ruin things with him.

"The BDSM scene isn't about pain or humiliation. Not like we traditionally think about those things. It's about trust and pleasure." He was choosing his words carefully. "What brings that pleasure is just different than what people think of as normal. Some people are wired to only experience pleasure in a soft touch, in gentle love-making. They only want tenderness and a slow pace. Other people are wired differently. We crave other forms of sensation, and need different stimuli."

He paused, then took off his sunglasses so that I could see his eyes. I did the same, understanding that we needed to connect for this conversation.

"You can't imagine the levels of pleasure you can attain

when you give yourself over to your true desires." His voice softened. "Or maybe, after last night, you have an idea."

I shifted in my seat. I knew what he meant. The orgasms I'd experienced during our time together yesterday were like nothing I'd ever felt before.

"As for your first question," he continued. "It's a complicated answer because there are so many aspects to BDSM that it can't be looked at too broadly."

I nodded as if I understood what he was saying when, in reality, I had no clue. Fortunately, he explained himself.

"I'm a dominant person, Carrie. It's part of my personality. I like to be the one initiating the action." He grinned suddenly. "Though I have to admit, I have liked it when you've started things."

I smiled back, the tension in my body easing slightly.

"But, for the most part, when I'm having sex, I want to be the one deciding how things go," he continued. "That doesn't always mean the same thing, though. I don't have to be... bossy. I can feel in control even when I'm asking what you want."

"And the spanking?" I had to ask the question. Domination was one thing. I'd already decided that I liked it, and knowing how he viewed dominating me made me feel much more relaxed about it. The B, S, and M part of BDSM, however, still worried me.

Gavin turned back towards me. "I'm not hardcore, if that's what you're worried about." His tone was gentle. "What I do like are the things that intensify sensation, that take what a person could think of as mildly painful and convert them into pleasure. When it's done right, spanking can be as arousing as oral sex, and not just for the dominant."

My breathing quickened. He'd started using the same voice he used when he was telling me all the things he wanted to do to me. My body couldn't help but respond.

"I promise you, I'll never do anything you aren't comfortable with," he said. "But I'd be lying if I said I hadn't been thinking about some of the things I'd love to introduce you to."

I reached for my bottle of water, my mouth dry.

"I want to tie you to the bed and use a flogger on all those delicate little bits until you climax."

Fuck. My eyes widened.

He reached forward and gently cupped my breast, brushing his thumb over my nipple and making it harden under the fabric of my dress.

"I want to use clamps on your nipples, show you the edge of pleasure and pain."

My nipples throbbed, as if I could already feel the pinch of rubber or metal.

His hand moved up to the base of my neck and his fingers played with a few loose curls there.

"I want to use all sorts of toys on you, make you orgasm again and again until you beg me to stop. There are so many things I want to do to you, for you. Take you to heights that will leave you gasping for air." He sat back, taking his hand with him. "But I meant what I said, Carrie. I'll never ask you to do anything you don't want to do, and I'll never hold it against you. No matter what we're doing, as long as we're together, I'm happy."

He picked his fishing pole up again and settled back in his seat. I watched him for a moment before doing the same. The conversation was over. I'd gotten my answers. I trusted him to do as he promised, but now I needed to decide how far I truly wanted to go. It was a lot to think about.

TWENTY-FOUR

We enjoyed the rest of our afternoon on the yacht, but it had ended up being more quiet and thoughtful than I'd originally anticipated. As we headed back in, my thoughts turned away from my conversation with Gavin to the upcoming party. I'd have been lying if I'd said I wasn't nervous.

"Are you okay?" Gavin's voice was soft.

He was standing behind me, but not touching me. He hadn't touched me since we'd had our little talk, but I could tell it was his way of giving me space. We had jumped into this relationship with both feet, and there was still so much that we didn't know about each other.

I took a step back, closing the distance between us. When I leaned back against him, I heard him sigh. His arms slid around my waist and he put his cheek on the top of my head.

"I was worried I'd scared you off," he admitted.

"Not a chance." I put my hands on his arms. "I still don't know what or how far I'm willing to go, but I'm not running away."

His arms tightened around me. "Is that all that's got you so quiet?"

I shook my head. "I'm nervous about the party. You said it was even fancier than the gala, and that was the fanciest thing I'd ever been to." I paused, then admitted the whole truth: "I don't want to disappoint you."

"You never disappoint me." The words were fierce. "Never."

A thrill went through me. I'd told him something similar when he'd planned an elaborate dinner date on the roof of his building, complete with three men playing strings. Now I knew that he felt the same way.

"I did think you might be a bit apprehensive," he said. "So I booked a make-up artist and a hairdresser to help you get ready. They're meeting us at Howard's and they'll make sure you're every bit as stunning as I know you can be."

"Thank you," I said. My anxiety started to leak away.

"Not that I think you need make-up or a gown to be beautiful," he added. His voice dropped. "Seeing you standing in front of me last night, nothing covering that amazing body... You took my breath away."

I closed my eyes. I wasn't sure how to respond to that. Another "thank you" seemed so inadequate.

"Then again..." His words took on a teasing note. "I don't want anyone else to see you that way, so a gown and all the trimmings will be the way to go for the party."

I laughed. I understood what he meant. He looked good – better than good – in his tux, but he looked even better without it. That wasn't a sight I wanted to share with anyone else.

"After the party, though," he continued, "I want to get you out of that dress and into bed."

I could hear a note of uncertainty and knew where he was coming from. For all he knew, I wouldn't want to have sex with him until I figured this whole kink thing out. I didn't have that kind of self-control when it came to him. I'd make sure we didn't go any further than I was comfortable, but I wasn't about to cut him off completely.

"That sounds wonderful," I said. "Any chance we can cut out early?"

He laughed, and the sound sent vibrations through me. I loved that sound. It was strange, I thought, how pretty much everything about my relationship with Gavin had been completely ass-backwards from how I usually did things, but the connection I had with him was stronger than anything I'd ever felt before. I should've been questioning it, second-guessing myself for falling so hard and so fast, but I pushed all the negative aside. I'd made my choice. I was with Gavin. It didn't matter how it had happened, only that we belonged together.

I was a little disappointed when we arrived back at the mansion and Gavin said he wouldn't be staying with me to get ready, but I went with one of Howard's staff, who showed me to the bedroom Gavin and I would be sharing. It wasn't as big as the suite back at the hotel, and the view wasn't as spectacular. I didn't care about that though. As long as I was with Gavin, it didn't matter where we were.

"Ms. Summers." A tall, elegant brunette greeted me as soon as I stepped inside the room. "I'm Rose, your stylist for the evening."

I smiled and shook the hand she offered. "Call me Carrie, please." Another woman stepped forward to take my hand when I was done. She was short, probably barely five feet tall, and curvy.

"I'm Glory. I'll be doing your make-up."

I nodded. For a moment, we stood there, and then I spoke, "I've never done this before, so I need to know what you want me to do first."

Two hours later, I stood in front of a full-length mirror while Rose and Glory finished up. The dress Krissy and I had chosen was a deep, rich green, so Glory had done my make-up to match. My eyes looked huge and even darker than normal, and my lips a wet shade of red that was dark enough to complement my skin, but not so red that it looked like it belonged on a hooker.

Because of the Miami heat, the air conditioning would be on full blast, allowing me to wear my hair down. Normally, I wasn't fond of it that way since my curls had a tendency to go a bit wild, but Rose was a magician. She tamed the curls and twisted half of my hair back so it'd be off my face, but left it hanging down so that it reached the small of my back, just below where the dress's open back ended.

One of the reasons I'd liked this dress was that it had a modest neckline, showing just a hint of cleavage, but the back was daringly low. Like my gala dress, this one was long, but it didn't have the slit up the side. Instead, it hugged my legs, hips, and waist. I could walk in it as long as I took small to normal-sized steps and moved slowly. If I tried to hurry, it wouldn't end well.

I was just slipping on my four-inch heels – a concession to the walking difficulty – when the door opened and Gavin entered.

"The guests are starting to arrive," he said. His eyes lit up as Rose stepped out of the way and let him see me. "Wow."

I smiled. "Rose and Glory did an amazing job, didn't they?"

He nodded, still not taking his eyes off of me. "Ladies, you've outdone yourself. I'll be sending bonuses with the second half of your payments."

They thanked him, but I wasn't sure he even heard them. The only reason I saw them leave was that they had to cross into my line of sight to do it. Gavin and I were too busy looking at each other to acknowledge their exit. He was wearing a tuxedo, but I thought it was a different one than he'd had before. This one had a small bit of color. His tie was a dark shade of blue that would've looked black if it hadn't been next to his jacket. The cut of the jacket was different too. I didn't know enough about men's fashions to be able to name it, but whatever it was, I liked it. Even more than his other one, this tux showed off his physique.

"You look magnificent," he said.

He held out his hand and I took it, electricity racing along my nerves as my palm slid across his. When he raised his hand to his lips and kissed the back, my heart did a little skip.

"But," he added. "Even all of this can't compare to how you looked last night."

My insides gave a pleasurable squirm.

"That, however, is just for me to enjoy."

I nodded, not trusting myself to speak. If I opened my mouth, there was a good chance we wouldn't make it downstairs and all of this preparation would've been for nothing. Still, it was tempting.

"Shall we?" The expression on Gavin's face told me he was thinking along the same lines.

We switched from holding hands to having my arm hooked through his as we descended the stairs. I felt like one of those girls in those movies, who goes to her prom or a party where she makes this grand entrance down a staircase. I didn't have a spotlight or a theme song, but I did have a handsome man on my arm.

I was able to look around the room as we came down the stairs, taking in the crowd from a different perspective than I'd have once we reached the floor. Hundreds of people were milling around, going in and out of the various doorways that I remembered led to a sitting room, the dining room, and a third room that I couldn't name. I recognized a few people from the entertainment industry. A director, a couple of actors, and one of those people who are famous for being famous. I also saw entrepreneurs I'd seen in various business magazines and running charities, as well as a handful of politicians. And it wasn't only American politicians. I recognized at least one head of state from Europe and two from the Middle East. I'd seen pictures of them with the president. For everyone I had a name to attach, there were dozens more that I couldn't place.

Also weaving their way through the crowd were more than three dozen drop-dead gorgeous women in bunny costumes carrying trays of finger food. Every one of them looked like they were about three seconds away from falling out of their tops. Before we reached the bottom step, I leaned closer to Gavin and said, "Howard must think he's a certain celebrity playboy if he surrounds himself with women dressed as bunnies."

Gavin laughed, but there was an edge to the sound I couldn't quite place. "You're not far off," he said. "Sometimes I think he believes he's Casanova."

My smile tightened. As long as Casanova kept it in his pants and didn't try to seduce me, we'd be fine. I took as deep a breath as my dress allowed and fixed my smile. Gavin and I were heading into the throng, and our first stop would be to greet the host. Gavin steered me through the crowd with his hand on the small of my back. He could have just kept our arms linked, but I liked that he chose to use a more intimate gesture.

When we reached Howard, I saw that he was flanked on either side by the same two women who'd been flirting with Gavin at the gala. I felt the corners of my mouth tighten, but I behaved myself and greeted them both with smiles.

"Carrie, wow!" Howard's eyes lit up, then began their slow crawl down my body. "You look amazing."

"Thank you." I tried not to let him see how much I didn't like the way he was looking at me. Gavin said Howard flirted with all women. It was just the way he was.

"I'm serious," Howard continued. "I can't decide if you'd look better with the dress or without, and that's saying something."

I felt Gavin stiffen next to me. Good to know that even he felt Howard had crossed the line with that one. Howard, however, appeared completely oblivious.

"Have you met Delilah and Ellie?" He motioned to the blonde and brunette respectively.

"Unofficially only," I said. "They sat next to Gavin at the gala."

Gavin's hand slid from my back around my waist to rest low on my hip and very visible to the trio in front of us. The tips of his fingers, in fact, were resting dangerously close to the edge of my panties. A warmth spread through me, part arousal, and part pleasure at his making an unmistakable gesture of possession.

"That's right." Howard nodded. "Well, these ladies have been two of my most trusted employees over the past two years. I'd be lost without them."

Interesting. I seemed to remember Gavin referring to them as part of Howard's entourage, not as his employees. Before I could ask for clarification, a man in an expensive-looking tux approached. He made one of those small gestures that people do when trying to get the attention of someone they know but not wanting to interrupt.

"Oh, I'm sorry, ladies," Howard said. "Gavin and I need to speak with our associate for a moment." He leaned over and whispered something in the blonde's ear – Delilah, I was pretty sure – but I couldn't make out what it was. He then smiled at me and headed for the associate.

"I'll be back as quick as I can," Gavin said. He lightly kissed my cheek, then followed Howard.

"So, Carrie, you've managed to snag Gavin for a date to the gala and to this party." Delilah gave me a simpering smile. "He is quite the catch. After Howard, of course."

I refrained from rolling my eyes. Was she serious?

"Howard always has had quite the eye when it comes to spotting potential." Ellie sounded like she was spouting something from a brochure. I had no doubt Howard had coached her on exactly what to say.

Apparently, he thought that these two would be able to talk

him up. Not that it was surprising. He didn't strike me as the type who had much of an opinion about the intelligence of women, and these two were giving me a pretty good idea as to his usual type. I fully intended to use that against him.

"He must," I agreed. "After all, he found the two of you, didn't he?"

They both beamed.

Okay, no sense of sarcasm. This was going to be easier than I'd thought.

"What do you do for him?" I figured I'd try for a blunt question and see what I got.

"Oh, all kinds of things," Delilah said airily. "We go with him to parties like this and talk to girls."

"Talk to girls?" I hoped they couldn't hear the eagerness in my voice, or if they did, they misunderstood what it was for.

"Yes," Ellie said. "Girls like you. Ones Howard thinks are interesting and wants to bring into the business."

I wondered if Patricia Vinarisky had been one of those girls, and felt a flare of anger towards these two women. They might have been legitimately innocent in whatever it was Howard was doing, but I couldn't believe they'd willingly recruit girls for whatever Howard wanted.

"And what do these girls, the ones like me, do for Howard?" I asked.

Delilah and Ellie exchanged a glance that said they didn't like me asking such a pointed question. Did other girls just accept that it was a legitimate offer because they were so wowed by Howard and his bimbos?

"Well," Delilah answered, telling me she was the smarter of the two. "It depends. Some girls stay on here and others go to New York. I'll bet that's where he'll have you, since that's where you're from."

"There are branches of his business all over the world," Ellie added. "When he hires someone, he always looks for where they'll fit best."

"And what about you two?" I couldn't resist a bit of a tease. "Aren't you worried?"

"Worried?" Delilah spoke, but both women wore puzzled expressions. "About what?"

"About him finding someone to take your place."

They both flinched as if I'd slapped them. That was a bit of an extreme reaction, I thought. Apparently, I'd hit a nerve. That was good. That meant, if I kept pushing, they might say something they wouldn't have otherwise.

"Come on," I said. "You had to have thought about it. You're not getting any younger, and plastic surgery can only do so much, right?" I made my tone as understanding as I could muster. "You have to be thinking it every time he talks about hiring someone younger." I smoothed down the sides of my dress, drawing their eyes to my body. "Someone prettier."

Delilah scowled. "Howard knows how valuable we are."

"And he tells us every day how beautiful we are," Ellie added.

Neither one of them was giving me a very friendly look now. That was fine with me. I wasn't looking for friends. I was looking for answers.

"He trusts us," Delilah continued. "Trusts us to find him the right girls."

"He brings us to all of these parties," Ellie said. "And we get to meet rich and famous men from all over."

"So he doesn't keep you to himself?" I asked. "He shares you with his friends?"

I let the question stand as bald and rude as I'd meant it to sound.

They didn't get the opportunity for retaliation, however, because Howard appeared, and they switched back to their glowing smiles. Their eyes, however, shot daggers at me whenever Howard wasn't looking. That was fine. I didn't really care what they thought about me. I was more convinced than ever that Howard was up to no good, and that, despite the lack of evidence, he'd had something to do with Patricia's disappearance.

"So, ladies, did you talk about me when I was gone?" Howard gave what I assumed he intended to be a charming smile. "All good things, I hope."

I looked around. "Where's Gavin?"

"Oh, he had to step out for a moment to get something for our associate." Howard took a step forward so that he was no longer between Ellie and Delilah, but closer to me. "I have to ask, Carrie, have you given any more thought to coming to work for me?"

My eyes darted to one side, unable to make eye contact. It hadn't really been difficult to realize that I didn't want to work for Howard, but I didn't want to tell him now, like this. As uncomfortable as he made me, I couldn't think of a legitimate reason to turn down his offer in a public setting. So, I lied. "I've just been so swamped at work, with your case and all, I haven't had time to think about it." I purposefully reminded him that I was working for him already, albeit indirectly.

"Well, we'll just have to make time, won't we?" He lightly touched my arm. "Why don't you come by my Manhattan office on Monday morning and we can discuss it in greater depth then. I'd love to show you the many benefits you'd get by working for me."

A chill went over me and I could barely stop myself from shivering. If I did that, Howard might think I was actually cold and offer me his jacket, or worse, try to put his arm around me. I couldn't say specifically why, but I didn't think I wanted to know what benefits he had in mind. Somehow, I doubted he was talking about a 401k. Still, I wasn't going to be rude, and besides, I could use the opportunity to try to find out more about what he was up to.

"I'll see you at eight," I said.

"Excellent." Howard smiled. "I'll be waiting in anticipation."

I wasn't sure how I was supposed to respond to that, but, fortunately, I didn't have to, because another partygoer came up to greet Howard. I didn't want to attempt another conversation with Delilah and Ellie, and judging by their expressions, they didn't want to talk to me either.

I turned, intending to find a quiet place to be alone until I could find Gavin, but it wasn't necessary. He was coming out of the library, his expression serious, eyes scanning the crowd. When his gaze met mine, his face lit up and I knew he'd been looking for me. We made our way towards each other, and the moment our hands touched, I relaxed. None of that other stuff mattered. Only the feel of his hand around mine and the fire in his eyes.

TWENTY-FIVE

Three hours of laughing at jokes I didn't find funny and thanking men for telling me how beautiful I looked while they undressed me with their eyes was about all I could stomach. When a serious-looking man told Gavin that they needed to speak privately about an urgent manner, I saw my chance. I assured Gavin that I'd be fine alone, then made my way towards the back staircase the moment he was out of sight. Howard's tour of the house was coming in handy.

I crept up the stairs, hoping no one else had gotten this idea. When I reached the second floor, it was quiet. Still, I wasn't going to take any chances. I slipped off my shoes and carried them as I made my way down the hall. There had been one room on this floor that Howard had mentioned, but hadn't let me see more of than a quick glimpse through the doorway, and it was to this room I now headed.

His office.

If there was anywhere in the entire house that held his secrets, this would be it. If I could find some sort of paper trail connecting him to the anonymous women in his pictures beyond those few shots, maybe I could figure out what he was doing. More than that, if I could find proof he'd been in contact with Patricia after their brief encounter, I might be able to get the police to investigate Howard in relation to the girl's disappearance. It was a long shot, I knew, but it was all I had.

I fully expected his office to be locked, but I hadn't taken into account Howard's hubris. Men like him, ones with money and friends in high places, they always thought they were untouchable. He'd never dream that anyone would have the gall to sneak into his office. Even if he did think someone would dare such a thing, he struck me as the type of person who assumed he was smarter than everyone else and, therefore, he had nothing to fear because no one would be able to uncover his secrets.

I was determined to prove him wrong on both counts.

His office was just as pretentious as I'd thought it was at first glance. I didn't dwell on that though. I wasn't here to critique his décor. I needed to figure out where he hid his paperwork. Of course, he wasn't going to make it easy for me by having an ordinary filing cabinet with an easily pickable lock. No, Howard had gone with a state-of-the-art steel cabinet with a code lock. It looked like one of those safes in a hotel room, the kind where rich people hide their jewels while on vacation.

I sighed in frustration. The keypad was numeric and it appeared to be eight digits. Actual word passcodes were so much easier to figure out because often there were commonly used ones that didn't require any personal knowledge. People like Howard would use words like "god," "power," "money," and "sex." Numbers, however, were nearly impossible without knowing things like birthdays and anniversaries. Not that Howard would use his anniversary, I reasoned. I knew it was pretty much hopeless to try to guess, but I did a couple common ones. All zeroes. One, two, three, four... Then backwards. Not surprisingly, none of them worked.

I turned towards his desk. Maybe I could find something there that would give me a clue as to what his passcode could be. I was careful as I looked through his papers, making sure only to touch with the very tips of my fingers and putting back anything I moved. If I couldn't find evidence of a crime, I didn't want him being suspicious that someone was looking into him.

After several minutes of searching, I still had nothing, and I knew I was running on borrowed time. Either Gavin would figure out I was missing or one of the security guards would venture up to this floor and find me. I had to get out before then, but I was reluctant to leave with nothing.

As I turned, something on the bookcase caught my eye. *The Art of War*. That was the book Howard had in his library, the one that had belonged to his mob boss great-grandfather. Well, not the exact same book. This one was a newer edition, one purchased to be read rather than one to be put on display. Had Howard bought it to feel closer to his ancestor or had he wanted to have the same mentality towards business that had allowed his family to run a vast empire for generations? I didn't think either one was a particularly good reason.

I reached for it, not really sure why I was doing it. Maybe I wanted to see if it was dog-eared and highlighted versus barely touched. It didn't matter, though. As soon as I opened it, a newspaper clipping fluttered to the floor, catching my attention. I picked it up, intending to put it back into the book, unread, but then I saw the picture of a beautiful young woman with blond hair and a sweet smile.

I recognized her.

Camille, Gavin's late fiancée.

I set the book down on the desk and began to read the article.

TWENTY-FOUR-YEAR-OLD CAMILLE TURNER *was struck by a hit-and-run driver yesterday afternoon as she and her fiancé, Gavin Manning, were out for a walk. The actions taken by Manning kept Turner alive until paramedics arrived and saved the life of his unborn child, a girl who was delivered via C-section at the hospital less than an hour later. Turner was officially pronounced dead minutes after her daughter was born. A hospital spokesman assured us that the baby, though a week early, is doing well and showing no signs of trauma from the accident. The only witness, Manning, gave the police a description of the vehicle as a black Bentley, but was unable to provide any additional details as he had been focusing his attention on Turner and their child. The police are asking anyone who may have any information about the incident to please call their local precinct.*

MY BRAIN DIDN'T KNOW what to register first. Gavin had been responsible for saving his daughter's life, but he hadn't been able to save the woman he loved. As the only witness, whatever information he'd given the police had been their only leads. If he'd gotten a license plate number, they might have been able to find the person responsible, so he had to feel guilty about that. Then, there was the huge, glaring fact that he'd failed to mention to me.

A black Bentley.

Why hadn't Gavin told me it was a Bentley? Had he not thought it was important after all these years? And hadn't he thought the same thing I was thinking right now? Howard loved Bentleys, had a lot of them. I was sure that had been true five years ago, too. Or had Gavin just dismissed the idea that his friend could be involved because a car preference wasn't enough evidence? The thing was, now it wasn't just the fact that Howard owned a black Bentley. Howard had a newspaper clipping about the accident tucked away in a book. Why would he have it if it didn't mean something?

Another thought occurred to me. This article had been written the day after the accident. Howard and Gavin hadn't known each other then. It was possible, I supposed, that after Howard had met Gavin that he'd tracked down the paper, but it seemed like an awful lot of trouble when he could've just read it online. He had no reason to find, cut out, and keep it.

Unless he'd had something to do with the accident. Black Bentleys weren't exactly uncommon in the city, but they weren't so prevalent that the odds of its being a coincidence were high.

Had Howard killed Gavin's fiancée? I was close enough to being a lawyer to know that what I had was circumstantial, and any good defense attorney would be able to spread reasonable doubt. Besides, I didn't want to destroy Gavin's friendship based on a theory, albeit a compelling one. I needed more.

I looked back at the cabinet-safe. I needed to get inside. Surely, if Howard was guilty of anything, the evidence would be in there. I just needed to figure out the right code. I looked back down at the article. Written June fourteenth. A snapshot of Gavin's tattoo flashed in front of my eyes. Six thirteen. The day of the accident.

My eyes widened. It couldn't be that simple. I walked over to the cabinet anyway. It wouldn't hurt to try it out. My fingers were trembling as I put in the eight digits: zero six one three two zero zero eight.

The click was louder than I expected, and I jumped. It had worked. I could barely believe it.

I opened the cabinet and saw row after row of files. I didn't have the time to go through all of them. I just needed to find my smoking gun. I started to flip through the folders, looking for something that could connect Howard to Camille's death. My fingers, however, stopped above another name.

Patricia Vinarisky.

I grabbed it. If I could get evidence about her, I could get a warrant, and if Howard had something about Camille, I could find it then. I started to look through the file. It was similar to what Gavin had given me, but there were dozens more pictures of Patricia, and they weren't exactly similar to the professional ones Gavin had. These were of the girl in various outfits, each one more risqué than the next, eventually getting her down to her underwear, then even less. At least half a dozen pictures were of her naked, a couple just standing, looking uncomfortable, but the rest had her in various lewd poses.

I flipped them over, and about half had dates written on them. Dates that were much closer to the day she disappeared than the ones I'd seen. I felt a flare of excitement. This was good. None of the pictures had Howard in them, but the fact that he had possession of them, particularly the sexual ones, meant that I could reasonably speculate that he had something to do with her disappearance.

Behind the pictures were two sheets of paper stapled together. At first glance, it looked like some sort of inventory or information sheet, almost like the one Gavin had in his folder. There was one major difference between the two, however. I couldn't read what this one said because it wasn't in English.

I may not have been able to recognize the language, but I'd seen enough news in the past ten years to be fairly confident in thinking it was a Middle Eastern language of some kind. Arabic perhaps. I'd need to show it to a translator to be certain. The only question was, how was I going to get these papers out of here? I definitely didn't have any room to smuggle them out in my dress. If I'd had my phone, I could've taken pictures and mailed them to myself, but I'd left my phone in my purse... It was in the guest room in this very house. I could get it, come back here, and take the pictures. No one would think it was odd that I'd decided to get my phone. Or at least I hoped they wouldn't. There was still the risk of being caught sneaking back into the office, but it would be worth it. I had to know what had happened to Patricia, if Howard was involved, and now, if he had something to do with Camille's death as well.

I was just starting to put the folder back into the cabinet when I heard it. Voices. I moved faster, hoping they'd walk past. Then I heard them stop directly outside the door. Shit. This was bad. I looked around for a place to hide. If Howard caught me in here, I didn't know what he'd do, but I didn't think it'd be good. Panic began to fill me as I saw the doorknob turn.

TWENTY-SIX

Howard
June 13th 2008

This was not the way I'd wanted to spend my day. It was a beautiful June afternoon in the Big Apple, but the atmosphere around me and my lunch companion was anything but pleasant. Earlier this month, after almost seven years, suspects in the attack on this city were arraigned. Today, there were rumors of a breakout of more than two hundred Taliban members from prison. Neither of these things made New Yorkers more inclined to be friendly to the Saudi man across from me.

I wasn't talking to him at the moment, however. No, I was on my cell phone trying to figure out how much more damage control was going to be needed for the disaster that had happened several hours ago.

"Were you able to move the car without being seen?" I kept my voice low even though the surrounding tables were empty. One could never be too careful.

"Yes, sir, Mr. Weiss." Gene was my fixer, the man I called

when things went to hell like they had earlier today. "And I heard from my police contact, too."

"And?" I asked impatiently.

"There's a witness."

I swore, my hand tightening on my phone.

"Sounds like he didn't see much," Gene continued. "It's the woman's fiancé. He was so busy with her, all he could tell the cops was that it was a black Bentley. He didn't even get a single letter on the plate."

I relaxed a little. Bentleys weren't exactly common, but I was hardly the only person in the city who owned one. I owned more than one, in fact. If we played our cards right, this could go away.

"Tell your contact to keep you informed," I instructed. "If the witness remembers anything else, anything that could come back on us, take care of it."

"Got it."

The call ended and I pocketed my phone. I turned back to my business partner, a smile on my face. It was almost all genuine. "Everything is clear. We can move on as planned."

"Excellent," he said in his heavily accented English. He leaned down and retrieved a suitcase. He slid it across the table to me. "The price we agreed upon."

I opened the case, my smiling widening into completely genuine as I saw the neat little bundles of bills. "It is always a pleasure doing business with you," I said as I closed the briefcase.

Now, if the little incident went away, it would turn out to be a good day after all.

TWENTY-SEVEN

Carrie
Present Day

SHIT, shit, and double shit. I silently cursed as my brain scrambled to figure out what to do. If I didn't act fast, I was going to be caught with my hand in the proverbial cookie jar. Except the cookie jar was a locked filing cabinet, and instead of a cookie, I was holding in my hand the file of a missing girl. A file that contained some pictures that would be pretty good circumstantial evidence saying that Howard Weiss had been in contact with Patricia Vinarisky around the time of her disappearance.

I shoved the file back into the cabinet and closed it, hoping it locked automatically. Now I had to find somewhere to hide. The voices in the hallway had stopped in front of the office door and someone was turning the doorknob. Thankfully, the person on the other side of the door paused.

I ran across the room as quickly as my elegant evening gown

and high-heeled shoes would let me. The door on the other side of the office led to a closet or bathroom, either one of which was fine with me. I just needed to be somewhere out of sight.

I ducked inside without looking behind me. The room felt bigger than I'd originally assumed, but I didn't take the time to see why. All of my attention was focused through the thin crack in the door. I'd considered closing it all the way, but a part of me felt the need to know what was happening.

The door to the office opened and I watched two people enter. One was Howard Weiss, the handsome billionaire whose office I'd broken into. The other was his personal assistant, Annie. Like all of the other women I'd seen with Howard, she was beautiful. Tall, slender, with honey blond hair and light blue eyes. She could have been a model.

At first, I was so focused on hoping they didn't look my way that I completely missed the angry expression on Howard's face. It wasn't until he spoke that I realized he and Annie were in here for something other than a quick grab of some papers or taking a memo. Something had happened while I'd been away from the party.

"How in the world do you lose a person?" His voice was low and angry, more so than I'd ever heard it before. The charming mask that he wore all the time had slipped away, and even though he still had his classic movie-star good looks, there was something ugly about him.

"I double-checked the flight manifests myself, sir. She was checked in." Annie sounded nervous.

Howard took a step towards his assistant, his eyes darkening to almost black. "I don't give a fuck if she checked in. I want to know why, when my client went to the airport to pick up his package, she wasn't there."

I pressed my hand over my mouth to stifle my gasp. Was I hearing correctly? Or was I just reading into it because I didn't trust Howard?

"Do you have any idea how much money this is costing me?" The rage in his voice had slipped away and now his tone was flat, and it was somehow more frightening. "My top girls, like her, bring in thirty thousand a night in Saudi Arabia. She was supposed to serve my client for three months. Do the math, Annie. That's a hell of a lot of money."

"Yes, sir." She nodded, her face pale.

"And it's not just the money." He stepped around behind her, using his body to turn her towards his desk. "You know Saudi Arabia is my biggest country of export. That's why we have a partner there. We don't want to disappoint him, do we?"

When he put his hands on either side of the desk, encircling Annie in his arms, my stomach clenched. What the hell was he doing? This wasn't flirting or even inappropriate comments, this was full-blown sexual harassment.

"No, sir." Anna's face turned even paler.

"If I can't provide assurances to my clients regarding delivery of their merchandise, they're going to go elsewhere."

He put his mouth against Annie's ear as his hands moved up to take her wrists. He put her hands flat on the desk. I couldn't see all of her face, but I could see enough to notice how her expression had changed. She didn't look annoyed or frightened now, more like she knew what was coming and wasn't sure how she felt about it.

"If they go somewhere else, Annie, that would be very bad." Howard's voice was almost too low for me to hear. He slid his hands up Annie's hips, over her ribcage, and then around to cup her small breasts through the thin silk of her dress.

I swallowed hard, wanting to look away but unable to actually do it. Annie wasn't fighting to get away, but rather arching her back, pushing her breasts further into his hands.

"I want to keep you here with me, Annie."

Howard dropped one hand, moving it low enough that it was out of my line of sight. I was able to see, however, the material of the dress shift, and then Annie caught her breath. I didn't need to see what was happening to know where Howard's fingers were now.

"But I need a replacement for my missing girl and unless you can find one for me, I'll have to send whoever I happen to have on hand."

Annie made a noise half of protest, half of pleasure. Her face was flushed, her eyes closed.

"And I'd have to make sure they know I punished the person responsible, so I'd be forced to hurt whoever is being sent." He wrapped his free hand in her hair and pulled, yanking her neck back until she gave a cry of pain. "I'd have to mark their skin with a cane, and still, my client will likely negotiate for their time and inconvenience."

He pulled his hand from between her legs and she made a sound of frustration. He pushed her forward until she was bent over the desk. He ran his hands over her body, his fingers flexing and squeezing.

"Because of your mistake, I might even have to give them that replacement permanently." One of his hands went back up her skirt, this time from behind, and she yelped in pain, her nails scratching over his desk. "Do you know what they do to their permanent girls? The ways they fuck them? How many men use them at a time?" He chuckled, and I could see on his face that even though he was angry, he was enjoying himself. His hand moved under her skirt, continuing to do whatever it was that was hurting her.

"What about that new woman, Carrie?" Annie asked, her voice strained.

I caught my breath. She couldn't be talking about me.

Howard scowled. His hands both moved to the front of his pants, but I wasn't really paying attention to that now. I wanted to hear why Annie had said my name.

"Carrie's not ready yet," he said. "I thought for sure she'd be groomed by now. Gavin has really disappointed me. I'm starting to doubt that he's the one to take over as my recruiter after all."

TWENTY-EIGHT

My head spun and, for a moment, I was afraid I was going to pass out. I stayed at the door, staring into the office, but I barely registered what Howard was doing to Annie now. Her cries and his grunts were background noise to the chaos in my mind.

Howard was selling women. He'd probably sold Patricia. The women downstairs recruited for him. Gavin recruited for him. Everything between us had been a lie. Every touch, every kiss. It all fit. He'd been grooming me for Howard, teaching me how to submit and obey, conditioning my body to respond to commands. His comment about spanking made perfect sense now too. I was learning obedience. Next, he needed to teach me how to enjoy pain.

I put my hand over my mouth and tried not to throw up. My stomach was churning, the champagne I'd drunk threatening to make an appearance. I forced myself to take slow, deep breaths. I couldn't leave any evidence that I'd been here. Howard was just as dangerous as I'd thought, but now I couldn't even count on Gavin to protect me. He was part of this.

A sharp cry of pain drew my attention back out in time to

see Howard finish. Annie was slumped over the desk, her face turned away from me so I couldn't see her expression. She had to hate what he'd done to her, had to want him to pay. Maybe I could get her to talk to me, give me the evidence I needed. I wanted everyone involved to pay for what they were doing to these women. My nausea faded as my anger flared. I wanted everyone to pay.

Howard took a step back and I heard Annie suck in a sharp breath of air. He didn't bother to fix her dress, but rather slapped her ass hard enough to make her jump. "Good girl."

My hands curled into fists. If I thought I could physically take him, I would've been out there in a minute, but all that would do would give him one more victim. I knew self-defense, but this dress would hamper any sort of movement I tried to make. No, I had to bide my time. I needed that file, and I needed to see if he had any more records of what he was doing. When he left, I was going to grab as much as I could carry and then figure out what to do next.

A knock at the door startled all three of us. Annie straightened, a pained look crossing her face before it became blank. Her make-up wasn't even smudged. For a moment, I thought maybe they'd just been role-playing, that he hadn't really hurt her, but then she took a step and I saw her wince.

"What is it?" Howard asked sharply, raising his voice to be heard through the door.

I wondered if whoever was out there had heard the end of what had just happened and what they thought about it.

"Sir, one of your guests has a concern regarding the origin of the fruit being served. He's worried about whether or not it's organic."

"Are you fucking kidding me?" he snapped. He wheeled on Annie, who flinched a little. "Since apparently none of my employees know how to do anything on their own, I need you to go handle whatever the hell this is and then come back."

She nodded without looking at him and started for the door. When he spoke again, she paused.

"And, Annie, darling, remember, if this situation isn't resolved, what I just did to you is going to seem like a picnic compared to what will happen."

I saw her shoulders stiffen, but she gave no other outward sign that she'd heard the threat. How could she let him do that to her? Hurt her, threaten to sell her off? And it wasn't like she was some escort he'd hired or one of those bimbos downstairs. That would've been bad enough. Annie was his assistant. She had a legitimate job with him and he hadn't even hesitated to hurt her. I was no psychologist, but I could tell this hadn't been the first time he'd done this. She couldn't actually care about him, could she? Was that why she hadn't gone to the police? Or, the thought came to me, was it something more basic? Howard wasn't only rich and with friends in high places, but his family's history meant he probably had friends in low places too. Even if someone did believe her, she'd never be safe. I realized that meant the same for me. If I tried to follow through with this, there was a good chance I could get hurt. I could just walk away, tell Mimi that my relationship with Gavin had ended and I couldn't be objective. I'd stay away and pretend like none of this ever happened.

The thought was fleeting and immediately followed by the images of Patricia, that sweet-looking girl, and how she'd been degraded and used. I knew now that those pictures didn't even tell a small portion of her story, and if she was still alive, she was experiencing things worse than I'd just seen. I squared my shoulders and set my jaw. No, I wasn't going to let fear of what could happen to me keep me from doing what was right.

I turned my attention back to Howard. He opened the filing cabinet and began shuffling through its contents. I took a moment to look around while he was occupied. I needed to know more about my surroundings in case he decided he needed something from wherever it was that I'd hidden myself.

I'd been right when I'd thought the space I was in was too big for a closet. It was actually a small bedroom. Well, more accurately, a room with a bed, a double that took up most of the room. The only other thing was a small table to one side of the bed. There was another door, and what little I could see in the dark interior told me that it led to a bathroom. A bathroom off of his office made sense, but if I hadn't just seen what Howard had done to Annie, I would've been puzzled by the bed. After all, he was in his house. It wasn't like he needed it in case he worked too late. I knew, though, that this bed wasn't for sleeping. I had a feeling if I looked closely, I'd find the same kind of restraints on this bed that I'd seen on Howard's yacht and at the club.

A noise from the office pulled my attention back. Howard had set a stack of files on his desk and was putting them into a briefcase. I hoped that meant he was about to leave, even if he was taking the files with him. As long as I could get out of here in one piece, I could figure out a way to find those files again. Howard struck me as the kind of man who'd never deign to destroy anything, no matter how incriminating. He was more of the "keep a trophy and brag" type.

He turned towards the bookcase and my heart started to pound. I knew where he was going even before his fingers brushed over the spine of the book. He frowned as he pulled it out, and I felt a stab of fear. Had I put it back in the wrong place?

Shit.

He opened the book and I could see his body tensing.

The article. What the hell had happened to the article?

With panic threatening to take over, I watched him looking around. When he bent over, I knew he'd spotted it. Would he think that it had just fallen when he'd opened the book and he hadn't seen it, or would he realize that someone had been snooping? The moment he straightened, I knew that he was suspicious. I needed to hide better.

I started towards the bathroom, but stopped. I didn't know if it was just a toilet or if there'd be a shower I could hide in. And what if the shower doors were glass? No, I needed somewhere else.

My eyes fell on the bed, then dropped lower. There wasn't much room, but it was the best I had. I dropped and wiggled underneath. The frame scraped against my back, but I could fit. I pushed myself back as far as possible and waited.

What seemed like forever passed, and then the room flooded with light. I scrunched back into the shadows, trying to make myself as small as I could. I could see his feet as he entered the room and crossed to the bathroom. The light went on there as well. I heard running water, then the light went out again. He stood in the middle of the room for a moment, then walked back towards the door. The light went out and I sighed in relief. Still, I stayed under the bed.

I might not have been able to see Howard anymore, but I could hear him as he called out for Annie to come back in. I really hoped he wasn't going to bring her in here for a second round, this time right above me. I wasn't sure I could handle that. He didn't, however. Instead, he told her that she would be flying back to New York tonight and she was to take the files to his Manhattan office.

"I want you spending the rest of the weekend giving me a short list of replacement candidates," he added. "I'll make the final decision on Monday. And remember, if I can't find anyone suitable, you're going to be taking a little trip."

I heard a sound that I didn't want to try to identify, and then I heard the door close. I stayed where I was, straining my ears to hear anything that might indicate whether or not Howard had left the room as well. When several minutes passed and I didn't hear anything, I slid out from under the bed. I brushed off my dress and crept over to the door. I peeked out and didn't see anything. It was time for me to return to the party. I just hoped I could lie as well as I thought I could. If Gavin suspected I knew the truth, I didn't know what he'd do.

TWENTY-NINE

"Are you sure you're okay?"

I grimaced and nodded my head. The concern in Gavin's voice was tearing me up. How could he pretend to care like that? It was beyond cruel.

From the moment I'd left Howard's office and headed back down to the party, I'd known that I might be able to smile and make nice, but the moment Gavin had touched me, it had taken everything in me not to recoil. My body was torn, wanting to respond to his touch, to the pleasure I knew he could bring, but I was at the same time repulsed by what I'd discovered. When he asked if I was feeling all right, I'd realized that I had a cover.

The remainder of the weekend, I'd played sick. It had been painful having to watch him hover and act like he wanted to take care of me, but I just reminded myself how much worse it would have been to have followed through with our plans. If I couldn't stand having him touch me in a nonsexual way, I never could have gotten through a kiss, much less fucking. And that's what it had been, I reminded myself. No matter how tender he'd pretended to be, how often he'd said he wanted to pleasure me, it had all been a scam. He'd fucked me over as thoroughly as he'd fucked me physically, and I refused to let myself consider that it could be anything else.

The only thing that kept nagging at me was the story about his fiancée and daughter. If I hadn't seen the article, I would've just assumed he'd lied about the whole thing, that the initials and date meant something else. Maybe that he was married or the very least had a girlfriend. But I'd seen the article, and everything he'd told me matched. Sure, there'd been a couple of details he'd left out, but nothing contradicted his story.

It hadn't been until the early hours of the morning, after he'd fallen asleep in the chair next to the bed, that I'd realized what the truth most likely was. All that Gavin had told me about Camille and his daughter was true up to the reasoning behind why he didn't have custody of Skylar. I was willing to bet that when Howard had approached him after Camille's death, he'd given Gavin purpose all right. He'd given him a job where he could make a lot of money and, twisted and bitter as he'd become over Camille's death, Gavin had chosen that over his daughter. I still hadn't been able to figure out how a father, especially one of a little girl, could not only allow such horrible things to happen to others' daughters, but participate in preparing them for it. What made it even worse, I had thought, was that he'd used the story of what had happened on women like me, ones who wanted to see a vulnerable side to the big, strong man. Ones who were stupid enough to fall for his bullshit.

I'd still been berating myself for being so gullible when I'd fallen asleep. I'd kept up the charade all through the next day and was doing it now even on the plane. Gavin had kept asking me if I needed to go to the emergency room, but I'd managed to keep finding excuses as to why I didn't need to go. Now, as we were heading home, his hovering was getting worse. I was pretty sure he'd thought it was either something I'd eaten or a stomach bug, but it had been more than twenty-four hours and I was still telling him that I wasn't feeling well and that I didn't want to be touched. I knew I was going to have to come up with something better.

"I really think I'm on the upside of this." I gave him a weak smile. "If I'm not better by morning, I swear, I'll have Krissy take me to the doctor."

He leaned over me and I avoided looking at his eyes. It was bad enough that he could lie with his face and his body. The fact that his eyes had fooled me made everything so much worse. His hand brushed over my forehead and I closed my eyes, hoping he'd think it was because I wanted his touch rather than because I couldn't lie with my eyes like he could. The sick thing was, part of me still did crave his touch.

Tears burned at my eyelids and I fought to keep them back. If he saw me crying, he'd know it was something more than just me feeling sick. I'd made it this far. We were only a few minutes out. Once we landed, a car would take me home and then I'd be safe.

One of the other things I'd been thinking about while I'd feigned my illness had been how much to tell Krissy. The heartbroken girl inside wanted to fall into her best friend's arms and sob out the entire story, but the harder me, the one forged by this betrayal, wanted to keep it all to myself. I told myself it was because I didn't want Krissy to get hurt, but if I was being completely honest, I knew it was because I wasn't sure that I wanted justice over revenge, and I didn't know what side of that argument Krissy would take.

I'd finally decided on something halfway between. I would continue the lie I was telling Gavin, and tell Krissy that I wasn't feeling well. I'd then spend the rest of the evening in my bedroom, pretending to rest. I'd get up before her and leave a note saying that I had to stop by Howard's office to pick up some files for Mimi. I didn't want to get her involved by telling her what was going on, but I also wasn't going to be dumb enough to walk into the lion's den without a bit of insurance. If things went smoothly, she'd never know what had happened until it was all over. If things didn't go smoothly... well, I was counting on Krissy to worry and tell someone where I'd gone.

With my plan firmly in place, I gathered my strength and waited for the moment I was alone to finally succumb to the tears that had wanted to come since the moment I'd learned the truth.

THIRTY

I didn't have any problem getting up before Krissy because I hadn't really slept at all in the first place. I'd thought that maybe I could cry myself to sleep, let the toll of the last couple days take over. I'd had times in my past where emotional exhaustion had let me sleep when nothing else could. This time, however, I couldn't get my brain to shut down enough to doze for more than a quarter of an hour or so at a time. Then I'd wake up, the same old thoughts repeating over and over in my head. Finally, when my clock said that it was five o'clock, I decided it wasn't worth it to keep lying there, waiting for the five-thirty alarm.

I got up and headed for the bathroom. I'd showered the night before, but ever since I'd heard Howard say that Gavin was grooming me, I hadn't been able to shower enough. I felt like there was a film of filth covering my skin and, no matter how hard I scrubbed, I couldn't get rid of it.

I dressed for work, but in one of my old boring outfits. Since I'd started seeing Gavin, Krissy had been able to convince me to put a bit more color and sex appeal into my work attire, but I didn't want that today. I wanted to go back to the way I'd been before I'd met him. So, a plain skirt that stopped just above my knees and a tailored, but not sexy, white blouse. I'd gotten rid of the pantyhose because Krissy had said there was no good reason to keep them, so thigh-high stockings were the only option I had other than bare legs. I pulled my hair back and pinned it into place. No make-up other than what I needed to cover the bags under my eyes. And, finally, sensible shoes. A modest heel that made me look professional but not enough of a heel to draw attention to my legs.

I looked at myself in the mirror. The young woman I saw peering back at me was familiar, but not the person I'd been seeing over the past few weeks. She looked like the girl I had been before. Confident in the courtroom but timid in life. The girl who'd only talked to the handsome stranger because her friends had pressured her. The girl who'd enjoyed sex but had never really had a problem going without it.

I knew I couldn't be her again, but I wanted to. I wanted to go back to who I'd been, pretend that none of this had happened. Now that I'd been with Gavin, I knew I could never experience sex the way I had before. He'd played my body like a musician playing a fine instrument. He'd made me feel things I'd never felt before, want things that I hadn't realized I'd wanted, and now that I knew these things, I couldn't un-know them.

I closed my eyes against the tears I could feel coming and took a deep breath. No crying. I'd done my crying the night before and I was done. I had a job to do, and it had nothing to do with Howard's divorce case.

I was going to take the bastard down.

With that thought firmly in my head, I headed out to the living room... and saw Krissy waiting for me. She was seated at our kitchen table, still wearing her cute little bunny pajamas, feet pulled up on the seat and a mug of coffee in her hands. She looked half-asleep, but I knew the caffeine would change that fast.

"Oh, hey." I tried to keep my voice nonchalant. "I didn't wake you, did I?"

She shook her head. "I was hoping we could have breakfast together and talk."

I tensed. Had she figured out that I'd been faking sick?

Then she grinned and I knew it wasn't about me. "I've been wanting to tell you about this insane weekend I had since you got home, but I wanted to let you rest last night."

I glanced at the clock. I could spare a few minutes. "I don't have time for a full breakfast, but one cup of coffee won't make me late. I just have to get some files from Mr. Weiss before work." I went and poured myself a cup while Krissy began telling me her story.

"So, I figured since you were off on a sex-adventure all weekend..."

I winced at her phrasing, but my back was still to her, so she didn't see my face.

"...I was going to have a little fun of my own."

I really hoped she wasn't going to regale me with tales of her sexual exploits going from one guy to another. Krissy wasn't a slut, but when she wanted to have a wild weekend, she could get pretty crazy. I'd once seen her make out with three different guys and take a fourth back to our hotel room. Granted, we'd been juniors on spring break at the time, but still.

"I called up Pete to have that cup of coffee you promised him."

I turned towards her, not trying to hide the surprise on my face. "Detective Pete Connors? The hot geeky guy you didn't want to see again. The one who lives with his mother and goes to comic book conventions."

"That's the one." Krissy sighed and turned in her seat so she was facing me when I sat down. "You reminded me how gorgeous he was with his golden hair and green eyes. And, of course, that body. He really does take the fitness part of his job seriously."

Out of all of the guys Krissy had been involved with for longer than a one-night stand, I'd liked Pete the best. He wasn't like any other guy Krissy had dated, which was, of course, the problem. Krissy tended to gravitate towards rich men who had more money than class. I was honestly surprised she hadn't liked Howard.

"Anyway, we go out for coffee and the next thing I know, we're back at his place."

"His place?" I almost smiled. "With his mom?"

Krissy held up a hand. "Let me tell my story."

I nodded and began to sip my coffee. I wasn't hungry and didn't think I could force myself to eat with these knots in my stomach, but the warmth of the liquid and the rush of caffeine did me good.

"Well, our coffee date turned into me trying to loosen him up by taking him to a bar for something stronger than an espresso. I challenged him to a drinking game, but apparently he can hold his liquor better than I thought. We were both a little buzzed and when we were walking out to catch a cab, I kissed him."

I raised an eyebrow, but didn't say anything.

"It was the alcohol," she protested. "And he just looked so cute with his hair falling in his eyes and those tight jeans showing off his firm ass. I couldn't help myself. It had been too long since I'd gotten laid."

I couldn't stop a smirk. I had to duck as a balled-up napkin sailed across the table towards me.

"Anyway," Krissy continued as she glared at me. "He has the basement at his mom's house set up like an apartment. There's a separate entrance and everything. So we go down there and start making out." She gave a dramatic sigh. "I don't know how a comic book geek ever got that good at kissing."

My smile this time wasn't about amusement at Krissy's expense, but just the enjoyment of the moment. I'd almost forgotten how it used to be. Us sitting down to breakfast while she told me about her latest conquest, often while said conquest was wandering around the apartment, half-naked, looking for his pants. It was always me living vicariously through her sex life, wondering what it would be like to have someone make me sound the way Krissy's partners made her. I wished things had never changed, that I'd never even laid eyes on Gavin that day at Huggins. I wouldn't be sitting here, hoping I wasn't going to throw up when I stole files from my firm's client. I wouldn't have this pit in my stomach that burned every time I thought about how Gavin had used me.

"Carrie?" Krissy sounded concerned.

I pulled myself back. "Sorry, continue."

For a moment, I thought she'd see right through me and ask what was really going on, but she didn't. She just continued with her story.

"Anyway, he's rambling on about how beautiful I am and I finally have to tell him to shut up and get on with it. And holy shit, does he." Krissy shivered and I knew it was because she was remembering how good it had felt. "I swear, he'd been good the last time we were together, but this was phenomenal. I came twice just from him going down on me and then when we started fucking... It was amazing. He rubbed on all the right spots and I saw stars."

My face flushed. I'd forgotten how detailed she liked to be in her retellings.

"We must've done it in three different positions and I came every time. I've never had that many orgasms that weren't fake or courtesy of myself. I ended up nearly passing out, and trust me, it wasn't from the alcohol." She sighed. "And then it was morning." Her expression of bliss faded.

I was puzzled, and a little annoyed. Was she seriously going to regret her amazing night with Pete just because he was a bit of a geek? I wanted to tell her that was a stupid reason. Better someone who liked comic books and didn't have his own place than an asshole like Gavin.

"I woke up to his mother coming downstairs and asking if we wanted breakfast. She was making heart-shaped pancakes."

I choked on a laugh and Krissy scowled at me.

"It's not funny, Carrie. I was buck-ass naked, half-lying on top of her equally naked son. His bits were covered but I gave her an eyeful."

Now I did laugh, and, after a moment, she joined in. "What did you do?" I asked.

"What do you think I did?" She grinned at me. "I asked if she had strawberries to go on top."

We laughed even harder and I was surprised by how good it felt. It reminded me of something I'd nearly forgotten. No matter how much damage my heart took, my best friend always had my back, and she would cheer me up, even if she didn't know she was doing it.

As I got up to put my cup in the sink, I was grateful I'd taken the time to talk to her this morning. I'd needed something positive to get my mind off of what I was about to do. I could tell by the look on Krissy's face that we were going to have a more serious version of this conversation at a later time, but for now, we were good. I didn't know exactly what she was thinking, but I had a pretty good guess that she wasn't sure how she really felt about Pete and wanted my advice. I wasn't sure I was the best person to ask, but that was another conversation I didn't have time for now.

I said I'd see her later at the office and then headed downstairs. I took a cab to Howard's office, again partly out of convenience but also because I wanted a record of where I'd been and where I was going. If Howard reported me stealing from him, my leaving a trail might backfire, but I'd followed enough cases where people disappeared without a trace that I was willing to take the chance. If Patricia had made sure her moves could be easily traced, she might not have disappeared, or at least would've been found by now.

When the doors opened on the top floor, I fixed a smile on my face and walked into the reception area in front of Howard's office. Annie was sitting at her desk. I hadn't seen her since that incident in Howard's office. When I looked at her now, all I could picture was how he'd bent her over the desk and used her.

"I'm here to see Mr. Weiss." I made my voice professional and chose my words carefully. I wanted it to sound like I was here on business.

"Mr. Weiss isn't in yet," Annie said brightly. Her eyes didn't meet mine though, and I wondered if she was thinking about what Howard had said regarding me not being ready enough to be the replacement "package." "He should be here shortly, if you'd like to wait."

"Thank you." I turned and walked to the chairs that sat across from Annie's desk. So far, so good. I'd hoped Howard wouldn't be in this early and I'd been right. I picked up one of the magazines and pretended to read it while I scanned the room, looking for any way I could get into that office before Howard showed up. At least I had a cover story. He had asked me to come to his office this morning to discuss his job offer. Obviously, there was no way in hell I was even considering it, but it would at least keep him from being suspicious as to why I was there.

I was starting to get concerned that I'd never find a way in when Annie stood and walked away from her desk. I didn't know where she was going, but that wasn't my concern. Before I could talk myself out of it, I got up and hurried over to the door. For a moment, I was afraid it was going to be locked, but it wasn't. The doorknob turned easily and I pushed the door open. I glanced behind me and didn't see Annie, so I slipped inside.

The office was just as neat as the one in his mansion, though I doubted this one had a side room with a bed. Then again, maybe it did. Not that I was eager to find out. I just wanted that briefcase. Fortunately, it was sitting on the desk... right next to a stack of files. Forgetting that I wasn't supposed to be here, that I was trying to find evidence to incriminate the man I'd been falling in love with, I crossed to the desk with only one thing on my mind: Patricia. If I didn't have anything else, I needed her file. Her father deserved to know that he was right about her not running off, and the file would at least give the police somewhere to start looking again.

I started going through the pile. I planned on taking all of them, but I had to make sure hers was there first. A wave of relief went through me when I saw it. I picked it up and opened it to make sure that the contents were there.

That was when I heard noise behind me.

An arm wrapped around me.

A cloth came towards my face, the sickly sweet chemical smell telling me this wasn't going to end well.

Before I could scream or move or fight back, my vision grayed, then the darkness swallowed me.

THIRTY-ONE

My head was pounding before I was even fully aware that I was waking up. My tongue felt thick, my mouth dry, filled with a cloying medicinal taste. I almost gagged as the darkness that had enveloped me started to recede. I managed to stop myself from making any noise. I couldn't remember what had happened, but I knew it hadn't been anything good. I searched my memory for clues and it all came back to me in a rush.

Files at Howard's office.

Someone grabbing me from behind.

Fuck.

Now I wanted to know if it had been Howard or Gavin who'd grabbed me.

Before I opened my eyes, though, I needed to further assess my situation. I didn't feel any pain other than in my head, and that was fading. At least that was good. As I continued to take my inventory, I realized that I was lying on my back. My arms and legs were spread out and I felt something around my wrists and ankles.

Panic flooded through me. I was tied up, spread-eagle, and

since the surface beneath me was soft, I was willing to bet I was in a bed.

Shit.

I tried to stay calm by telling myself that at least I was wearing clothes, but it wasn't working. I just kept thinking about how I was tied up and all of the horrible things it could mean.

I heard a soft chuckle and tensed. It wasn't Gavin. I knew that now. That meant it had to be Howard. A flare of anger burned through the panic, and I let it. I thought of all of the things Howard had done and let myself get more and more angry. Then, when all of the fear had been replaced, I opened my eyes.

He was sitting on the edge of the bed, looking down at me with a cold smile and colder eyes. I quickly looked around and saw that we were in the members' room at club Privé. He hadn't taken me back to his place, which was good. Being here was bad, but not as bad as it would've been if I'd been someplace completely unfamiliar. I knew the layout of the club and if I could get free, I could escape.

"I was hoping it wouldn't take you long to wake up," he said. He reached out and brushed the back of his knuckles across my cheek. I jerked my head away, half-expecting him to hit me. Instead, he just laughed. "This is going to be fun."

I swallowed hard and tried not to let him see how much his words freaked me out.

"I knew you were there, by the way," he continued in a conversational tone. "Back at my mansion, in my office."

I couldn't stop the look of surprise. He'd known? Why hadn't he done something then? I'd obviously been somewhere I didn't have permission to be. He could have easily thrown me out.

That was it, I realized. He hadn't wanted to make me leave the party. He'd wanted me here, like this. What I didn't understand was why he hadn't just tied me up back at his place. No one would've noticed that I was gone, and it could've been an easy excuse that I was sick. Why wait the whole weekend and let me come back to the city?

"I can see those wheels turning in that pretty little head of yours," Howard said.

Now he didn't just look like one of those old-time movie stars. He sounded like he was spouting some of their cheesy dialogue. How did he get women this way?

"Did you really think I wouldn't have cameras outside my office and that my security staff wouldn't let me know the moment someone went inside?"

Embarrassment mixed with horror flooded me. How could I have been so stupid? Of course he'd have cameras, if not in the office, then outside of it.

"I didn't know exactly what you'd been looking for, but when I saw the book had been moved and the clipping was on the floor, I knew I needed to give you something to come after." He shook his head. "I'd told Gavin you weren't right for us, that you were the kind of person who meddled in things that didn't concern her. You ask too many questions, and don't know your place."

At least he running his mouth was keeping me pissed off enough to not give in to the fear hovering at the edges of my mind.

"I figured that if you saw me tell Annie to take the files to my Manhattan office, you'd suddenly decide to take me up on my offer to talk about a job." He ran the tip of one finger down the underside of my arm. "I got there early and told Annie to pretend I wasn't there yet. I knew that as soon as she gave you the chance, you'd come in to get those files. Even if they weren't what you'd been after originally, you wouldn't be able to resist snooping. You thought you were so clever, but I was one step ahead of you. I'm always one step ahead."

"You're a bastard, you know that?" It was hard to come

across as tough tied to a bed, but I thought I managed pretty well. "Preying on innocent girls. Raping them. Selling them to the highest bidder."

"You see, Carrie, that attitude is exactly what Gavin was supposed to fuck out of you." He leaned closer so that his mouth was against my ear. "I do have to ask though, before I get too caught up in our fun and games. Did you like what I did to Annie?"

I didn't say anything, but he didn't seem to actually want a response.

"That little show was all for you, you know. Since I knew you were there, watching, I wanted you to see that I can do what I want, and no one can stop me."

His tongue flicked against my earlobe and I shuddered in revulsion. Up until that moment, I'd been telling myself that he'd just tied me like this to restrain me, that he wasn't going to do anything. Now I knew that was a lie.

"Not that she wanted me to stop," he continued. "All of my girls are trained to love what I do to them, what I have them do to me."

"I saw her face, Howard." I spoke through gritted teeth. "Trust me, that wasn't enjoyment I saw."

He grabbed my hair and yanked on it, twisting my head around so that our faces were less than an inch apart. "Then why is she sitting there in my office instead of going to the police?"

"Because she's scared of you," I said. "But I'm not."

He laughed and released my hair as he sat up. "You think that was the first time I've fucked her? How do you think she got the job? I don't hire anyone who doesn't bend over and spread them in the interview." He stood. "Well, women anyway. I don't do men."

He reached into his pocket and pulled out a pocketknife. My heart began to pound. Maybe he wasn't going to rape me.

Maybe he was just going to kill me. At the moment, I wasn't sure which one to hope for.

"Shall we move this along?"

I realized now that he'd already taken off my shoes and thigh highs while I'd been unconscious. Easier to tie my ankles, I supposed. I would've wondered why he hadn't just stripped me completely, but I already knew the answer. He wanted me to be awake when he cut off my clothes. He got off not only on the power, but on the fear and pain as well.

He ran his free hand up over my calf, then over my skirt and up to my blouse. I tried to jerk away when his hand reached my breast, but there wasn't anywhere to go. He grabbed one, squeezing hard enough that I let out a hiss of pain, then did the same to the other.

"Do you have any idea the time and effort that goes in to training someone for what I have them do?" He lowered the knife and cut off the top button. "I'm not some pimp who grabs girls off the street and turns them out to any trick with ten bucks. I only cater to high-end clients with refined taste."

"So, you're a high-class pimp?" It probably wasn't a good idea to backtalk to someone with a knife just above your chest, but I couldn't just lie here in silence. I may not have been able to move, but I could talk, and words had always been my go-to defense mechanism.

Howard scowled. Apparently, he didn't like my question. "My girls don't just lie on their backs and take it. I groom them to learn how to read a man's desires and respond accordingly. I do train some for specific purposes, ones whose masters want to humiliate them, I don't degrade, leaving that pleasure to my client. Ones who are to be left intact, I don't fuck. But most of my clients are looking for women who can and will do whatever they are told without complaint."

The last button fell away and my blouse was hanging open, exposing my bra and a pale strip of skin down my stomach.

Howard leaned down and put his knife through the thin cotton, easily ripping up one sleeve, then the other. He let the ruined shirt lie in pieces under me and moved down the bed.

"You saw firsthand some of that with Annie," he said. He began to cut my skirt off. "I groomed her to please me, but in a pinch, she could do the same for my clients. Do you want to know the things I've done to her?"

He was trying to get a rise out of me, and I knew I shouldn't respond, but I couldn't just do nothing. I really didn't want to hear what he'd done to his assistant. I shook my head, but it didn't stop him, just like I'd known it wouldn't.

"The first time I made her take off her clothes in public, she cried." He pushed the two halves of my skirt away, leaving me in just my bra and panties. "I bent her over my knee and spanked her for it right there in that park."

I squeezed my eyes closed, as if I could block out his words. Then I felt his hands on me, the cold metal of the knife against my skin, and had to open them. He wasn't trying to cut me; it was only the flat of the blade. He was touching me though, running his hands over my legs and stomach, never touching anything covered by my underwear.

"She learned quickly." He sounded almost proud. "I rarely had to punish her, and never as harshly as the first time. She'd refused to go down on me at a restaurant, even after I'd told her that she would be punished for saying no."

His hands now moved to my breasts. I pressed my lips together as he touched me. I wasn't going to give him the satisfaction of a response. Not for this. I would fight him later, but this I could endure.

"I took her into a storage room in the back, took off her panties, pulled down the top of her dress and tied her to one of the shelves." He slid the knife under one strap and pulled, cutting through the material. He did the same to the other side. "I let everyone who worked there use her, and then they called their friends. I sat and watched, listened to her scream and beg and plead with me to stop them. They took her every way you can imagine. Two, three at a time. I had to have her carried to my car when they were done."

If he'd meant this to scare the shit out of me, it was working. I'd known he was a sick fuck, but this... it was worse than I'd imagined.

"The next time I told her to blow me in public, she just opened her mouth... then swallowed."

My stomach roiled. If I'd eaten anything, I would've thrown it up. Somehow, I doubted even that would've stopped him.

The blade slid between my breasts and I held my breath. He didn't even nick me as he cut the last bit of cloth keeping my bra in place. It fell off on its own, exposing my breasts.

"I'm going to have fun with these." He used the tip of the knife to poke my nipple. He didn't break the skin, but the threat was still there. "Do you want to know what I'm going to do to you?"

After what he'd told me, I knew it was going to be bad, but I didn't answer him. Of course I didn't want to hear it, but it wouldn't matter what I said. He was going to tell me anyway.

"You need to be punished," he said as he ran his hand over the length of my body. "And if I had the time, I would spend days with you, teaching you your place." He cut one side of my panties, then the other. "I would make you beg for what was done to Annie."

I clenched my hands into fists as he removed my last article of clothing.

"A natural blond, I see." He smirked. "Not too much hair to bother me, for this anyway."

He put his knife back in his pocket and walked over to one of the chests. I remembered what was in that one. He opened the drawer and pulled out a pair of nipple clamps, metal with jagged teeth.

"First, I'm going to put these on you. We really should work up to them, use soft ones until your body's conditioned to enjoy pain, but I don't have the time. These have a nice chain I can use to pull on them whenever you're bad."

When he turned to the wardrobe, I tried tugging on the restraints, but they didn't give. He came back to the bed a moment later, his arms full. He set the clamps down and then began to lay out an array of dildos ranging from medium to the insanely massive one I'd seen when Gavin and I had been in here that first night. It was bigger than Gavin's cock, and that was saying something. He was almost too big for me. What Howard had would hurt, no matter how much he stretched me first.

"I'm going to fuck you with every one of these, working up to this beauty. We want to make sure you're nice and loose." He put his hand on my stomach, just below my belly button, but not quite between my legs. "Then I'm going to flip you over and spank your ass until it's black and blue. I'll probably use a belt or one of the paddles. I won't stop until you beg me to fuck your ass, and trust me, you will."

His fingers slid just a bit lower so that they were skimming over the top of the thin layer of curls that covered me.

"Maybe I'll even use some of these on your ass." He motioned to the dildos on the bed. "If you're a good girl and can prove to me that you're going to behave, I won't kill you. Instead, I'll send you to my client in Saudi Arabia whose package was lost. You'll be a gift to him. One he can keep." He removed his hand and leaned down to whisper in my ear. "I hear that the things he does to his permanent girls ruins their bodies and their minds." He straightened and smiled down at me. "But that's getting ahead a bit, isn't it?"

His gaze traveled up and down my body, as if he had a thought in his head and was trying to decide what to do with it.

"This isn't right," he said finally. "After all, I'm not the only one you've been so rude to. Gavin should be here to enjoy your punishment as well."

"No, please." I couldn't stop myself from speaking. I couldn't bear to have Gavin here, have him watch and know that he was enjoying watching Howard rape and abuse me.

Howard smiled. "That settles it. I'll go get him." He started towards the door, then stopped and turned back. "By the way, there's no point in trying to scream for help. In case Gavin hadn't told you, the room's fully sound-proofed." He pointed towards the lights above the bed. "Oh, and there are cameras everywhere, recording everything that happens in here, so feel free to struggle all you want. I'll enjoy watching the tapes later."

He left and as soon as the door closed behind him, I let the tears come. I screamed, knowing no one would hear me, but unable to keep it inside any longer. I pulled at my restraints as the tears ran down my cheeks, but I wasn't thinking about escape. I couldn't think about anything but the anguish and panic flooding me. No one was coming to save me. This was going to happen and nothing I could do would stop it.

THIRTY-TWO

I had no idea how much time had passed because there were no clocks in the room, but I knew that I'd been screaming long enough for my throat to hurt. When I stopped, a sense of calm came over me. Actually, it wasn't really calm; it was more a lack of feeling anything. No fear. No panic. No anger. Nothing. It was as if by allowing myself to have what was basically a breakdown, I'd bled away the emotions that had overwhelmed me.

I didn't know how long this feeling would last, only that I had to take advantage of it while I still could. I tested my restraints again, but this time more methodically. I pulled on one leg first, though I didn't have high hopes for the restraints around my ankles. Slipping my feet out would require a decent amount of give. After I confirmed that I didn't have any room to move with my left leg, I tried my right with the same result. Frustration crept in, starting to chase away the emptiness. I knew other emotions would soon follow. I pulled with my left hand. I had a bit more movement, but it was still too tight for me to be able to slip out.

"Come on!" I growled, switching my attention to my right. Time had to be racing by. I didn't know where Howard had gone to get Gavin, and that meant I had no way of knowing how much time I had before they came back.

I twisted my right hand and felt the leather slip on my wrist. Hope flared so sharply inside me that it almost hurt. I rotated my hand back and forth, gauging just how far I could get. My skin burned from the friction, but I didn't care. If I could get it only a little further, I had a trick up my sleeve that could make the difference...

The door opened and I stopped. If Howard caught me trying to escape, things would go from bad to... who was I kidding? Things really couldn't get much worse than this. My heart thudded painfully against my chest as I saw Gavin follow Howard into the room.

"All right, what's this big surprise that couldn't wait..." Gavin's voice trailed off as Howard stepped to the side and let him see me.

I didn't want to look at him, but if I had to go through this, I was as sure as hell going to make sure he looked me in the eye. He didn't even try to conceal his shock.

"What the hell, Howard?"

Howard grinned and crossed over to the bed. He picked up one of the dildos. "She's been quite the problem child, Gavin, and needs to be punished. I was going to do it myself, but I figured that she's caused problems for both of us, so we should both get to enjoy ourselves. Maybe even take her for a ride at the same time." He held out the toy. "I just want her ass first. Why don't you start warming up her pussy?"

Gavin didn't take the dildo, but that didn't make me think any better of him. After all, he was bigger than that particular toy. Maybe he wanted to do it himself. I glared at him, but he wouldn't look at my face. In fact, he was staring at a spot to one side of my head, his expression blank.

"What'd she do?"

That was what he had to say? Anger boiled up inside me,

proving that it hadn't disappeared, only slept. "You fucking asshole!" My voice was rough.

"I told you not to bother screaming." Howard sounded vaguely chiding, as if I truly was a misbehaving child. He turned towards Gavin. "She's been playing detective. Snooping around my business... our business."

"I see. And this is what? You getting in some fun before you kill her?"

I wanted to keep yelling obscenities and insults at him, but the nonchalant way he was talking was making it hard for me to breathe. I'd known about his betrayal, but to see it in his face like this was so much worse.

"I promised that if she was good, I wouldn't kill her," Howard said. He gave Gavin a sideways glance, as if measuring him for something. "I, or I should say, *we* have a client who could make good use of a naughty girl. He knows a thing or two about taming disobedient women."

"A client? Are we talking about 'The Caretaker'?"

Howard looked surprised. "You know about him?"

What were they talking about?

Gavin answered Howard's question without looking at either of us. "I saw him mentioned in some papers a few weeks back and figured it must be the handle for your top client. I never found his real name though, or where he's located." Now he looked up at Howard. "If I'm sticking my neck out to help you here, don't you think it's fair you let me in on who he is and where you're sending her? I don't want to risk her coming back one day."

I felt sick. My body slumped down on the bed. He hadn't just been playing me. He was willing to let Howard sell me. Gavin really hadn't felt anything for me. Tears burned against my eyelids.

Howard furrowed his brow, but nodded. "Fair enough. His name is Abdulla Mahaj, one of the richest people in Saudi

Arabia. He's more like a partner than a client, but you'll learn more about that as you take on more responsibilities." Howard glanced at me. "Shall we get started?"

Gavin didn't move or speak. I saw some emotion playing through his eyes, but couldn't identify what it was.

"Fine. I'll do it." Howard started to turn towards me, the flesh-colored toy in his hand.

Gavin moved then, faster than I'd seen him move before. His hand went around Howard's throat and he threw the smaller man across the room. I stared, open-mouthed, as Gavin crossed to Howard in just a few long strides and put his hand on Howard's neck again. He picked Howard up and shoved him back against the wall, raising him high enough that Howard was on his toes.

What the hell was happening?

"Finally!" Gavin's face was inches from Howard's and he was practically spitting the words into the other man's face. "You have no fucking idea how long I've waited to get that name, your precious Saudi connection, and I think you know why."

The pieces fell together in my shocked brain even as Gavin confirmed them.

"He was the driver who killed my fiancée, and he was driving your Bentley."

Howard's eyes widened and his mouth opened and closed, as if he wanted to say something, but Gavin wasn't letting him.

"For years I'd been looking for the car that killed her, but found nothing. I already knew it couldn't have been you since you had a rock-solid alibi at the time of the 'accident.' You were giving a business presentation in Manhattan that day and at least a hundred people saw you. It wasn't until you approached me about opening the club together that I stumbled on some-thing that changed everything." He smiled, but not a nice smile. "That's right. I checked you out. With all those barely legal women you dated, I knew you were a sick bastard, and I wanted to find out just how sick before getting into more business with you. Using the exact same software you helped me finance when we first met, I hacked into your computer. I went through some of your old emails, and imagine my surprise when I found an email from just before the accident confirming a meeting with your mysterious Saudi... and you offering him the use of one of your Bentleys for his stay. I dug deeper, and there it was, right in front of me: an email from him thanking you for the 'clean up.' It didn't take much deduction to figure out he was the driver who'd killed Camille, and you'd helped with the cover-up."

I'd been right. Sort of. Howard had been involved with Camille's death. I just hadn't realized that Gavin had known already.

"The problem was, I'd gotten the information under less than legal circumstances, and the emails were vague enough that I knew that by themselves, they wouldn't be enough evidence. I needed more, but I couldn't find much else." Gavin continued, "I knew I had to gain your trust and get the name of your Saudi guy. Unfortunately, you were good enough to keep your sex-trafficking business with Abdulla under wraps. I had no idea what you were really doing, what you were using me to do, finding women with your 'desired personality traits.'"

My stomach twisted as I realized what his words meant. He hadn't known the truth. He wasn't a part of selling these girls. Then it hit me. Howard had known I was in his office from moment one. What he'd said about Gavin grooming me had been a lie. Gavin might have been using Howard's attraction to me to get closer to Howard, but he hadn't been grooming me for Howard's twisted enterprise.

His voice was thick with disgust and contempt. "I'd thought you were a horny old bastard who liked them barely legal, but when Carrie couldn't find any information about some of the girls, I got suspicious. A couple days ago, I did some more digging into your files, and this time, I struck gold."

I startled when he said my name, but neither he nor Howard looked at me.

"I found the location of one of the girls. Wouldn't you know, Melissa was in Miami, stashed in a cheap motel, far from your mansion. She was being prepared for a 'shipment.' The digging also finally led me to your dark secret. It was right there in your files. Every single detail about all the women. Their locations, what you had them do for you. The only thing still missing was the name of your Saudi connection."

Howard looked furious, but that could've been because his face was starting to turn red from lack of oxygen.

"I flew into Miami early Friday and met up with Melissa. I had to warn her about your plans abroad for her. She had no idea, and told me everything. How you'd made her dependent on drugs and slowly introduced her to the degrading work of servicing your perverted clients. Now, she's talking to the cops, the FBI, Interpol, and whoever else wants a piece of your ass." The triumphant note in Gavin's voice was impossible to miss. "I'm sure they'll be coming for you soon, but I'm glad she didn't have your partner's name. He's mine now."

Gavin had saved the girl that hadn't shown up at the airport. The one that was supposed to be sent to Saudi Arabia. The news hit me hard enough to make me catch my breath. Even if he'd used Howard's interest in me to try to get on the inside, I couldn't hate him, not when he'd risked everything to rescue this girl. Saving her could have resulted in him never finding out the name of the man who'd killed Camille, but he'd done it anyway. The man I'd fallen for wasn't all an act.

"As for you." Gavin's voice lowered to a near growl. "I was going to just let the cops deal with you, but walking in here and seeing Carrie–"

To my complete and utter shock, his voice broke on my name.

"I'm going to break every fucking bone in your body."

I shivered, and not because of the temperature. I hadn't known Gavin could sound like that.

"You took one woman I loved away from me. I'll be damned if I let you get away with hurting this one."

I was still trying to process what this all meant when Gavin's body suddenly jerked and he cried out in pain. He staggered backwards, clutching his arm. Howard dropped to the floor, his bloody pocketknife in his hand. He reached behind his back even as he got his feet underneath him. Gavin took a step forward, then froze. The gun in Howard's hand wasn't big, but it would be enough to do the job.

"Now," Howard wheezed. "We're going to have some real fun."

THIRTY-THREE

The gun was pointing straight at Gavin. "I was going to bring you into my business as a partner." Howard straightened and steadied his gun hand. "I'd originally befriended you to keep an eye on you, but then I saw all of that potential and realized that we could do great things together. I was doing all right before you came along, but your software made finding women so easy."

Gavin looked like he was going to be sick, and I didn't think it was because of the cut on his arm. I didn't blame him. He'd just found out that something he'd created had been used to find victims for Howard and men like him.

"I suspected you wouldn't have the balls to do what needed to be done though," Howard continued. "Then I saw you with Carrie and hoped that you were starting to do what I'd suggested you do months ago and sample the goods. That's why I brought you here. It wasn't just to make it worse for her, but because I needed to know that you hadn't developed any real feelings for her. If you were willing to help me punish her, then I would know I could trust you, train you, make you my replacement one day. It seemed my faith was misplaced."

My heart was pounding in my chest but I didn't want to let myself hope. Just because Gavin didn't want to help Howard rape me didn't mean he actually had feelings for me, only that he was a decent human being. What Gavin had said – it could've meant a lot of different things, and I didn't have the time to try to figure it out now. I needed to stop listening to Howard talk and start working on getting free. I began to twist my right hand back and forth, the friction burning my skin, but I didn't make a sound. What I did next was going to hurt a lot worse than this.

"About Melissa – I'll have one of my people in Florida do the dirty work. She might talk to the police now but not for long. I know a couple of people who'd love to have some one-on-one time with a piece of ass like her." Howard shifted his stance so that he was angled away from me. "You two, I'm going to take care of personally."

Gavin clenched his fists and took a step forward, but Howard shook his head. "You really don't want to do that."

The restraint was loose enough now. I gritted my teeth and applied pressure to my thumb. I felt the pop, and gut-churning pain ran down my arm. I gave myself a few seconds, knowing I needed to be fast once I got one hand free. I took slow, steady breaths as Howard continued to talk. He really did love the sound of his own voice.

"I'm going to get a pair of handcuffs and you're going to cuff yourself to that chair." He motioned with the gun. "I want you to have a front row seat to what I'm going to do to your little bitch. When I'm through with her, I'm going to make sure you're unrecognizable."

I closed my eyes and began to pull my hand through the loop, fighting back whimpers from the pain in my dislocated thumb.

"It's too bad, really," he said. "Abdulla would've loved her, and he might've been able to find some uses for you too. He doesn't fuck men, but he knows plenty of people who would like nothing more than to be able to abuse a rich American man. The stories he's told me would make you sick."

"I'm going to kill you." The words were flat.

Howard laughed. "You're not going to do anything to me. Not for your fiancée, not for yourself, and not for Carrie. You're going to watch her die a slow and painful death, and there won't be anything you can do to stop it."

The blood flow back down my arm and into my fingers was almost as painful as the thumb, but I'd gotten used to it enough that I could push it to the back of my mind. I popped my thumb back into place by pushing it against my chest, and then I reached up to the other restraint. They weren't made for keeping actual prisoners, so from the outside, they were quick to release. It took only a few seconds to get my left hand and both of my feet free. I thought for sure Gavin or Howard would've noticed what I was doing, but both men were still focused on each other.

"I'm not going to let you hurt her," Gavin said.

"And if you try to stop me, I'm going to shoot out your kneecaps." Howard lowered the gun. "It won't kill you, but it'll be painful as hell and you won't be able to run."

Gavin took a step forward and I knew he was going to rush Howard. I didn't know how well Howard could shoot, but I wasn't about to take any chances. I grabbed the first thing I could lay my hands on and swung it as hard as I could at Howard. The giant, heavy, and solid rubber dildo hit him in the back of the head hard enough to make him stumble to the side. I then shoved him as hard as I could and he fell back against the wardrobe. The sound his head made when it hit the wood was loud and satisfying. He slumped to the ground, unconscious.

"Carrie."

Gavin's arms were around me before I could react. He

pressed me against his body tight enough that I almost couldn't breathe, and I felt hope stirring inside me.

"I am so sorry." His face was pressed against my neck and I could feel the wet of his tears. "I am so sorry."

I closed my eyes and slid my arms around his waist. I desperately wanted this to mean that he felt what I felt, but I couldn't give in to that, not yet. For all I knew, he could just be apologizing for getting me into this mess.

He pulled back and put his hand on my cheek. His eyes were still shining with tears. "If he'd have hurt you, I never could have lived with myself."

"I'm okay." That wasn't entirely true, but it was the best I could do at the moment.

He stared at me for a moment, then bent his head and took my mouth in a kiss so fierce that I gasped. He took advantage of my parted lips and slid his tongue inside my mouth. His hands ran over my body, reminding me that I was still naked, but I didn't care. This wasn't the kiss of a friend or a kiss of apology. His lips and tongue, his entire body, held the same primal need as mine. The need to know that the other one was alive and safe. I ran my hand down his arm, and he hissed, pulling back. I looked at my fingers and they were slick with blood.

"You're hurt." My voice came out a little dazed. My head was still spinning from that kiss.

"And you're naked."

I looked up at Gavin and gave him a half-smile. "You just now noticed?"

His expression was serious, bringing me out of my lust-induced haze. Right. This wasn't the time or place. He pulled off his shirt and held it out to me. I slipped into it. He was enough bigger than me that it actually covered everything important. In fact, it was longer than some dresses I'd seen.

"I meant what I said." Gavin brushed his fingers along my

cheekbone. "I don't know what I would've done if he'd..." His eyes narrowed. "He didn't hurt you, did he?"

I wasn't about to tell him what had happened before he'd arrived. Not now, anyway. I opened my mouth to lie, but the words died before they reached my lips.

Gavin let out a cry of pain and looked down. Howard smiled up at us as he yanked his knife out of Gavin's calf, raising it to strike again. I kicked out, knocking Howard away, but he rolled with it this time and came up with his gun in hand.

"Move!" Gavin grabbed my hand even as I saw Howard raise the gun.

My legs obeyed before my mind processed what was happening. I let Gavin pull me out the door and we ran down the hall. I heard a muffled sound of a gunshot behind me. The room was soundproofed all right. We headed straight for the stairs. Howard was shouting after us as we disappeared through the door. Fear was sharp and metallic in the back of my throat, and the sound of blood rushing in my ears was almost deafening.

We ran into the main room and started to cut across. We were less than a third of the way across when Gavin stumbled for the first time. I grabbed his arm, trying to help him.

"Go," he said.

I shook my head. "No."

"Dammit," he swore. "Carrie, please."

His leg buckled as we reached the middle of the floor and his foot slid on the blood that had been trailing behind him. Howard's knife had gone deep. I bent to try to help him up and heard the stairwell door slam open.

"Go!" Gavin shoved at my hand. He looked up at me, pleading. "Please."

A gunshot echoed and I felt the air above me move. Howard was getting closer, and the next shot might not miss. But I couldn't just leave Gavin to die. An idea – something completely and utterly insane – popped into my head. I stuck my hand in Gavin's pocket, ignoring his questions and look of complete surprise. I grabbed what I wanted, then turned and ran.

I hit against the wall, jarring my hands and sending a jolt of pain up my injured thumb. I turned, praying that Howard would wait until he got closer to Gavin to do anything. Gavin pushed himself backwards, but didn't try to get up. Without him saying a word, I knew it wasn't because he couldn't stand, but because he was trying to draw Howard's attention away from me, giving me time to escape.

Fuck that.

"You son of a bitch." Howard was breathless. He may have had the pretty movie-star face, but he clearly didn't keep up with his cardio. "How dare you! I gave you everything!" He pointed his gun at Gavin as he moved closer.

Now Gavin pushed himself to his feet, the look on his face saying that he wasn't about to let Howard shoot him on the ground.

Every inch of me was tense as I waited. Just a little more. I heard the click as Howard prepared to fire. No more waiting. I jammed Gavin's key into the lock, turned it, and hit the button.

With a soft whirr, the gears beneath the floor began to turn and the floor started to move. I saw surprise flash across Gavin's face, but his reaction was brief. Howard's was not. He let out a sound I could only describe as a squawk and nearly tripped over his own feet trying to move away from the widening gap. Gavin didn't even hesitate. His fist hit Howard square in the jaw, sending the older man reeling backwards. The floor had opened enough that Howard fell into the water beneath with a splash. His gun landed on the floor several feet away.

I breathed a sigh of relief and ran back out to the floor. I threw my arms around Gavin and pressed my face against his bare chest. I could feel his heartbeat and concentrated on that steady sound. His arms wrapped around me, his hands moving up and down my back, palms hot through his shirt. My body started to respond to his touch. Even after all I'd been through, he could still have that effect on me.

"Help!" A gurgling cry from the pool pulled our attention from each other to Howard.

He was thrashing around in the water, going under, then sputtering as he resurfaced. "I can't swim!"

"Too bad." Gavin's words were hard.

I looked up at him. I had to admit, part of me wanted to leave him there. If Gavin and I ran outside and just left Howard to drown, we could tell the cops that we'd just kept going. But it would be murder, and we were better than that.

"We need to help him." I reluctantly stepped away from Gavin and started towards the edge of the pool. "We're not killers."

Gavin walked with me, though the expression on his face clearly said that he wasn't so sure.

"Besides," I added, "I think Howard deserves to make friends with all of the nice guys in prison who have issues with people like him."

Gavin reached down and grabbed the back of Howard's shirt. He lifted the other man over the edge and tossed him to the floor.

"Thank you!" Howard gasped. He staggered to his feet, a grateful expression on his face. "You won't regret it. I'll make sure it's worth your while." He started blabbering.

He must not have heard what I'd said about him making new friends in jail.

"I have plenty of money. I can make you each a full partner."

I looked at Gavin and saw my own incredulity on his face. Was Howard serious? Did he think that saving his life meant we were going to let him go? That his money could pay us off?

"No hard feelings." He held out a hand.

That was it. I took two steps forward and kicked him squarely between the legs. He dropped to his knees, mouth opening and closing, but no sound coming out. I swung my already damaged right hand and hit him as hard as I could, straight on the jaw. He fell to the floor, eyes rolling up. The dull throbbing in my hand and foot were overshadowed by the extreme satisfaction I felt with the damage I'd inflicted.

I turned towards Gavin and found him staring at me with wide eyes. "Guess I should never piss you off."

I smiled. "That's probably a good idea."

THIRTY-FOUR

"You call the cops while I call the airport."

I gave Gavin a puzzled look. "The airport?"

His expression was grim. "I'm taking a little trip to the Middle East."

I took a step towards him and put my hand on his arm. "You have a name. You have evidence. Let the authorities handle it."

"He killed Camille."

The pain in Gavin's eyes made my heart hurt. I reached up and put my hand on his cheek. "I know he did, but if you go after him, you could lose everything." I could see the war of emotions playing across Gavin's face. I added, "That man took one parent from your daughter. Don't let him take another."

He closed his eyes and slowly let out a breath. "You're right," he said. He reached out and pulled me to him.

I stayed there for a moment, letting myself soak in the feelings of safety and security. I wanted to just stay there, but unfortunately, Gavin needed a doctor and Howard needed the cops. I took a step back, but slid my arm around Gavin's waist. "Let's get you sitting down. You're bleeding all over the place."

I helped him over to a chair and then did all the things that you don't usually see the heroes do in a movie. Usually, the scene just cuts from them saving the day to the cops being there and taking the bad guys into custody – or body bags, depending on the film. Now I knew that in that in-between time, the heroes had other things to do. While Gavin made the call to the cops, I picked up Howard's gun and fished his knife out of his pocket. He was still out.

I put the gun and knife within arm's reach of Gavin, then ran upstairs to the room and retrieved a pair of handcuffs. They may have been lined with pink fuzz, but they were good enough to cuff Howard around the base of a table. Since the table was bolted to the floor, I felt pretty safe in assuming he wouldn't be getting away any time soon.

Once I finished all of that, I returned to attend to Gavin. He'd pressed some napkins against both of his cuts, but they were already soaking through. I went back behind the bar and found some towels that I was able to tie around his wounds. They would do until the paramedics showed up. With that done, I started to sit in the chair next to him, but he grabbed me around the waist and pulled me onto his lap. I wasn't going to complain, though I did make sure most of my weight was on his uninjured leg. Granted, the cut was in his calf, but it was propped up and I didn't want to put any extra stress on it. It was a bit awkward, but I didn't mind. I leaned back against him and wrapped his arms around my waist.

"First thing tomorrow, I'm calling my contractor to come in and tear down that room."

His words surprised me. I tilted my head back to look at him. The angle was awkward, but I didn't want to sit up. "Why?"

Now he looked surprised. "You were assaulted in that room. Almost raped and murdered. Why would I want to keep it?"

I gave him a half-smile. "But I also have some good memories in there too." I did shift this time, moving so that I was leaning on my side rather than back. It was easier to look at him then. And touch him. I put my hand on his chest. "Or have you forgotten?"

Gavin put his hand on the back of my neck and pulled me towards him for a kiss. When his tongue teased at my lips, I opened my mouth eagerly. My hand slid down his abdomen, feeling those strong muscles tighten under my touch.

He broke the kiss and pressed his forehead against mine. "I remember every detail of that night and the next morning. I couldn't believe I could feel that way again."

A thrill went through me. "Besides," I added. "What's a sex club without a private room?"

His expression sobered. "That's another thing. I think I should turn it into a regular club."

I understood what he was thinking along those lines. Howard had used the club as a front for his sex-trafficking business. Keeping it as it was just seemed wrong somehow, but I had an idea. "There are tons of regular clubs in Manhattan. Why don't you just tweak it a bit?" He raised an eyebrow in question. "How about a burlesque club for both men and women? A place where singles and couples could come together."

"That's a possibility," he said slowly.

"Maybe I could even help you run it." I grinned. "And maybe you should keep that room upstairs for just two very exclusive members."

He blinked, as if my suggestion startled him.

"After all," I teased. "What better place to introduce me to all of those pleasures you've told me that your world holds."

He kissed me again, his hand sliding up my thigh and under his shirt. I'd forgotten that I wasn't wearing anything under it. The heat of his palm as it ran over my ass reminded me. It was tempting to lose myself in the kiss, to let my body respond to his touch the way it wanted to, but a comment he'd made earlier had wormed its way back into my mind and I needed an answer. Reluctantly, I broke the kiss.

"Back in the room," I started. He tensed. "You said you'd found information on the missing women."

"I did." Now he just looked confused.

"Do you remember anything about a girl named Patricia Vinarisky?" I almost didn't want to ask. It seemed like too much to hope for, to find her. "Do you remember if she was still alive?"

Gavin thought for a moment. "There were so many names, I can't remember if she was one of them. But the files are all in the office." He handed me his keycard. "Go look. I'll keep an eye on Howard."

I took the keycard, kissed Gavin's cheek, and ran up to the office. The files were easy enough to find. He'd left them in a stack on the desk. I shuffled through them, my anger towards Howard returning as I saw just how many lives he'd ruined. Halfway down, I found it. I opened it eagerly, hoping to find a statement that she was alive, but that information wasn't in there. What was in the file was confirmation that Patricia had been delivered to the mansion of a rich sheik in Saudi Arabia over a year and a half ago. That was a long time, but I had to believe that she was alive. If she had half the fortitude of her father, she would have survived.

We'd be giving the files to the authorities, but I couldn't make Mr. Vinarisky wait any longer, not when I had something. I knew that the DA's office would be pissed if they found out I did this, but after what I'd just been through, a couple of angry lawyers just didn't seem that scary.

I picked up the phone, then realized that I didn't have the number. The computer was on, so it didn't take long to do a quick search and find it. Frank answered on the second ring.

"Hello?"

"Mr. Vinarisky? I don't know if you remember me, but my name's Carrie Summers."

"You were that lawyer who called looking for my daughter." His voice immediately hardened. "I still don't know where she is."

"I do." I blurted out the words, hoping he wouldn't hang up before he heard them.

Silence, then: "Say that again."

"I know where your daughter is, Mr. Vinarisky." I could hear the wail of sirens and knew I didn't have much time. "She's just outside of Medina in Saudi Arabia. She was sold to a local millionaire twenty months ago. I don't know any more than that. The authorities will have this information in just a few minutes, but she's not the only one."

"Wait – wait, what are you talking about?"

I didn't blame him for sounding so blindsided, but I couldn't take the time to explain. I told him the name of the man who had bought Patricia and added, "I'm sorry I don't have anything else, but I couldn't not tell you."

"Where are you getting all this from?"

I didn't answer his question or wait for a thank you. I didn't have the time. I hung up and picked up the stack of files. As an officer of the court – or at least an almost one – I knew that I should leave the files here for CSU to find, but I couldn't, in all good conscience, make these women and their families wait one minute longer than necessary. I took the files downstairs, arriving at Gavin's side just as the first officers entered.

The series of events that followed took on a surreal quality. The police took me away from Gavin so we could give our statements separately while the paramedics looked over us. Howard was quiet. They weren't going to be getting anything from him for a while. I tried to keep my voice even and matter-of-fact as I relayed everything that had happened from the moment I'd arrived at Howard's office, but it didn't work. I started to shiver when I got to the part about Howard cutting off my clothes, and one of the paramedics wrapped me in a blanket. My teeth were chattering, but I kept going, finishing with getting the files from the office. I skipped the part about calling Frank.

When I was done, the paramedic who'd been examining me spoke, "We need to get her to the hospital to do a rape kit."

"He didn't rape me," I said. "He just put his hands on me." The words were bitter in my mouth. "You won't get any evidence from a rape kit." That's when I remembered what Howard had said when he was leaving. "But you will get it from the cameras."

"Cameras?"

"I forgot," I said. "When Howard was leaving the room, he told me that there were cameras. I don't know if they have sound, but they'll show everything that happened." I didn't even have the energy to be embarrassed by the thought of people watching what Howard did to me, seeing me naked.

The detective started asking questions then, but I didn't hear the first two because that was when the paramedics were wheeling Howard out. I watched as they went by.

The cop repeated himself, "Ma'am, why were you at Mr. Weiss's office this morning?"

I chose a half-truth. "He asked me to come by to discuss a job with his company."

The questions kept coming and I could hear another detective doing the same thing to Gavin. I answered them all as truthfully as I could without implicating Gavin and myself in our less-than-legal activities to get the information. I was careful not to out-and-out lie, so that if the cameras did have sound, nothing I said would contradict what had really happened. I had to admit, I was impressed with how well my brain was working after what I'd just been through. Then again, it was probably just a coping mechanism, and my mind would go into shock like my body at some point in the near future.

"I'm not going to the hospital!" Gavin raised his voice enough for me to hear what he was saying.

I ignored the detective's protest and hurried over to Gavin's side, clutching my blanket around me.

"Sir, you really should have these stitched up." A baby-faced paramedic was arguing with him.

"You do it," Gavin said. "I'm not going to the hospital."

"Gavin." I took his hand.

"I just want to go home."

I could see the weariness in his eyes. He wouldn't rest in a hospital, I knew. He needed to be at home. I turned to the paramedic. "Can you stitch him up here?"

"We have this emergency stuff that's kind of like glue, but we only use it if we have to close a wound in the field," the medic answered reluctantly.

"Well, if you want these closed, I suggest you use it," I said. "Because, trust me, it's pointless to argue with him."

"Ms. Summers," the detective I'd left behind had walked over. "I do have a few more questions."

"Of course." I kept my tone agreeable enough even though I wanted to tell him to leave me alone so I could stay with Gavin. It would be better to get this done and over with rather than trying to delay things.

The FBI showed up before the detective was done questioning me, and I had to give my statement all over again. By the time they were finished, it was almost noon and Gavin and I had been telling our story for over two hours. I was just about to tell them that they'd kept us long enough, especially after what we'd been through, when they finally told us we could go. The FBI agent who'd been questioning me offered to have one of her agents take us to our homes, but we declined. Gavin had followed Howard here in his own car.

Gavin put his uninjured arm around my shoulders, helping me hold the blanket in place as we started towards the exit. I wasn't cold anymore, but I was still wearing only Gavin's shirt and nothing underneath, which didn't make the prospect of walking past dozens of cops, Feds, gawkers, and reporters very appealing.

We managed to get to Gavin's car without being mobbed and, once inside, I spoke, "I need to call Mimi."

Gavin gave me a puzzled look.

"I'm late. I need to tell her that I have to run home and shower, get dressed, before I can come in."

Gavin started to laugh, but the expression on my face must've told him I meant what I'd said. Concern replaced amusement. "Carrie, you're not going to work today. Not after what just happened."

I frowned. I had to go to work. "Mimi needs me there to help prepare her cases." I was vaguely aware that there was a perfectly legitimate argument against what I was saying, but I wasn't able to grasp it.

Gavin leaned across the seat and put his hand on my cheek. My eyes found his. "I'll call Mimi and tell her what happened."

Panic flared inside me. No, he couldn't do that. "No, I don't want her to know. She'll be mad."

Gavin brushed his lips against mine, a touch almost too brief and gentle to even be called a kiss, but it stopped me from talking. "No, she won't. She's going to be thankful you're okay, and she's going to tell you to take as much time as you need." He gave me a half-smile. "Besides, I have a feeling Howard's divorce case just got a whole lot easier for his wife."

I returned the smile with a soft one of my own. He was right. That whole mental shock thing I'd been worried about had just thrown me for a minute, making me delusional. "I want to call Krissy, see if she can come home early. I don't want to be alone."

A sad expression crossed Gavin's face and then disappeared

behind a blank mask. "Oh. Sure, I can take you home." He started the car.

"Gavin?" I touched his arm. "What is it?"

"I..." He seemed to be struggling to find the words he wanted. "I thought you could just come home with me, but I understand if you don't want to." He eased his way out onto the street, careful to avoid crushing the mass of media who had flocked to the sight of so many cops and Feds in the same place.

"Gavin." I waited until he glanced my way. "I want to."

Relief broke across his expression, so strong that it surprised me. I hadn't realized that he didn't want to be alone any more than I did. I was glad he wanted me to be with him. I loved Krissy, and I knew at some point, I would want nothing more than to curl up with my friend and cry, but right now, I wanted something that would eradicate the memory of Howard's hands on my body, and sex with Gavin would definitely do that.

THIRTY-FIVE

There is something to be said about the adrenalin rushing through your body when you think you are about to die or face a fate even worse. Surviving such an experience makes the endorphins go sky high. So, based on my previous experiences with Gavin, I had a pretty good idea of what to expect when we got back to his place. I doubted we'd even completely get undressed or make it to the bedroom. I had these images playing through my head of him picking me up as soon as we were inside his apartment, putting my back against the wall, unzipping his pants, and fucking me right there. Maybe we'd get to the couch, shedding clothes along the way, but it would be hard and fast, something almost frantic, fueled by our desire to forget about what had happened and almost happened today.

So, when he shut the door behind us and picked me up, I was prepared for whatever he was going to do. I was ready for anything. Anything except what actually happened next. Instead of tearing my shirt off and fucking me senseless, he kicked off his shoes, cradled me against his chest, and carried me into the bathroom, leaving the blanket on the floor, forgotten.

He walked right into his shower, both of us still fully dressed – or at least as dressed as we had been when we'd come in. Without letting me go, he turned on the water, giving it the minute it needed to warm before switching on the spray.

He looked down at me, droplets of water clinging to his eyelashes. He set me on my feet and gently touched my face. It wasn't until he spoke that I realized the shower wasn't the only reason his face was wet.

"Do you have any idea how terrified I was when I walked into that room and saw you there?" His thumb brushed my bottom lip. "It's been a long time since I've been that scared." His hand was trembling.

I took his hand and pressed my lips against his palm. "I need you to forgive me." I hadn't realized I was going to say the words until they came out. He might hate me when I was done, but I didn't want to lie to him, not when he was being so open and honest with me.

"Forgive you for what?"

I looked up at him, feeling my own eyes burning with tears. "I thought you knew," I said. "About the girls Howard was selling. I overheard him in his office at the mansion, telling Annie that you were supposed to be grooming me for him. I believed him. And then when you told him that you knew about what he'd done to Camille and that you had gotten close to him to find out the truth, I thought you'd just used me to get to him."

"You thought all of this we have together had been a lie?" Gavin had gone very still.

"I didn't know what to think," I said. "Everything between us had happened so fast and you'd been so persistent. I've never had a man want me like that before, and it was easier for me to believe that it was an act than to think that it could possibly be true. That this intense connection could be real... for you. It was always real for me."

I fell silent and waited for his response. My stomach was in knots. I'd thought the worst of him, believed lies and speculation. I wouldn't blame him if he didn't want to see me again.

"This," he said as he cupped the side of my face. "This is the most real thing I've felt in ten years." He lowered his head and gently kissed me. "None of it was fake, and I'm sorry I did anything that made it hard for you to believe me."

He was apologizing to me? I shook my head. "It wasn't your fault," I protested. "It was all me."

He put his finger on my lips. "How about this?" he suggested, "No more apologies. Forgiveness across the board, and we have a clean start."

I smiled. "I like that."

He returned the smile with that sweet one I loved so much. "Now, what do you say we get clean for our clean start?"

He looked down at me then, his eyes darkening at the sight of his shirt molded to my body. I couldn't help but drop my gaze, wanting to see his body's response. I wasn't disappointed. The jeans were tight and wet, leaving little to the imagination. My stomach twisted in anticipation.

He peeled the shirt off of me and tossed it aside. His pants came next. They were already ruined, with one leg cut so that the paramedics had been able to get to the cut on his leg. His boxers came off with the pants so that when he straightened, he was as naked as I was.

He reached for the shampoo and motioned for me to turn around. His fingers massaged the thick lather into my curls and I closed my eyes. My body was starting to relax at last. The chill that had come over me in the club was finally gone. I backed under the spray as Gavin washed his hair.

I was surprised as the shower continued. He conditioned my hair and washed every inch of me, his hands gentle and caressing, but never once did he try to initiate anything. Part of me considered taking matters into my own hands, but something about the way he was looking at me made me decide not to. There was something different about his expression, something deep in his eyes that hadn't been there before. It wasn't until I'd begun to wash him that I realized what it was.

He was taking care of me. Not like before with sex, where it had been about making sure I reached my pleasure. That had been great and had told me that he wanted to make sure I was happy. This wasn't the same. What I saw in his eyes was the kind of caretaking that came with something deeper. This was holding someone's hair back when they threw up and then cleaning them up after. It was bringing chicken soup and crackers. It was choosing to go to the theater on date night instead of spending the night out with the guys. It was giving up everything for that other person.

I slowly ran the soapy cloth around his side to his back. I swallowed hard around the lump in my throat and moved the washcloth across his broad shoulders. I'd believed his words with my head when he'd said this was real for him, but the last piece of my heart that had been holding back couldn't stand against the tenderness I saw in those eyes. And I didn't it want to. I closed my eyes, feeling two tears sliding down my cheeks and mingling with the shower spray. I slowly let out a breath, letting the last of my doubts and fears wash away.

By the time we were finished and drying ourselves off, I felt more at peace than I had in a very long time. At peace, but exhausted. Without a word, Gavin took my hand and led me to his room. He brushed out my hair and braided it, the simplistic style telling me that he'd learned by braiding his daughter's hair. Another surge of emotion went through me, but I didn't say anything. It wasn't the right time. The silence between us was what we needed right now.

He tossed our towels into a hamper and we slid, naked,

between the cool, clean sheets. He curled his body around mine and I nestled back against his chest. His arms went around my waist and I put my hands over his, careful not to jostle his wound. His lips pressed against the hollow under my ear and that was the last thing I knew for several hours.

THIRTY-SIX

When I woke up, two things struck me almost immediately. The first was that the clock said we'd been asleep for more than three hours. The second was that Gavin was still wrapped around me and was enjoying it. His flesh was slowly hardening against my ass.

I smiled and rolled in his arms so we were almost face-to-face. I still had to tilt my head for our eyes to meet, but it was close enough for him to bend his head and brush his lips across mine. His hands splayed across my bare back.

"Good... afternoon?" he said with a smile. "I trust you slept well."

"I did." My own smile faded a bit. "How are you feeling?"

"Better," he said. "I broke my arm when I was eight trying to show off on my bike. Not even close to as bad as that." His expression sobered. "What about you?"

"My hand's aching," I admitted. "I didn't realize Howard's head was that hard, and it probably wasn't a good idea to do that with the same hand I'd dislocated my thumb on."

"And... otherwise?"

I gave Gavin a puzzled look. I wasn't sure what he was asking.

He lifted one hand and gently ran his fingers down the side of my face, then over my arm. "It's not bothering you, me touching you like this?"

Now I was really confused. "I don't understand."

"I know that when someone goes through what you went through with Howard, they don't want to be touched."

"He didn't rape me, Gavin," I said.

"But he put his hands on you."

I could hear the anger in Gavin's voice and a realization hit me. "Is this why we didn't have sex before?"

"I wanted so badly to make love to you," he said. His voice was so earnest that it made my heart skip a beat. "But I didn't think you'd want me that way, not after what had happened. I was even worried about how much I could touch you in the shower."

That explained why he'd seemed almost hesitant while washing me earlier. I closed the short gap between us even though it meant bending my neck at an almost painful angle to still be able to look at him. I heard his breathing hitch and felt him swell even more.

"Howard did touch me," I said. "And even though I showered, I can still feel his hands. I need you to chase away those memories." I slid my arms around his waist and felt the muscles in his back tense. "Please."

He rolled us over so that he was above me, the majority of his weight balanced on his forearms, his body resting on mine from our bellies down. He leaned down and I could see his arms flexing with the effort of keeping himself in position as he kissed me.

It was slow and sweet, his lips moving with mine, slowly parting, and then the tip of his tongue tracing my bottom lip before darting inside. My tongue moved out to caress his and he made a sound in the back of his throat. His teeth scraped over my bottom lip and it was my turn to moan.

I tilted my head back as his mouth moved from mine down to my jaw. His lips burned a trail down my throat, gentle kisses that were at odds with what I was expecting. I remembered how he'd marked me before, sucking skin into his mouth until the blood rose to the surface. There was none of that this time.

Gavin shifted so that he was on his side, allowing him better access to my body. He ran his hand across my stomach and then up to my breasts. He covered one with his hand and I ran my hand up his arm, skirting the bandages. I loved the feel of his skin against mine.

"I promise you, Carrie," he said softly. "No one will ever touch you without your permission again."

I arched my back, pushing my breast against his palm. "You have permission. Please touch me."

He smiled and lowered his head to my bare breast. As his fingers teased my nipple, his lips moved over my soft skin, leaving wet, open-mouthed kisses circling up to my already hardening nipple.

"Ahh," I sighed as his hot mouth closed over the wrinkled flesh.

My eyelids fluttered as he began to suck. It was a slow, steady suction that went straight through me, a deep pull of pleasure. In the back of my head, I was waiting for teeth, for a sharp tug and twist by his fingers, but it didn't happen. By the time he switched to my other nipple and ran his hand down my side to my hip, I stopped thinking about what it had been like before and let the sensations of now take over.

I moaned as Gavin ran his tongue between my breasts and then down my stomach. His tongue swirled around my belly button before continuing its journey south. I opened my eyes as soon as I felt him nudge my legs apart. He looked up at me as he positioned himself between my thighs. He turned his head to one side and placed a kiss first on one inner thigh, then the other. I shivered with each contact, the anticipation of his mouth on me making heat coil in my stomach. He turned his gaze back to my face, keeping his eyes on me as he moved forward.

"Fuck," I gasped as he ran his tongue the full length of me.

He worked that thick muscle between my lips, dipping inside me before moving up to circle the little bundle of nerves that throbbed in need. I could feel the delicious pressure building inside me and knew that my release – the first of what I hoped would be quite a few – was near. He wrapped his hands around my hips as he pressed his mouth closer, his kiss tipping me over the edge.

My hips tried to move, to push themselves closer to that delightful mouth that was sending wave after wave of pleasure washing over me, but his hands held me fast. I reached down and buried my fingers in his silky hair, trying to accomplish what another part of me had been unable to do.

As a second orgasm rolled over me, one of Gavin's hands moved from my hip, and a moment later, I felt his finger at my entrance.

"Yes," I hissed as he slid it inside.

His tongue continued to flick over my clit, sending signals racing along my nerves, as his finger slowly pumped in and out of me. I was wet, but tight, and he took full advantage of that, letting the friction help work me towards a third climax. When he slipped a second finger into me, I closed my eyes and moaned.

"One more," he murmured against my flesh, the puffs of hot air on my sensitive skin making me shiver. "Come for me again."

I nodded. I wanted to. Every inch of my body was humming and I could feel it getting closer. Then he crooked his fingers and pressed against that spot inside of me. I exploded, my back arching up off of the bed as he applied just the right amount of pressure to keep me coming until spots danced in front of my eyes. I was vaguely aware that I was calling out his name, and then I dropped back to the bed, my body limp as he withdrew his hand from between my legs.

I tried to focus on my breathing and getting my limbs to work again as he crawled up my body until we were face to face. His cock nudged against my still-sensitive pussy and I drew in a shuddering breath.

Gavin kissed me gently and I tasted myself on his lips. It wasn't deep or long, just enough to not be chaste. "Are you sure you want this?" he asked. "We don't have to."

I reached up and wrapped my arms around his neck. "Make me forget."

His hand moved between our bodies and, a moment later, I felt the tip of him enter me. He slid inside, taking his time to let my body accept him one inch at a time. I hooked my legs over his, resting my ankles on the backs of his knees. I sighed as he came to rest, fully sheathed inside me. There it was, that completeness I craved.

His eyes locked with mine as he began to move. Each stroke was slow and deliberate, creating the perfect friction to fan the flames stirring inside me. He rubbed against my G-spot with every thrust, and it sent electricity across my nerves, igniting my cells. I knew something big was coming and I wasn't sure I could survive it.

I'd had the kind of orgasms that had made me scream, the ones that sent me into unconsciousness. They'd all built with a pressure that promised an explosion of ecstasy, and then delivered. This wasn't an explosion waiting to happen. No, this was a building inferno that threatened to consume everything.

Gavin moved suddenly, pulling me up with him until he was sitting and I was in his lap. He didn't lose contact as he wrapped my legs around his waist and pulled me against him so that our chests were pressed together. My nipples rubbed against his chest, making me whimper at the added sensation. The base of him rubbed my already sensitive clit with each movement and I shivered.

The new position brought us even closer, something I hadn't thought was possible. His arm ran up my spine, his hand cupping the back of my head, holding me against him. We moved together, almost as one, our bodies grinding against each other as the fire inside us licked across our skins, coating us, consuming us. His mouth took mine, our tongues mimicking the movements of our lower bodies.

All sense of time and place bled away. It was only Gavin and me, our connection, the way our bodies fit together so perfectly. Our lips moving, tongues dancing. Every place where we touched each other blazing with an inferno of pleasure.

I almost didn't recognize my orgasm as it began, the flames spiking, then spilling over. I tore my mouth away from Gavin's and cried out, my entire body shuddering with the force of my climax. It wasn't a sudden and massive rush, crashing over me like a wave, but rather the relentless pounding of the tide against the shore.

Gavin's arms tightened around me and his hips jerked against mine. I felt him come, pulsing inside me, filling me. He called out my name over and over again, crushing me against his chest.

What seemed like years passed before I dropped my head to his shoulder, my muscles twitching as the fire inside me began to cool.

I'd never experienced anything remotely close to what had just happened. Orgasms had been bursts of intense pleasure between the enjoyable friction that had brought me. Gavin had made me see stars, made me come so hard I'd passed out, made me scream. This had been something different. I'd felt like I'd been melted down, turned into molten lava, liquid heat. Somehow, it had been more intense, as if it had meant more.

I raised my head and found Gavin looking at me. The moment my eyes met his, the blue almost the same shade as a midnight sky, I knew that he'd felt it too. It hadn't been how we'd done it, what position, or the fact that it had been gentle. Everything that had happened had shifted something between us.

Gavin brushed back a few curls that had escaped my braid and shifted us so that we were stretched back out on the bed. He lay on his back and I curled up against him, resting my head on his chest. I loved hearing the sound of his heart.

We lay in silence for several minutes before I admitted that I needed an answer to the question that had resurfaced as I'd come down from my climactic high. "Can I ask you something?"

"Of course."

"That was amazing, but there wasn't any..." My voice trailed off as I realized I wasn't quite sure how to actually ask my question. "I mean, we didn't do anything..."

"You want to know why we didn't do anything kinky?"

I looked up to see him smiling at me. My cheeks burned, but I nodded.

"I don't need the S&M stuff to enjoy myself, Carrie," he assured me. "I like variety." He kissed my forehead. "Besides, I figure we have plenty of time to explore that in the future."

A thrill went through me at his mention of the future. Still, I decided to tease him a bit. I fixed my lips into a saucy grin. "Does that mean if I'm a bad girl tonight, you won't want to punish me?"

He raised an eyebrow.

I slid my hand across his stomach and down, wrapping my fingers around his softening cock. He sucked in a breath and I chuckled.

"If you want to play," he said. "I'm going to need my strength. We should get something to eat."

I gave him a mock pout and he laughed, leaning down to

take my bottom lip between his teeth, lightly tugging on it. I started to move on top of him, but just as things were about to get interesting, his cell phone rang.

I glanced at it, more out of habit than from actually caring who it was. I had other things on my mind, but as soon as I saw the number, I rolled off of Gavin and reached for it. He gave me a puzzled look, but as soon as I answered it, understanding crossed his face.

"Hello," I said.

"What the fuck, Carrie?!" Krissy's voice was too loud in my ear. "I've been trying to call you all day!"

"It's a long story, Krissy," I interrupted before she could get going. I glanced at Gavin.

"You fill her in. I'll go get us something to eat." Gavin kissed my cheek and then climbed out of bed.

I watched him walk across the bedroom, my thoughts straying until Krissy brought me back.

"Carrie, if you're ogling your boyfriend instead of talking to me, I'm going to kick your ass."

I grinned sheepishly even though she couldn't see me. "Sorry," I apologized. "So, here's what happened..."

THIRTY-SEVEN

None of this seemed real. Actually, not much in the past two weeks seemed like anything other than some very strange, and sometimes erotic, dream.

The rumors throughout the legal world were that Howard had royally screwed himself in thinking he could talk himself out of his charges by buddying up to the detective interrogating him. He'd gotten himself a reduced sentence on the sex trafficking charges in exchange for his client lists, but because his ego had gotten the better of him, he'd ended up admitting to a whole slew of other crimes that even his high-priced lawyer hadn't been able to make go away. Between the drugs he'd supplied to Melissa, my assault and attempted rape, his assault and attempted murder of Gavin, and the information linking him to covering up Camille's death, he wasn't going to be getting out of jail for a very long time, if ever. I'd also been hearing that some of his female staff had gone in to officially file complaints. I hoped Annie was one of them.

Of course, all of that had brought a lot of unwanted attention my way, so Gavin and I had been hiding out in either his place or mine, the timing depending on whether or not Krissy wanted the apartment to herself. We didn't walk anywhere and we definitely didn't go out to eat. I'd begun to feel sympathy for celebrities who complained about the paparazzi. I'd even missed participating in my own graduation ceremony because the press had gotten wind of it.

The only place outside of the two apartments where the media couldn't touch me was work. The first time someone had tried to sneak in to the office, Mimi had gone to a judge who'd slapped a restraining order on the reporter and ordered the press to stay at least five hundred feet away from the building. Mimi really was an amazing lawyer.

"Are you ready?" Krissy asked as she approached my desk. "It's your party, after all. Can't start till you get there."

When Mimi had heard I hadn't been able to go to my graduation, she'd decided to throw me a party at work. I'd dressed for the occasion, putting aside my usual wardrobe in exchange for one of the sundresses Gavin had bought me for our trip to Miami. That particular weekend had so many bad memories that I was determined to make new ones to overshadow the old. This would be my new memory in my cute mint-green dress.

"Have I told you how adorable you look in that?" Leslie asked as she joined Krissy at my desk. Dena followed closely behind.

"Thank you." I smiled, and it felt a lot less forced than the ones I had been giving to people. Aside from Gavin, my three friends had been my salvation through all of this. They'd treated me no differently than they had before. The only change was that the teasing that had previously been directed at my lack of a romantic life was now about my rich, sexy boyfriend.

"Mimi said she bought a red velvet cake." Krissy hooked her arm through mine. "Shall we go check it out?"

I nodded and we headed to the large conference room. There was, indeed, a red velvet cake with chocolate icing and "Congratulations, Carrie" in deep red frosting. It was huge. I'd never seen a cake that big before. My friends stayed close as our various coworkers came over to congratulate me, intervening whenever the conversation veered towards topics best left undiscussed.

I was just starting to try to figure out how I could get out of the rest of the party when Dena returned from the restroom by way of the outer office. She had a strange expression on her face as she approached me and said, "There's someone here to see you."

She didn't appear to be upset or concerned, so I followed her back out. Standing by my desk was an older man with salt-and-pepper hair, and a young woman who was looking at the floor.

"Ms. Summers?" the man asked.

His voice sounded familiar, but it wasn't until the dark-haired girl raised her head that I realized who they were. A chill ran through me. "Patricia?"

"Ms. Summers, we had to come down here and personally thank you for what you did." Frank took a step forward and extended his hand.

I took it, tearing my eyes away from the pale young woman long enough to see that her father had tears in his eyes.

"If it wasn't for you, she would still be—" His voice broke.

"You saved my life, Ms. Summers." Patricia's voice was soft. "And that's not an exaggeration."

Frank had regained control of his emotions. "After you called me, I made arrangements to leave on the next flight to Saudi Arabia, and then called the detective who'd been assigned Patricia's case to tell him that I had a lead and that I was flying out the next day. He tried to talk me out of going but I didn't listen. When I arrived, I went straight to the American embassy and, with their help, was able to convince the Saudi police to raid the mansion."

"There were four of us you helped rescue." Patricia took a

step towards me and started to raise her arms. She hesitated, as if unsure if I would hug her.

Of course I did. I could feel the tears streaming down my cheeks, but I didn't care. Everything that I'd been through, in that moment, was worth it. Even if it had just been Patricia, if no one else would've been saved, every second of torment would have been worth it.

We didn't talk long. I could tell Patricia was adjusting to being back and dealing with everything that she'd gone through. She had a good therapist and had found a support group for survivors like her. Her father was determined to do everything in his power to give her a good life, and I knew that would be as important as everything else. The support and love of family and friends would help her heal. And maybe then she could help others heal. I had a feeling Patricia would be the kind of woman who took her own tragedy and turned it into a way to help others who were suffering.

The Vinariskys left, and I had to stop in the restroom. I couldn't go back into the party until I'd composed myself better. That was a part of the story that only Gavin and Krissy knew, though I would probably share it with Leslie and Dena soon. I didn't want questions about why I looked so emotional.

When I came out of the restroom, Gavin was stepping off of the elevator. As always, the sight of him made my heart tighten and my stomach flip. He was dressed nicely, but nothing too fancy. Just a pair of dress jeans that hugged his body in a way that made my mouth go dry, because it only hinted at what I knew lay underneath. His short-sleeved dress shirt made his eye color pop, and was fitted tight enough to show that he was fit, but not so tight that it revealed every dip and curve of muscle. The man knew how to dress. Then again, I thought he'd look sexy in pretty much anything... and even more so in nothing.

"Earth to Carrie." He waved a hand in front of my face. "Where'd you go?"

I smiled up at him and wrapped my arms around his neck. His look of surprise made my smile widen. I'd been very clear about no public displays of affection at work. His arms automatically slid around my waist though he still looked confused.

"It's my party," I said. "And if I want to kiss my boyfriend, I will."

He chuckled and gently pressed his lips against mine. It was sweet and soft, exactly what I needed to finish calming my emotions after seeing Patricia. I'd tell him all about that later. Right now, we had cake to eat.

I took a step back and took his hand, threading our fingers together. "Let's go get some cake."

"Cake sounds good," he said. "But I'm thinking we cut out after we're done."

Now it was my turn to be confused.

"I want to take you on a little trip."

"Where?"

He smiled. "That's a surprise." He raised our hands and kissed the back of mine. "Let's see about that cake, make the rounds, thank Mimi, and get out of here."

"But I have to finish work."

"Nope." His grin widened. "Already cleared it with Mimi. She said you deserve it. So, what do you say?"

"I say, that sounds like exactly what I need."

Less than twenty minutes later, we were heading down to the lobby where, I assumed, he'd have one of his infamous town cars waiting.

I was wrong.

What was sitting in front of the building wasn't a town car, but a cherry red Italian sports car. A Ferrari, to be exact. I remembered him saying he preferred them to Bentleys, but I hadn't realized that meant he owned one. I'd never been one to fawn over cars, but even I had to admit that this one was a beauty.

"This is my 'outside the city' car," he said as he opened the door for me.

"So we're leaving the city then?" I asked as I slid into the passenger's seat. The leather was soft against my skin.

"No guessing." He closed the door and then walked around to the other side. He continued speaking as he got in. "Don't ruin the surprise."

I gave him a mock pout and he laughed. Not the sexy laugh that made things low in my belly tighten, but the one that was far rarer, the one that was open and joyful. I hoped finding the man responsible for Camille's death would give him some closure and allow him to laugh like that more often.

He reached over and squeezed my hand before starting the car and pulling out into the street. We didn't really speak until we passed the city limits, and then it was he who initiated the conversation.

"Now that you've graduated, are you planning on staying at Webster and Steinberg or do you have another firm in mind?" He glanced at me before returning his attention to the road. "I just realized that I'd never asked you that before."

He was right. We'd talked in vague generalities about things, but never specifics about what I planned to do after graduation and passing the bar.

"I appreciate everything Mimi has done for me," I said. "But divorce court isn't where I want to practice. I've always wanted to help the helpless, you know? Go after child abusers and wife beaters, that kind of thing; but I don't think I'm cut out to be a prosecutor either." I'd actually had this idea bouncing around in my head for a while, but this was the first time I was giving it voice. "I've been thinking lately that I want to fight sex trafficking by working for the victims, go after people like Howard not just criminally, but in every way possible. Fight to get laws passed for better protection and compensation for the victims."

Gavin put his hand over mine. "I think that's a great idea."

I sighed. "The only problem is that, because it's not a very lucrative business, there aren't a lot of firms that specialize in that kind of work, and none of them are hiring. I've been checking this past week."

Gavin was silent for a moment, then spoke, the hesitation in his voice making me turn towards him. "What about starting your own firm? Take cases pro bono. Maybe even spend some time digging into potential traffickers and gathering evidence for the authorities. You've proven you're good at that."

I gave him a puzzled look. "That would be great, but I'm going to be paying off my student loans until I'm forty as it is. I have to make a living somehow."

"You make a living through your partnership in the club," he said. "And you can even use it to weed out potential traffickers."

"Okay," I said slowly. I wasn't sure where he was going with this. "It still doesn't explain how I'm going to manage to not only pay my bills but fund a law firm with what I make helping run a club."

"You don't fund the law firm," he said. "I do."

I stared at him. He couldn't be serious.

He continued, "It's important work, Carrie. It means a lot to you, and I helped Howard run his business through the club."

"You didn't know."

His expression was grim. "I didn't, but it doesn't mean I shouldn't help put a stop to others like Howard." He lifted our hands and brushed his lips across my knuckles, sending little tingles across my skin. "Those seem like just a few of many reasons why this is a good idea."

He looked as if he expected me to argue like I had before, any time he'd spent a lot of money on me, but this wasn't for me, not really. Sure, it was letting me do what I wanted to do, but it was about the victims, the survivors like Patricia and the ones who never made it home to their families. I wasn't about to pass that up. Besides, I was getting more used to his generosity's just being a part of who he was.

I leaned over, putting my hand on his leg to steady myself, and kissed his cheek. "Thank you."

We went around a bend as I was starting to sit back, and the turn jostled me, causing my hand slid higher up his thigh, my fingers brushing against the bulge in his jeans. I heard him suck in a breath and my stomach clenched. I loved that an accidental touch could make him react like that.

The mischievous part of me, the one that had been growing bolder the more time I spent with Gavin, decided that it was time to come out and play. I didn't sit back, but rather leaned as close as my seatbelt would allow, pressing my breasts against his arm, and put my mouth against his ear.

"Wherever we're going," I whispered. "I hope it has a nice, big bed because I fully intend to show my gratitude for your offer." I flicked out my tongue, catching his earlobe with the tip.

The car jerked, then pulled off the side of the road, moving up behind a small cusp of trees. It was all so sudden that I barely had time to process it before the car was off and Gavin was turning towards me, his eyes blazing.

Oh. Apparently not waiting for our destination. The ache between my legs approved of that decision.

He wrapped a hand around the back of my neck, pulling me forward until our mouths crashed together. I made a noise in the back of my throat and his fingers flexed against my neck as his tongue pushed between my lips.

We'd had sex several times since the incident with Howard, and it had been great every time, but the edge that had existed before was gone. We teased about me being a "bad girl" and things like that, but never did anything about it. I kept telling Gavin that I was okay, that he didn't need to treat me like I was breakable, but I could feel him holding back. And it wasn't like before when he'd been testing what I liked. This was more that he was afraid he would do something that would hurt me, not physically, but emotionally. I appreciated that, but I was starting to miss the world he'd just started to introduce me to. I was actually craving something rougher, something driven by pure need.

This kiss promised everything I wanted and more, and I wasn't about to let him reconsider.

I sucked on his tongue, earning that near-growl I'd been missing, and I dropped my hands between us. I managed to get the button undone and his pants unzipped before he realized what I was doing. He took my bottom lip between his teeth, tugging lightly at the kiss-swollen flesh, and I slid my hand into his pants.

"Fuck." His mouth tore away from mine the moment I took him in my hand.

He was hot and hard, straining against the confines of his boxer-briefs, and I wanted nothing more than to free him – lower my head and take him in my mouth, feel him thrust up, running that silk-covered shaft over my tongue...

"Get out of the car."

I blinked, startled out of my fantasy. What?

He pressed his lips against mine hard enough to bruise. "Get. Out. Of. The. Car."

I drew in a shuddering breath, my panties instantly soaked. My fingers were shaking so badly I could barely unfasten my seatbelt, but I finally managed and climbed out of the car. Gavin was already standing on my side. He held out his hand and I took it. Without a word, he pulled me towards him. Just before I crashed into him, he turned me, pressing his hand against my back.

I didn't need him to say anything to know what he wanted. My entire body was thrumming in anticipation as I bent over the hood. Part of me couldn't believe I was doing this, out in the open, hidden from the road by only a few trees, but a louder part of me was screaming for him to just do it already because I was going to explode if he didn't.

Gavin pushed up the back of my dress and I waited for him to remove my panties. He didn't. Instead, he nudged my legs further apart and pulled aside the soft cotton material. There was no warning. No prep. One moment, I felt him at my entrance, and then next, he was buried to the hilt inside me.

I cried out, a sound that might have been a wail if I'd had more air in my lungs. I didn't though. I could barely get a breath as he immediately began to pound into me, his thrusts hard and deep, each one raising me up on my tiptoes and forcing the air out of my lungs.

I squeezed my eyes closed, trying to absorb the sensations. The heat of the metal beneath my hands, through my dress. His fingers digging into my hips. My pussy stretching around him. The almost painful pleasure racing through every cell.

And then there was more.

His hands left my hips. One slid between me and the car, delving into the front of my dress to find my nipple hard and eager for his attention. His other hand moved underneath me, his fingers finding that swollen bundle of nerves.

The instant he touched me, I came, but he didn't stop. Even as my body shuddered, tensing with my orgasm, he continued his ministrations, working me from one climax into another. Only as my second orgasm peaked did I feel his hips jerk against me. He came with a drawn-out groan, and I felt him pulse as he filled me.

His arms tightened around me as his body curled over mine. He pressed his lips against the hollow under my ear, sending another shiver of pleasure through me. We stayed like that for several minutes, his cock slowly softening inside me, one hand around my dress, the other between my legs.

"Are you okay?" he asked as he finally straightened.

I inhaled sharply as he slid out of me, the loss leaving me

feeling empty. His cum trickled down the inside of my thigh as I stood and adjusted my panties.

"Am I okay?" I echoed his question. "Are you kidding? That was amazing."

He gave me that shy little-boy smile I loved so much. "I wasn't sure... I mean, it wasn't..."

I put a finger on his lips, stopping the flow of words. "Just so we're clear. I like it when you take charge like that. I wasn't pretending before, or now."

Relief showed on his face.

"If you need any further proof," I said, grimacing as I took a step back towards the car. "Here it is: we need to find a store so I can buy dry underwear. I've been wet from the moment you kissed me."

His smile widened into a full-blown grin. "I think that would be a good idea."

Twenty minutes and a new pair of panties later, I knew where we were going and was glad I'd suggested stopping at the store. As soon as I saw the sign for Stamford, I looked over at Gavin. The look he gave me was all the confirmation I needed.

He was taking me to see his daughter.

I could feel the tension radiating off of him as we pulled up in front of a modest, two-story house. He looked over at me, but didn't say anything. He didn't have to. I knew he was nervous. I reached out and squeezed his hand. I was nervous too.

Then I saw her. This petite little blonde in a white and pink sundress. She burst out of the house, a smile lighting up her face.

"Daddy!"

He climbed out of the car and bent down to scoop her up in his arms.

If I'd still had any doubts about Gavin or how I felt about him, they would have disappeared the moment I saw the complete and utter adoration on his face when he looked at his child. No one could argue he'd given her grandparents custody because he didn't want her. I'd never seen anyone look at someone with so much love.

I climbed out of the car, my heart pounding, and walked around to where Skylar was chatting away. I hung back for a moment, and then she saw me.

She stopped talking and studied me for a moment with those eyes that were so much like her father's. She tilted her head to one side, and in that serious voice that small children have, asked, "Is she your girlfriend?"

Gavin smiled and stretched out his hand. "Yes, she is."

I took his hand, letting his touch ease my nerves. "Hi." I gave Skylar a smile.

"You're pretty," she declared. "I like you." She squirmed in Gavin's arms and he put her down. She looked up at me and put her hands on her hips. "We're having a picnic in the backyard and you have to push me on the swings." With that statement, she turned and ran around the back of the house.

"I guess I'm pushing her on the swings," I said.

Gavin chuckled and released my hand, sliding his arm around my waist. He pulled me against his side. He pressed his lips against my temple. "I love you."

We'd said similar things before, but this was the first time those three words had been stated in such a simple, declarative fashion. I could barely speak around the lump in my throat. "I love you too."

I tilted my head to look up at him and he bent his head, giving me a soft, sweet kiss. I slid my arm around his waist and felt something that I hadn't felt in a long time. I felt like I was home. Not because of this house or this neighborhood, but because of the man next to me.

"Ready?" he asked.

I knew he was referring to meeting Camille's parents and spending the evening with his daughter, but my answer meant so much more. I was ready. Ready to start the next chapter in my life. I nodded. "I'm ready."

We headed for the backyard, drawn by the joy of his child's laughter. Yes. I was definitely ready for this.

The End

**The Club Prive series continues in Krissy's story,
Chasing Perfection (Club Privé Book 3), available
now. Turn the page for a free preview.**

PREVIEW: CHASING TEMPTATION (CLUB PRIVE 3)

ONE

DEVON

As I used the expensive linen napkin to wipe the wine from my face, I was glad I'd ordered white instead of red. My dry cleaner would be able to salvage my dress shirt. I was still pissed, though. A perfectly good glass of Chardonnay wasted in a fit of childish temper.

"You're breaking up with me?" The beautiful blonde who was still in the midst of the previously mentioned temper tantrum had pushed back from the table and was now standing to deliver her indignant monologue. "Are you fucking kidding me?"

I opened my mouth to tell her to sit down and be quiet, but she didn't let me speak.

"After everything I've let you do to me?" Her face was starting to get that red, splotchy look that happened when fair-skinned women let their temper get the best of them. She looked around at the other diners, most of whom were no longer even trying to be polite and ignore the scene.

"I let you tie me up for your little games!" She was almost

shrieking now. "You fucking *spanked* me!"

Shit.

I could see the expressions on the other men and women, saw their eyes darting towards me. Some of them recognized me. That was not acceptable.

I stood and crossed to her in two long strides, putting just an inch between our bodies so we weren't touching, but she was forced to look up at me. I glared down at her and spoke in a low voice, the one that demanded submission.

"You are behaving in a manner most unbecoming, Miss Paine." As it always did when I was trying to control my temper, the faint accent that usually tinged my words thickened until I sounded more like the teenaged boy who'd first stepped off the plane from Venice. That just made me angrier. My next statement was nearly a growl. "You know what happens when you misbehave in public."

Her mouth snapped shut.

I watched her swallow hard and the anger in her face drained away, replaced by lust. I preferred that look on a woman's face. Lust was easy to control.

I took a step back and motioned for one of the waiters who'd been nervously standing in the shadows.

"Yes, Sir?" the man asked nervously.

"Bill me for the meal," I said. "And a bottle of wine for each table as an apology for the disruption of your guests' meals." I glanced at the waiter. "And add a thirty percent tip for your aggravation as well."

"Thank you, Sir."

I turned my attention back to my soon-to-be former lover. "Follow me."

I didn't bother to check if she was following as I walked towards the exit. I kept my eyes forward, my head up, expression blank. The only thing that betrayed what was bubbling under the surface was my lips pressed in a thin line. I stepped out into the balmy autumn night, not pausing to see if she was coming. I walked around the corner and into the narrow alley that separated the expensive Beverly Hills restaurant from the boutique next door. Less than a minute later, she appeared, stepping into the alley without a moment of hesitation.

"Face the wall, palms flat against it."

I could see her fingers trembling as she did as she was told. She knew what was coming, and the fact that she was here meant that she accepted it, wanted it. She was always free to walk away at any time. I knew she wouldn't, though. They never did.

I closed the space between us and slid my hands under the hem of her shirt. I had instructed her to wear the two-piece dress combination rather than a full dress for just this reason. Of all my lovers, Sami had been one of the most contentious – and not always in an enjoyable way – requiring far more discipline than the others. It hadn't been a difficult decision to end our... encounter.

I pulled down her skirt and tapped her bare calf. She lifted one leg, then the other, kicking away half of the twenty-five hundred dollar garment. The top came down to the middle of her ass, leaving the rest of her bare. Like all my women, she didn't wear panties in public. I preferred easy access at all times. I only allowed those who needed it to wear a bra. Sami didn't.

I wasn't interested in her breasts at the moment, however. I ran my hand over the firm globes of pale flesh and felt her tense. I smiled and drew my hand back.

The first crack echoed in the alley, sounding louder because of the silence between us. She didn't make a sound until my hand made contact for the third time, the skin on her ass already starting to turn a delightful shade of pink.

"Ahhh..." It wasn't exactly pleasure, but it wasn't pain either. Sami was in that place where the two were starting to join, but her body hadn't sorted out how it wanted to respond.

I spanked her harder, reminding her that this was a punishment for her behavior. It wasn't meant to truly hurt her, but she needed to feel it. My palm was starting to sting and I was starting to wish I'd thought to bring a belt. Used correctly, it worked as well as a flogger to bring my submissive right to that edge.

I didn't stop until her breathing began to hitch and I could see the moisture between her legs. Only then did I reach into my pocket for one of the little packets I kept on me at all times. I tore it open, unzipped my pants and rolled the condom down over my throbbing cock.

When I stepped up behind her and nudged her legs further apart, I could feel the heat radiating off of her ass. She wasn't going to be able to sit comfortably for days. I lined myself up and thrust into her pussy with one hard stroke.

She keened as I buried my full length inside her. She was wet, but still so tight that it was almost painful for me, but I didn't stop. I grabbed a handful of her hair as I began to pound into her. I could feel her body quivering around me as I tugged on her hair. For as much as she'd made it sound like I was the one who wanted it rough, she got off on it just as much as I did.

I could feel the pressure building in my stomach and knew I was close. I'd been wound too tight from the moment she'd started her tantrum, and spanking her had just made it that much worse. I put my mouth against her ear.

"Come if you can, but I'm not helping you."

She growled in frustration, but I ignored her. My own release was too near. I lowered my head to the place where her shoulder met her neck and took some of the skin there into my mouth, sucking on it, nibbling it with my teeth. We were done, but I'd make sure she'd remember our last time together.

She was making whining little mews now, pushing back to meet my thrusts, forcing me even deeper. I put my hands on her hips and held her in place as I slammed into her, biting down on her neck as I came. She wailed, her body shaking around mine, further proof that I wasn't the only one who liked what I'd done.

I closed my eyes for a moment, letting the waves of pleasure wash over and through me. I let out a breath and took a step back, hearing her hiss as I slid out of her. She staggered, as if her legs couldn't hold her, and then rolled so that her back was against the wall, propping her up. She gave me a cat-ate-the-canary kind of smile.

I discarded the condom and tucked myself back into my pants. I pulled out my wallet and withdrew a twenty. "Here." I tossed it towards her. "Take a cab."

I saw the shock settle over her and resisted the urge to roll my eyes. Had she really thought this meant we weren't done?

"Danny will be your agent from here on out. I don't want to see your face again." I turned and started towards the street where my car would be waiting.

I'd just reached the sidewalk when she screamed out, "Asshole!"

I didn't acknowledge it as I thanked the valet, tipped him, and climbed into the driver's seat. Sami was right. I was an asshole, but that's the way it had to be. Two weeks was my usual, four at the max. No attachments. Ever.

Besides, I reasoned as I started towards home, Sami was just another no-talent, wanna-be actress, anyway. The best she could ever hope for would be bit parts in cheap, made-for-TV movies before she made the inevitable transition to adult films. She'd do okay there. She had a nice body and was a decent enough lay, though not as good as she seemed to think she was.

Women like her were a dime a dozen. They all came to Hollywood with the same idea, that their pretty face and tight pussies would let them sleep their way to the top. And I was the top. I was DeVon fucking Ricci, one of the biggest agents in Hollywood. Nothing could touch me.

TWO

KRISSY

I leaned against the edge of my best friend's desk, watching as she put the last of her things into a plastic container. Leave it to Carrie to be overly organized. We were complete opposites that way and I knew my disorganization annoyed her as much as her tidiness annoyed me.

Damn, I was going to miss her.

Carrie Summers had been my best friend since we'd met at Columbia six years ago. We'd been roommates in the dorm, then moved into an apartment after we'd been hired at Webster and Steinberg. We'd met Dena and Leslie here, and the four of us were close, but Carrie and I were closer. Sometimes, I thought that we were more like sisters than friends, and I knew she felt the same way.

"I can't believe we're having cake again." I sighed, putting a bit of drama into it. "It's only been two months since we had cake for your graduation party." I gave her a shrewd look. "You just wanted to feed that sweet tooth, didn't you?"

Carrie gave me a soft smile, the same smile that she'd been

wearing since she'd started making these plans. I loved Carrie, but she'd always been a bit uptight. She'd always been the one who'd needed coaxing to follow her heart and her dreams. Now, she was leaving one of the largest divorce law firms in New York to start her own pro bono law practice helping people who'd been abused, specifically focusing on the sex trafficking industry.

"I'm going to miss you," I said. As soon as I said the words, I wished I could take them back. They hadn't come out as light-hearted as I'd intended, and sincere emotions weren't something I liked showing in public.

Carrie paused in her packing and looked up, giving me a puzzled look. I had to drop my gaze down to where my fingers were tapping at the edge of the desk. I couldn't meet those dark eyes. Not when it was finally time to tell her.

"What do you mean you're going to miss me?" she asked. "I'm only going to be four blocks away. We can still have lunch together every day and meet after work for drinks whenever you want. That's the joy of being my own boss. Flexibility."

I pushed back my thick, glossy black hair. It was past my shoulders now and I was thinking it might be a good idea to cut it before I left. There was a big difference in the weather from here to where I was going.

"Is this about me moving in with Gavin?"

Carrie's question made me look up, startled. I hadn't thought she'd take it that way.

"I thought you said you were okay with it."

I straightened. "I am," I assured her. "I am. Gavin's smoking hot, and a really good guy. I'm glad that you're moving in together."

I was telling the truth. For a while after they'd first met, my approval of Gavin had fluctuated, but once the whole truth had come out, I'd been more than happy to put my stamp of approval on their relationship. Some people might've thought they were moving too fast, but I knew Carrie. She never would've made this decision if she wasn't sure about him, and I'd given her my full support. She deserved to be happy, and so did he.

Carrie folded her arms over her chest and her eyes narrowed. "Well, something's weird with you. What is it, girl? Spill."

Dammit. Why did she always have to be so insightful when it came to me? I'd wanted to ease into this, but like most of my life, I'd fallen into it. "I'm probably leaving the company, too," I said slowly. Carrie's eyes widened. "And that's not all," I continued. "I'm most likely leaving New York as well."

Carrie's jaw dropped and she stared at me for nearly a full, uncomfortable minute. Then her mouth snapped shut and she gave me a suspicious look. "Are you saying this because I'm moving out? If you don't want me to go or you think I'm moving too fast with Gavin, just say so. He'll understand if I change my mind."

Was she serious? I rolled my eyes. "Really, Carrie? Come on. You know me better than that," I said. "I think you and Gavin should definitely move in together. The truth is, there's a job as an associate looking my way."

I saw shock, then hurt, cross her face.

"You've been keeping this a secret from me for how long? Why?"

"I applied three months ago," I said. "And then I had the phone interview two weeks after that. Understand why I didn't say anything?" I saw her doing the math in her head and then watched her frustration with me fade away as she realized that I hadn't told her because she'd had enough going on at the time. "I haven't exactly gotten it yet. Besides, I didn't even know if I'd get called out for a face-to-face interview."

"And that's what this is? Not a definite, but an interview?"

I nodded. "They said it was down to just three applicants

now. I think I have a good shot." I paused, then added, "And even if I don't get it, I might look out there anyway."

"Out there?" Carrie echoed. I knew she was still putting the pieces together and had just understood that when I said out of the city, I hadn't meant Jersey. "Where's the job?"

Here was the part I really hadn't been looking forward to. "On the West Coast."

Carrie took a slow, deep breath, letting it out before she asked her next question. "You mean you might move to San Francisco or some place like that?"

"Not San Francisco," I said. "Hollywood."

"Are you nuts? You want to go be some divorce lawyer in L.A.?"

I shook my head. If she hated that idea, she was really going to hate this one. "The offer's from a talent agency."

She frowned. "A talent agency? What, are you trying to become an actress or something?"

It was a mark of our friendship that I took pride in her snide remark. I found it comforting that I'd rubbed off on her over the years. "No, smart-ass," I said. "One of the biggest talent agencies in Hollywood needs another associate in their legal department. Remember that guy, Kenny, who used to work here?"

"The one you made out with in the elevator and then bragged about it over drinks?" Carrie's lips twitched into a grin. "Yeah, I have a vague recollection of him."

I laughed. Even with as kinky as she and Gavin had gotten, Carrie was still hesitant to talk about sex anywhere that wasn't our apartment. Or, based on what I'd heard through our thin walls, the bedroom. "We did a little more than make out, but yes, that's the one. He's been trying to get back in my pants ever since. His cousin works at the agency and told him they were looking for another associate. He figured it'd be a good reason to call."

"Did you go out with him again?" Carried asked.

I shook my head. "No way. He wasn't that good, or that hot." I ignored the judgey look she was sending my way. She might keep her mouth shut about it most of the time, but I knew she didn't approve of the way I handled my romantic life. "But I did decide to send in my résumé and now they want me to fly in for an interview."

"When are you leaving?"

"Monday morning. The meeting's at noon."

"I'm happy you have this opportunity," Carrie said. Her eyes were bright with tears. "But if you get this job, am I ever going to see you again, or is this it?"

I rolled my eyes again. "Of course we'll see each other." I playfully pushed at her arm, trying to lighten the mood. This is exactly what I hadn't wanted. "I'll come visit. Or, here's an idea. You and Gavin can move to LA. Start your little sexy club out there. Give me a good place to scope out all those California hotties."

"Krissy." Carrie said my name with a combination of affection and irritation.

"And your pro bono business can be just as effective on the West Coast. There are plenty of young women being abused in California. Trust me. Probably more than in New York."

Carrie frowned. "That's not funny."

I held up my hands in a gesture of surrender. I knew I'd crossed the line as soon as the words had left my mouth. "I know, I know. Crude," I said. "But I'm pretty sure that's a true statement."

Carrie nodded, and her expression shifted to one of sadness. "What am I going to do without you?"

I put my arm around her shoulders. If she started crying, I was going to start and I didn't particularly like the idea of walking around for the next hour or so with red eyes.

"Come on," I said. "Let's go get some of that cake. I heard

Mimi ordered the same as last time: Red Velvet with cream cheese frosting."

Carrie gave a laugh that had a sniffle in the middle of it. "She *always* orders Red Velvet..."

I laughed and started to walk us both towards the conference room. I hadn't told Mimi about the interview yet. That was another conversation I didn't really want to have. I pushed down the butterflies that wanted to make an appearance. I wasn't usually the nervous type, but even I had a bit of anxiety about this one. It would be my first big venture completely on my own. Going away to college didn't really count. This was the first adult move I'd be making, and it would be across the country, all by myself. On the one hand, I was excited by the prospect of a change, of soaking up the sun in LA, rubbing elbows with all of the beautiful people; but on the other hand, I'd miss all of my friends. No matter what I told Carrie, I wasn't sure how often I'd be able to make it back across the country. I didn't want to lose the people I cared about, but I didn't want to pass up this chance.

I forced thoughts of myself to the back of my mind as Carrie and I entered the conference room. This wasn't the time or place. This was Carrie's moment to say her good-byes and get her well wishes. My time was coming.

THREE

KRISSY

I'd flown before, but I'd never been so thankful to have my feet firmly on the ground. I carefully made my way through the corridor, walking more steadily than some of my fellow passengers, most of whom looked just as green as I felt. Despite the anxiety and nausea caused by our turbulent six-hour flight, I also saw smiles on many of the faces as we stepped into the LAX terminal.

I stopped as I stepped into a patch of sunlight. I tilted my head back and closed my eyes, letting myself soak it in. I'd left a cloudy and overcast New York at seven thirty in the morning and arrived in sunny Los Angeles at ten thirty, thanks to the time zone changes. I had thirty minutes before my interview, so I headed to the bathrooms first to freshen up. My phone said only three hours had passed, but I probably looked like the full six the trip had taken.

Not even that thought could take the smile off of my face. My queasiness had settled, proving that it had only been the turbulence and not nerves. Now I was ready. Not just ready. I was excited.

I was here. Los Angeles. The City of Dreams. This was the only place in the world where your handyman would give you his screenplay after fixing your air conditioner. In New York, there were the waiters and waitresses who were waiting for their big break on Broadway or as 'serious' writers, but in Hollywood, pretty much everyone wanted to be something more.

I had only my carry-on with me since I was only staying for a couple of days, which meant I didn't have to stop at the baggage claim. That was good. I wanted to have the time to make myself look presentable. No, I amended. I wanted to look good. I stepped into the bathroom, put my bag on the counter and got to work. The company had offered to put me up in a hotel for two nights so that if they wanted a second interview, I wouldn't have to fly back out in two days. They'd been very accommodating.

When I was sure that my tanned skin looked flawless and my thick black hair was behaving itself, I smoothed down the skirt of my sensible business suit and headed back out into the main lobby. This time, I went for the line of people waiting for pick-ups. Sure enough, there was a man in a black suit holding a sign with my name on it. I grinned when I saw that they'd actually spelled it right. Points to Mirage Talent. I don't know how many job offers I'd turned down because they spelled my name wrong or tried to make it Kristine or Kristen. Nope. It was just Krissy, and if they couldn't take the time to learn that, I didn't want to work for them.

"Ms. Jensen." The driver inclined his head as I approached. "May I take your bag?"

A slightly snarky and very inappropriate comment popped into my head, but I held my tongue. Even if the driver was kinda cute in a tall and gawky kind of way, I wasn't going to risk a potentially awesome job for a one-liner.

"Thank you," I said as I handed over the bag. It wasn't very heavy, but it was on the bulky side, so carrying it always made me feel like I was walking lopsided, especially in the four inch heels I'd chosen for today.

I was a little over average height even without the shoes, and they put me a nice five foot ten. That was a good height, I'd found, for meeting new clients and potential employers. Tall enough so that I didn't have to strain to talk to taller men, but not so tall that I ended up towering over most of them. I'd also found that the heels complemented my figure. I was just a touch too curvy to be considered slender, but the heels made my legs look longer and thinner.

I felt good as I followed the driver to a black Town Car. I'd felt the admiring looks from men, and a couple women, as I'd passed and knew that I'd chosen the right ensemble for the day. I wanted admiration, not cat calls. Attractive but professional was always the right call for first impressions. If I got the job, I'd take a lay of the land and figure out where I was on the fashion scale.

The driver didn't say a word as he eased into the infamous LA traffic and began to make his way towards Mirage Talent. I stared out the tinted windows, completely enchanted by the skyline. It was so different than New York or Chicago. The sky seemed so much bigger here, the sun brighter. I hadn't realized just how much I was going to love it. I'd told Carrie that I might look around for another job out here if I didn't get the one at Mirage, but I'd only been half-serious. Now, after less than half an hour in California, I was certain this was where I wanted to be.

The car pulled up in front of an impressive building with the Mirage logo on the front of its steel and glass exterior. I took a deep breath, feeling a small flutter of nerves in my stomach. I had to admit, the place was a little intimidating.

"My bag?" I asked the driver as he opened the door.

"I'll be the one taking you to your hotel, Miss, so the bag is safe in the trunk." His face was carefully blank, the kind of professional expression that told me, despite his youthful appearance, he'd been doing this for a while.

"Thank you," I said as I started towards the front doors.

It took all of my self-control not to gawk at the lobby as I walked inside. It was done in the same steel and glass style as the exterior, but inside it was even more impressive. People expected the outsides of buildings to be like that, but the inside made it feel like something sleek and modern. It was the exact opposite of the old-fashioned antiques and art work of Webster and Steinberg. I'd never been very fond of that style. This, however, this I liked. I could work here and love every minute of being in this building.

The receptionist beamed at me as I approached and I wondered if she was really that friendly or if it was an act. If I was back in New York, I would've leaned towards fake, but she seemed genuine.

"Hi." I returned her smile with one of my own. No way was I going to get the reputation as the bitchy New Yorker. "I'm here for an appointment. Krissy Jensen."

"Of course, Miss Jensen," she said. "If you just keep going through that set of doors, you'll come to the reception seating area. Have a seat in there and you'll be called as soon as they're ready for you."

The seating area was just as gorgeous as the lobby. Across from the set of doors I'd just come through were two more doors, also steel and glass, but these were frosted so that I couldn't see what lay behind them. To my left was a huge leather couch and, across from it, separated by a massive glass coffee table, were two large leather chairs.

A handsome young man was already sitting in one of the chairs, so I headed for the couch. I picked up a magazine off of table and opened it without really looking at it. I stole a glance at the man across from me, and then took a second look. He had the white blond hair, blue eyes and tan that I'd always associated with California guys, the kind of guy who looked like he'd be just at home on a beach, wearing shorts and carrying a surfboard, as he was sitting across from me in khakis and a button-down shirt.

"Who's your agent?"

It took me a moment to realize that he was talking to me.

"Oh, I'm not here for...I'm an attorney." I smiled at him. "I'm here for a job interview."

"Ah." His teeth flashed white against his tanned skin and I wondered how often he had to bleach them. No one had teeth that white.

"I'm Krissy Jensen," I said.

"Taylor Moore." He leaned across the table and held out a hand.

I took it, giving him a firm and brief handshake. Normally, I would've been all over that, but I didn't think it was smart to hit on a client, or at least someone who was the client of my potential employer.

"You know," he said as he leaned back. "I have to admit, I wouldn't have pegged you for a lawyer."

I raised an eyebrow. If he was going to flirt, I wasn't going to encourage him, but I wasn't going to say no, either.

His grin widened, showing dimples. "Women in LA who look like you are models or actresses." His gaze ran over me, the light in his eyes saying that he was definitely being more than polite. "I'm guessing you're under five eight, so probably not a model, even though you're gorgeous enough to be one."

He got points for saying I was too short, not that I was too...curvaceous.

"So I guessed an actress."

"Wrong, but very observant," I said as I set aside my magazine.

"And you're not from around here," he commented. "I thought I'd caught an accent before. Now I'm sure. Where are you from?"

"New..." I paused. "Born and raised in Chicago, but I've been in New York for a while."

He nodded. "I'm from Wisconsin." When I didn't pry with a question, he offered more information. "I came out here after high school to be an actor. I've done a few commercials. Local stuff, so you wouldn't have seen me in anything...yet. I've got things in the works. Who are you interviewing with?"

I had to admit, I was impressed. He was definitely into me, but he hadn't asked yet if I was married or had a boyfriend. Most guys would've asked that question first or second, not wanting to waste their time with someone who was already taken.

"The head of the legal department. Mr. Duncan."

He nodded. "That's good. It's a good thing it's not with DeVon."

That didn't sound good. I knew DeVon Ricci was the head of the company, but I hadn't done a lot of research on him. I'd focused on Duncan, since that's who I had to get through first. If I made it to the second interview, then I'd planned to start looking into Ricci. Now I wasn't so sure I'd made the right choice. Maybe I should've checked Ricci out first.

"What's wrong with Mr. Ricci?"

Taylor shrugged. "Let's just say DeVon has his own...unique style." He sounded like he was being very careful with his word choices. "If you were interviewing with DeVon, I think he'd scare you off and I want you to stick around."

I gave him a polite smile. "Thank you." I straightened. "But I wouldn't be too worried," I added. "I don't scare easily."

"Miss Jensen?" A petite red-head came through the frosted glass doors. "Mr. Duncan will see you now."

I stood and smoothed down my skirt. "It was nice to have met you."

"And you," Taylor said. His eyes ran down my legs. "I look forward to seeing more of you very soon."

The heat in his eyes suggested he wasn't just talking about seeing me again around the agency. When he said more, he meant *more* and it took all of my self-control not to fire back with a double-entendre of my own.

"Have a good day," I said as I followed the red-head through the doors. I could feel Taylor's eyes on me as I walked. I was pretty sure he was staring at my ass, so I put a little more swing in my hips than I normally would have. Might as well leave him with a good impression.

I was definitely liking Hollywood.

"Mr. Duncan?" The red-head knocked on an open door at the end of a corridor.

I caught a glimpse of an elevator to my left. A sign next to it said "Private." That must lead to the mysterious Mr. Ricci, I thought as I walked into the office.

An attractive man in his mid-fifties stood on the other side of a very expensive-looking desk. He had such light-colored hair that, at first, I wasn't sure if it was blond or white, but then I realized that he had been blond, but his hair was streaked with silver, giving it a strange, dual-colored look. His eyes were intelligent and a pale gray that contrasted strongly with his tanned skin. My boss back home would've been all over this guy.

"Mr. Duncan." I gave him my best professional smile as I held out my hand.

His handshake was brisk, but not rude. That was good. Too many men either snatched their hands away like they were afraid I'd read something into their touch if they lingered too long, or they purposefully lingered, turning the shake into a holding.

"Please, have a seat." He gestured to the chair across from his.

I sat carefully, crossing my ankles and tucking my feet under my chair. My skirt was an appropriate length for work, but I didn't want to take any chances on flashing my prospective boss. He didn't seem like the type who'd appreciate the view. And I was grateful for that. I didn't want someone more interested in what was between my legs than what was between my ears.

"You have quite an impressive résumé for someone so young, Miss Jensen," he began.

The interview was like something out of a dream. He asked specific questions and seemed pleased with the answers I gave, though not overly exuberant about them. Another good sign. He wanted to make sure I knew that I'd done well, but didn't want to show any sort of sign as to how I measured up against the competition.

"I do have to ask, Miss Jensen," Mr. Duncan said as he set down my résumé. "Do you have any desire to become an actress, model or celebrity of any kind?"

The question surprised me, but I didn't let it show. "No, Sir," I answered promptly. "I've never wanted to be in the spotlight like that. Put me in a courtroom in front of a judge and jury, and I'll be a star, but I don't want to be in front of a camera."

He gave me a partial smile. "That's very good, Miss Jensen. You understand, in our business, we get a lot of attractive young people who see this place as a stepping stone, but not to rise in the legal department. They think that they can use us to get their 'big break' and that is not something we encourage."

"I understand." I nodded, thankful that I was being completely honest. "I'm not interested in any of that. I want to rise in the company, but as a lawyer, not as anything else." I decided that bold was a good idea. "In fact, Sir, I'd like to see myself sitting in that desk one day." I let one side of my mouth twitch up into a half smile. "Many years from now, of course."

Mr. Duncan gave me a full smile, his eyes twinkling. It was good to know that the serious face wasn't all there was to him. "That's very good, Miss Jensen." He stood and I did the same. "While we do have other interviews to conduct, I would like you to come in tomorrow for a second interview."

I tried not to let how excited I was show. "Thank you, Sir."

"And, Miss Jensen," he added. "You are one of our most promising candidates."

Now I couldn't stop the smile. "Thank you." I almost sounded like I was gushing and I forced myself to rein it in.

"Your driver will take you to your hotel. Enjoy the rest of your day here and be back at nine tomorrow morning, prepared for a more in-depth interview. We are only conducting two second interviews, so it is imperative that you come fully prepared."

I wasn't sure, but that sounded to me like a warning. Taylor's comment about DeVon Ricci came back to me. As I walked out of the office, I wondered if that's what Mr. Duncan had meant. Was I going to be meeting the big boss tomorrow? And if I was, what could he possibly have planned that I would need to prepare for? I had to admit, the thought did make me a little nervous.

I set my jaw as I walked back out into the California sun. I wasn't going to let it bother me. I knew I was perfect for this job and nothing was going to keep me from making sure everyone at Mirage Talent knew it too.

FOUR

KRISSY

I had a feeling my driver was taking the scenic route to the hotel. I wasn't minding, though. I'd never seen anything like this city before and even my excitement over how well the interview had gone couldn't distract me from the view. When we finally pulled up in front of the hotel, I was eager to get to my room, shower and head out into the sunshine. I hadn't eaten much that morning, not liking to fly on a full stomach, and I was starting to get hungry. I couldn't wait to see what Los Angeles had to offer.

I thanked the driver as he handed my bag to the valet waiting at the entrance. This was a nicer hotel than any I'd been to in New York, but it was impossible to compare them, really. New York was stone and history. No matter how updated their buildings were, they always had a sense of being old, especially the swankiest hotels. This one was modern, with clean-cut lines. If New York was 'old money' then this was new, and I loved it.

"Miss Jensen, you've been upgraded." The clerk at the desk gave me a pleasant smile.

"Excuse me?" I knew I couldn't have heard her correctly.

Mirage was a wealthy company and they obviously liked to show their potential employees a good time, but a hospitality suite at a hotel like this was already above and beyond.

"You've been upgraded to a top floor suite," the woman clarified.

"By whom?" I didn't mean to sound rude, but it was a bit of a shock. I mean, my interview had gone well, but this was ridiculous.

The clerk's smile faltered for a moment, then came back, steady as ever. Definitely a wanna-be actress. "Mirage Talent, of course," she said. She slid a keycard across the desk. "Marcus will help you with your bag."

"That's okay," I said. "I can take it from here." I held out my hand and, after a moment, was handed my bag. I just wanted to be alone to process.

When I got off on the top floor, I still hadn't figured out why I'd been upgraded. Maybe tomorrow was just a formality, I thought. This could be their way of welcoming me to the company. If it was, wow. I smiled. Whatever the reason, I was going to enjoy it.

I took half a dozen steps into the room as the door swung shut behind me, and that's when I realized I wasn't alone.

In the center of the room was a massive couch and my trio of visitors were centered around it. I stared at them for several seconds, unable to believe what I was seeing. Two were women: one a red-head, the other blonde, neither of them naturals. I could tell because, unfortunately, neither of them was clothed. One was on all fours on the couch, her ass towards me as she kissed the man sitting on the couch. The other woman was kneeling between his legs, running her hands up and down his thighs. He, at least, appeared to be clothed. Not that it made things better, because while he was kissing the red-head, he had one hand between her legs, two long fingers sliding into her. His other hand was on the blonde's breast, pinching and twisting one rose-colored nipple.

I processed all of this in the time it took for me to regain my voice and to overcome my shock.

"Excuse me." My voice came out stronger than I'd expected. "What are you doing in my room?" And, as I always did when I was mostly at a loss for words, I said exactly what I was thinking, no matter if it was appropriate or not. "Are you having some kind of orgy in my hotel room?"

The man on the couch rolled the red-head onto her back so that she was lying across his lap, her legs spread so that I could see more than I wanted to. His fingers slid back inside her and she moaned, writhing on his lap.

"What else would it be?" The man had a faint accent; Italian, I thought. "Come join us."

I looked at him now, my temper flaring. Who the hell did he think he was? "Join you? No fucking way." I sneered at him. "You couldn't handle me."

I let my eyes rake over him, taking in the wild black waves of hair that fell across his forehead, the rich brown eyes. He was handsome, with strong features rather than the pretty-boy look Taylor had going on. His shirt was unbuttoned, revealing a firm, defined chest. He was lean but his body was cut in a way that would usually make me wet. The fact that he was still fingering the red-head and the blonde was crawling up next to him, her large breasts swaying as she moved...that all kinda pissed me off, so arousal wasn't exactly my emotion at the moment.

"Get the fuck out of my room before I call security." I gave the women my most derisive glare. "And take your bimbos with you."

His eyes flashed, but the corners of his mouth twitched like he was amused by something. When he spoke, however, his voice was flat. "You don't know who you're talking to, do you?"

"Yeah," I retorted. "An asshole."

He laughed, sliding his fingers out of the red-head's pussy. He held his hand out to the blonde, barely glancing at her as she began to lick his fingers clean. The red-head made a protesting sound, but he ignored her, too. "I like your smart mouth," he said. "Duncan will definitely be pleased with you."

I frowned. Duncan? He couldn't mean Leon Duncan, the head of the legal department at Mirage Talent, the man I'd just interviewed with.

"Oh, that's right. We were never properly introduced." He stood, spilling the women off of his lap.

I couldn't stop my eyes from flicking down over his torso to his narrow waist, my curiosity getting the better of me. I tried very hard not to lick my lips at the impressive bulge at the front of his tailored, gray slacks.

"Krissy."

My name brought my attention back up with a snap. I could feel heat creeping up my cheeks.

"I'm DeVon Ricci. Your new boss."

My stomach plummeted. Fuck. What kind of shit-storm did I just walk into? I shook my head, refusing to believe it. "I never met DeVon Ricci. How do you know who I am?"

He grinned and held out his hand. The hand that had been between the red-head's legs. No way in hell was I going to shake that. I folded my arms across my chest. He dropped his hand and used it to gesture towards the coffee table in front of the couch.

"I was watching your interview. Duncan has a webcam on his computer that allows me to watch all of his interviews. I find it saves time weeding out the candidates."

"So, what is this, then?" My hands curled into fists, my fingernails digging into my palms. "I join in the fun and I get the job?"

He raised an eyebrow, a gesture that usually went straight through me. I wasn't going to let this one do that. I focused on how pissed I was.

"Well," he said. "I never give out guarantees." He ran his gaze down my body in that slow way that said he was imagining how I looked naked. "But it might put you at the front of the line." His eyes were darker as they met mine, and I knew he'd liked what he saw. "That is how my last assistant got hired."

His voice was dripping sex, promising pleasure I couldn't imagine. Damn, he was hot. I shifted my weight from one foot to the other. Too bad he was a complete tool. There was no way in hell I was joining in. "Like I said." My voice was even, but I could hear the fury in every word. "This is my room, so I'll give you and your bimbos thirty second to get the fuck out before I call security. I have another important interview tomorrow and I'd like to relax."

DeVon's eyes narrowed as he studied me for a moment and I held his gaze. I had nothing to be ashamed of here and I wasn't going to look away first. Finally, he glanced over his shoulder and held out his hands. "Ladies."

The women stood, bending over to pick up what I assumed were their clothes. They pulled skimpy dresses over their heads, not bothering with any undergarments. I really hoped that was because they hadn't been wearing any. I didn't want to sit down and find a pair of panties under the cushions. I glanced at the couch. On second thought, I'd just sit in one of the chairs.

DeVon let the women leave first and then he paused, turning back towards me.

"Congratulations, Miss Jensen." His tone was serious now, no hint of flirtation. "If you had joined us, you wouldn't be getting to stay here in this lovely suite preparing for your interview tomorrow. You would be on your way back to New York. Mirage Talent does not hire women who use sex to get ahead."

I gaped at him. Seriously? The whole thing had been a set-up? I wasn't sure if I should be relieved, horrified or even more furious. I chose the latter. I scowled. "I thought you said that's how your last assistant got hired."

A glint appeared in his eyes and one side of his mouth tipped up, giving me that sexual smile again. "There is always the exception to the rule." He stepped into the hallway, getting the last word in as the door closed. "She was fucking hot."

FIVE

DEVON

The thing I hated the most about what I'd done was the fact that I'd had to carry my jacket in front of me while I waited for my hard-on to go down. I was glad Krissy Jensen had turned me down — my lips twitched at the memory of how pissed she'd been — but it definitely made for an uncomfortable ride back to the office.

I was still thinking about the way her dark eyes had flashed when Leon Duncan stepped out of his office before I could get on to the private elevator to my office. I was turned towards him when something flew through the air, narrowly missing my face.

"You bastard." Leon's face was red. "You were spying on me!"

Sometimes, I wondered if complete honesty was always worth the trouble. I looked down to see the webcam I'd had installed shattered at my feet. I looked back up at the head of my legal department and spoke in a cool, even tone despite feeling anything but cool.

"You will do well to remember that I am your employer, and

calm the hell down." I waited for a moment to see how he responded. As I'd hoped he would, he took a slow breath and some of the color receded from his face. "If you look over the contract you signed – and you wrote, may I remind you – there is an entire section that states all company property may be monitored at any time at my discretion."

"I-I thought that was to keep people from surfing for porn or making personal calls on company time." Leon was flustered, but I didn't know if it was because he'd just realized that he'd thrown something at his boss, or because I was right and he had no legal standing to be mad.

"That is the main reason," I admitted. "But it allowed me to monitor the interviews." I paused, then added, "And that's all I monitored. I wasn't spying on you, Leon. I wanted to see the remaining candidates before they did their interview with me."

Now he just looked puzzled. The man was great at the legal stuff, but he wasn't a businessman. His brain just didn't work that way.

"Why?" Leon asked. "Whoever I hire isn't going to be working directly under you. She'll be in my department. You've never been interested in who I hired before."

"This time, it's different," I said. I didn't have to explain myself, but Leon was a good man. When he wasn't throwing expensive electrical equipment at my head. I wanted him to understand. "I don't want to keep thinking so narrowly. There could be potential among these candidates. Maybe someone who could rise above just being a lawyer sitting behind a desk."

Leon raised an eyebrow. "Like who?"

"Krissy Jensen," I answered immediately. She'd been the only one who'd struck me as anything special. "There's something about her." *Something more than a tight ass and nice tits*, I wanted to add, but that wouldn't have been appropriate.

Leon shook his head. "Jensen, really? She's good, I'll give you that. And I like her attitude, but Melissa Tomes is much better qualified. I'd put Ms. Jensen as a runner-up, but Ms. Tomes scored higher on every test. She has to be first choice."

I had crossed the distance between us before I'd realized what I was doing and it was all I could do not to grab the front of his shirt and yank him up onto his tiptoes. That would've been a bit extreme, I thought.

I spoke slowly and clearly so that he would understand me. "It's not about test scores or experience. Someone could look good on paper, but be as exciting as a pile of dog shit. In fact, that is your first choice. Melissa is books and ass-kissing. We work with people and we need to hire people with skills in that field. Someone with fire in their veins and steel in their backbone. *That* is what Krissy Jensen brings."

I turned and walked back to the elevator, catching a glimpse of Leon's face, pale and mottled with pink from the sudden change from anger to intimidated. My entire body was thrumming with energy as I got onto the elevator. Maybe I should have gone to the gym, I thought. I was way too tense. I should've known better, getting wound up like that without any release.

I was two steps into my office when I realized that I wasn't alone.

Cheri was leaning against my desk, completely naked. The skimpy dress she'd worn out of the hotel was lying in a chair.

"What the fuck are you doing here?" I snapped. "How did you get here before me?" I looked around, fully expecting a blonde to appear. "Where's Tina?"

Cheri grinned at me as she ran a hand over one pert breast, cupping the firm flesh. "She had to leave to see her dentist or something, but I snuck in while you were talking with Duncan. You really should get better security."

"I'll keep that in mind," I spoke through gritted teeth. I was pissed, but I couldn't quit looking at her fingers playing with her nipple.

"Do you mind that I came to see you?" She pushed herself off of the desk and walked towards me.

"Yes, I fucking mind! Get the hell out!"

Cheri's smile widened as she leaned against me. I should have taken a step back, but I could feel the heat of her blazing through my clothes and all of the pent-up tension I had from the hotel came rushing back. Never one for subtly, she ran her hand over my crotch and my blood went straight south.

"You seem tense," she teased. "Do you need a massage?" Her hand slowly rubbed the bulge in my pants.

I closed my eyes and clenched my hands into fists. I could feel myself swelling under her hand. "Fuck," I muttered.

Then her hand was gone and I opened my eyes. I wasn't sure if I wanted her to have left or still be there, offering herself to me. I was strung so tight that I wasn't entirely sure I could remember my name. If she'd left, I'd have to spend a couple minutes in the bathroom before I'd be any good at work.

She hadn't left. She'd just moved to her knees. When she saw me looking down at her, she reached for my zipper. As she opened my pants, she licked her lips, leaving no doubt as to what she intended to do.

Aw, hell. How was I supposed to say no to that?

I buried my fingers in her hair as she pulled my cock out of my pants. I was so hard it almost hurt, and I knew I wasn't going to last long. Cheri was tall, making access to her mouth easier than it would've been on someone shorter, like Tina.

"Open your mouth," I growled.

She did as she was told. She knew exactly what I wanted. I shoved the first three inches between her lips, groaning as she swirled her tongue around my swollen shaft. There was no way I would last long at all.

"I'm going to fuck your mouth." My accent had thickened as my need grew.

"Please."

Cheri only managed that single word before I was shoving her head down the length of my cock. She'd given me a blow job before so I knew how far she could take me. I took her to that point over and over again, using her hair to pull her off of me before shoving back into that hot, wet cavern. I looked down at Cheri, her mouth stretched wide around me, my cock glistening with her saliva, and suddenly, it wasn't her red hair and porcelain skin I was seeing.

Thick black hair between my fingers.

Large, dark eyes peering up at me from between thick lashes.

Krissy.

My entire body shuddered as I came without warning. I jerked back, the last of my cum splashing across Cheri's face. I stared down at her, my heart pounding in my chest. She grinned at me as she got to her feet, licking her lips and wiping her hand across her face.

"I got no problem swallowing, hun, but warn a girl next time." She chuckled.

What the hell?

"Get out."

Cheri looked startled, but I didn't care. I grabbed her dress from the chair and threw it at her. "Get dressed and get the fuck out!"

She scowled at me as she pulled on her dress, but she didn't argue. I barely even noticed when she closed the door behind her.

What the hell? I sank into my chair, my hands shaking. I never lost control. I WAS control. But something about the thought of having Krissy on her knees, her lips around my cock...

I slapped my hand against my desk, letting the sting clear my head. Whatever it was, it was done, and it wouldn't happen again.

SIX

KRISSY

I was torn between wanting to open the door and throw something at my maybe-future-boss, and getting on a plane to go back home. I didn't do either. Instead, I carried my bag back to the bedroom and then went into the bathroom to clean up. My stomach was growling and a glance at a clock told me it was almost two, which meant five on the East Coast, and I hadn't eaten anything substantial yet today. I needed to get something to eat or I was going to end up with a massive headache.

As I headed down in the elevator, I kept thinking about what had just happened. I knew there were bosses who pressed for sexual favors but I'd never heard of one who wanted to be told no. I supposed it was a good thing and I should be grateful DeVon – Mr. Ricci – hadn't been serious, but I still wasn't sure how I felt about what I'd walked in on. I mean, I was no prude, but that had been...too much.

I shook my head. I didn't want to think about DeVon and his naked women. I had changed out of my interview clothes and into a cute little dress that Carrie's boyfriend, Gavin, had been nice enough to buy for me one of the times I'd taken Carrie shopping. It was a warm, gold color that complemented my skin tone and it accentuated my curves, drawing attention to my narrow waist as much as my bust.

"Hi." I gave the concierge a bright smile. Judging by the expression on his face, I'd chosen the dress well. "I was just wondering if you could recommend a good lunch restaurant."

"Of course."

I was impressed at how well he did not staring at my breasts. I didn't know many men with that much self-control. For a second, I wondered if DeVon would've pretended not to notice, or if he'd openly ogle. I was willing to bet the latter.

"There are several excellent restaurants at Sunset Plaza. Clafoutis is quite well-regarded."

"Thank you," I said. I started to turn away when he spoke again.

"Would you like a complimentary ride?"

Surprised, I nodded. "Thank you. That would be great."

It wasn't until I was in the hotel's town car, heading for Sunset Plaza, that I thought to wonder if this was another test by Mirage, or just something nice the hotel or the company did.

No, I told myself. I wasn't going to second-guess every decision I made, worried about what Mr. Ricci would think. I was going to do what I knew was right and not worry about anything else. I wanted this job and I really wanted to live out here, but I wasn't about to compromise anything I believed. No job was worth that. And accepting a complimentary ride from the hotel was far from unethical.

When we arrived at the Plaza, the driver opened the door for me and asked if I wanted him to wait or if I'd prefer to call the hotel for a pick-up. I chose the call option, not knowing how long I was going to linger over lunch, or if I'd take a walk when I was done. I'd chosen flat sandals rather than heels just for that reason.

Several restaurants sat next to each other, each one looking just as good as the last. I spotted the one the concierge had mentioned and decided to take his advice. It was absolutely gorgeous and had an array of tables out on a patio where I'd be able to enjoy the sunshine and people-watch.

Their menu was amazing. I almost couldn't decide. Finally, I chose the Gazpacho – a seasoned cold tomato soup with garlic croutons – a turkey club with everything on it, and a side of garden vegetables.

As I settled in under the partial shade and began to eat, I watched the beautiful people of Hollywood walk by, sporting the latest fashions, arms linked as they chattered away about the latest gossip. It was nothing like watching New York sidewalks. Everyone there was so busy, hurrying from one place to the next. There was a sameness about them. Not because everyone in New York looked the same, but they all had the same harried expressions, whether they were in a three-piece suit or wearing leather. It was all important business. Here, there was a mixture of those rushing and those taking their time, but even the people in a hurry didn't carry themselves with the same briskness I associated with the people of big cities like Chicago or New York.

Then there was the traffic. I'd heard horror stories about LA traffic, and having lived in the Big Apple, I was no stranger to cars parked bumper to bumper. I didn't know if it was the time of day or where I was, but it wasn't too bad. The main difference between the two cities, however, was the type of car. Back home, every other car would be a yellow taxi. Here, every second or third car cruising by was a Ferrari, Lamborghini, Porsche or another exotic car that cost more than I made in a year. Hell, some of them were worth almost twice as much as I made in a year.

I knew the saying about the grass being greener on the other side of the fence, and I'd worried that I was trying to do that to LA, but that's not what it looked like to me from here. I was sure there'd be disadvantages to living here, just like there were negatives about every place, but sitting there, enjoying the more relaxed atmosphere and the warmth of the sun, I couldn't see it. Being here just made me all the more determined to get hired at Mirage.

"Krissy!"

I blinked, startled out of my reverie by my name being called. From the sound of it, it wasn't the first time. I looked around, trying to figure out who I knew out here who could possibly be yelling for me. I spotted him even as he came towards me. Blond hair, tanned skin and that impossible smile.

"Hello again, Taylor." I returned the smile. He was off-limits for anything sexual or romantic, but a talk wasn't unethical.

"Here I was thinking I'd have to make an excuse to go back to Mirage just so I could see you again." His eyes ran over me and he gave a low whistle. "Much better than what you were wearing before. Not," he hastily added, "that there was anything wrong with you before. It's just that dress..."

"Were you just walking by, or coming to get something to eat?" I asked the first question that popped into my head so he'd quit talking about the way I looked. Normally, I loved a compliment, but I couldn't flirt back. It wouldn't be right, not when I still had a chance at the Mirage job.

"I come here all the time," he explained, his eyes returning to meet mine. "I live two blocks that way." He pointed, then gave me another charming grin. "I share a house with three other actors. It's not much, but it's home." He looked down at the empty seat across from me. "Would you mind if I joined you?"

I knew it was probably a bad idea, but I wanted some conversation and I didn't know anyone else here. I could keep it platonic and almost business-like. Lawyers went to dinner and out for drinks with clients all the time. It was fine. As long as it didn't cross the line.

The waiter who'd taken my order was coming with my main food, so Taylor and I waited to start a conversation until Taylor's order had been taken. He motioned for me to go ahead with my meal, for which I was grateful. The soup had been amazing, but it hadn't been even close to filling.

"How did your interview go?" Taylor asked as I took a bite of my sandwich.

Wow. This was good. I took a moment to savor the bite before answering Taylor's question with a see-sawing motion of my hand. After I swallowed, I told him a very brief part of the story, mostly how well things had gone with Mr. Duncan but I also mentioned showing up in my room to find DeVon Ricci on the couch. I didn't mention that he was with two naked women or what he had been doing to them, rather choosing to keep it professional and simply say that I'd kicked him out.

Taylor laughed at that, his eyes lighting up. Damn, he was hot. "I did warn you about DeVon."

I nodded and chuckled. "You did."

The waiter returned with Taylor's lunch, some sort of steak sandwich that looked just as good as my turkey one. If I did move out to California, I had a feeling I'd be back here.

"I can't believe you kicked him out of your room," Taylor said before taking a bite of his food.

I shrugged. "It was my room and he was being quite rude."

"Would you kick me out?" Taylor teased.

I chewed slowly on the mouthful I'd just taken. If we were back home or I was just visiting, I knew what the answer would be. Hell, no, I'd ride you like a pony. Unfortunately, that's the kind of answer I most definitely could not give here.

I tried for something safe. "I'd call security on anyone who showed up in my room unannounced and uninvited." I kept my tone flat so it wouldn't sound like I was flirting. I didn't want

Taylor to be mad, but I also didn't want him to get the wrong idea. I changed the subject, asking him questions that would be appropriate for a lawyer-client relationship. Details about his work. Where he hoped to be in five years. The kinds of things I could ask anyone without getting too personal.

The problem was, Taylor kept trying to make the answers personal. When I asked about what he saw in his future, I didn't specify his career and he took that latitude to joke about being with a beautiful lawyer. It wasn't that I didn't appreciate what he was saying, but it wasn't making things any easier for me to keep professional.

"Did you rent a car?" he asked as he handed the waiter a credit card with the bill.

I shook my head as I did the same with my bill. I was glad Taylor hadn't tried for an awkward 'I'll pay that.' "The hotel has a car service." I took out my phone. "All I need to do is give them a call."

"Why don't you let me take you back?" Taylor offered.

"I couldn't," I protested.

"Nonsense," he said. "Why have to wait around here for the driver to come get you when I have a car right over there?"

It made sense, I had to admit. I nodded and, after the waiter returned with our receipts and cards, I followed Taylor to a mid-sized Audi. It was nice, but older, definitely more of an up-and-comer type car rather than something an established actor or a mega-star would have. The inside smelled like fast-food and the pine-scented air freshener that hung from the rearview mirror. I couldn't help but smile. Every college guy I'd dated had a car that smelled the same. It was typical bachelor with a menial type job. I suddenly realized that I didn't know what Taylor actually did for a living. If he was only doing local commercials, he had to have either a trust fund or a 'day-job.' I was betting not many kids from Wisconsin had trust funds.

Before I could ask, he looked over at me and asked his own question. "Do you have anything planned the rest of the day?"

I shook my head.

"I was wondering if you'd like to see the ocean. The sun will set in a couple of hours and it's absolutely beautiful over the water. It's not something you'll want to miss."

I hesitated. I really did want to see the ocean and a sunset over the Pacific sounded amazing, but I wasn't sure it was a good idea to be in a car, alone, with Taylor that long. At least eating, we were in public. I didn't want to give anyone the wrong impression.

"It's a half-hour drive," Taylor said, as if he could read my mind. "We'd have some time to enjoy the view, then I could get you back to the hotel before it was even really dark. Plenty of time to rest for your second interview."

After another moment, I nodded. "Let's go."

SEVEN

KRISSY

The Santa Monica Pier. I'd seen it in movies, but it was even more beautiful in real life. The Ferris wheel against the backdrop of blue sky. The sounds and smells that could only be found in a place like this. All of it was everything I'd ever dreamed.

We walked slowly, sometimes talking, sometimes just enjoying the setting sun. Just before the sun reached the horizon, the lights came on, turning the pier into something almost magical. We stopped at a distance so that I could get the entire panoramic view.

I sighed as I leaned against the railing. The smell of salt water mingled with the other scents and I could hear the gentle lapping of water beneath my feet. It was the week after Labor Day, so most of the vacationers had gone home, leaving the pier virtually empty, at least by New York standards. If you weren't pressed shoulder to shoulder with complete strangers, it was almost empty.

I was watching the sun slowly starting to disappear when it

happened. Taylor put his hand over mine. I jerked back automatically, turning towards him.

"What do you think you're doing?"

He shrugged, giving me a grin that I was fairly certain he was used to charming the pants off of women. If I hadn't wanted this job so badly, it might've worked for me, too.

"Maybe I'm off here, but I could've sworn I was sensing some attraction."

Dammit. I hadn't been as careful as I'd thought.

"I was under the impression that you liked me."

I sighed again, this time not out of contentment. "I do like you," I confessed. "But you're a client of Mirage. I can't date a potential client." I laughed. "Look, if this was New York and I'd met you there with no strings attached, or even here under different circumstances, I totally would've jumped your bones. But I'm trying to make something of this opportunity." I gave him an apologetic smile. "Sorry."

He took a step towards me, closing the distance down to just a foot between us. "Come on, Krissy." His gaze was heated as it ran down my body and back up again. "I'm just one small client with Mirage, not even close to their top one hundred. They don't give a shit about whether or not we hook up." He reached out and ran the tip of his finger down my arm. "I swear, I won't say a word. No one will ever know."

"I'm sorry, Taylor." I kept my voice cool and firm. "It's not going to happen." I turned my back on him to watch the rest of the sunset. I really hoped he'd take the hint because I wanted to enjoy my view for a bit longer.

He was silent as he moved to stand next to me, but I didn't sense any animosity, which was good. He kept a respectful distance as we finished watching the sunset and I was able to relax and let myself absorb the beauty of what I was seeing. We stayed standing there for several minutes after the last sliver of sun had disappeared, waiting for the first of the stars to begin to come out. The lights from the Pier kept them from being as bright as I knew they'd be out in the country, but it was still far more than I'd ever seen in New York or Chicago.

Finally, I pushed back from the rail and broke the silence. "I should be getting back."

He nodded and flashed me a polite smile that made me feel like perhaps things would be okay between us. That was good. As bad as it would be to date a client, I had a feeling Mirage wouldn't look too fondly on a client being pissed at me either.

We made small talk on the ride back to my hotel, keeping it light and nothing personal. By the time he pulled up in front of the hotel, I had regained the sense of wonder I'd had when I'd first stepped off the plane.

"So," he said as he flashed that beautiful white smile again, "What do you say to a night-cap in the bar?" He winked at me. "Or in your suite?"

He was like a dog with a bone.

"You're super cute and very persistent." I kept my voice polite. "But I can't do this. You're a client and I'm taking this job possibility very seriously."

If anything, his grin widened. "But what if you don't get the job?"

Now I was annoyed. Persistence was one thing, but if he kept pushing it, even his pretty face and rock-hard body weren't going to be enough to keep me from saying something I'd regret. "If I don't get it, and you're ever in New York, look me up." I opened the door. "I'm sure you'd be fun for a couple days." I didn't wait to hear a response, but rather climbed out of the car and headed for the front doors.

I really hoped that put an end to it. I so didn't need a client stalker.

EIGHT

KRISSY

This time when I was called out of the reception area, I was taken to the elevator I'd seen yesterday. The receptionist didn't say a word as we reached the second floor and the doors opened. She just gestured for me to go ahead without her. Based on what I'd seen yesterday with Mr. Ricci, I had a feeling he was the type of man who appreciated a strong woman. At least professionally. Something about him told me that in his personal life, it might be a bit different.

I stepped off the elevator and knocked on the heavy wooden door now directly in front of me.

"Come in." An annoyingly familiar voice came from the other side of the door.

As I stepped inside, I saw that DeVon's office didn't look like the rest of the building. Instead of glass and metal, his office was dark with a heavy curtain covering what must have been a window at his back. He had heavy wooden furniture that matched the door I'd knocked on. The color scheme was dark brown and a deep red that almost looked like blood. It looked like something out of a *Godfather* movie. Or a vampire flick.

DeVon was sitting behind his desk and didn't get up when I closed the door behind me. I really hoped that wasn't his normal way of behaving and he wasn't only being an ass to me because of yesterday. I walked towards him, waiting for him to look up from the paper he was reading and greet me. He didn't. In fact, all he did was point to one of the chairs in front of the desk.

I was tempted to take the other one, just to see what he'd do, but I didn't. As much as he annoyed me, being intentionally antagonistic wasn't a good idea. No matter how much I wanted to.

I crossed one leg over the other, folded my hands in my lap and waited. I was normally impatient and impulsive, at least according to my friends, but when it came to a battle of the wills and sheer stubbornness, winning trumped everything else.

Finally, after what was probably a good ten minutes, he closed the paper and set it aside. His expression was unreadable as he looked at me. "Krissy Jensen, I liked how you handled the situation yesterday."

Apparently, he didn't believe in opening with small talk. That was fine with me. The less time I had to spend with him, the better. He might have been pretty to look at, but I wasn't fond of the attitude.

"That was a test, you know."

No shit. I didn't say that, of course. "I figured that much. A little unusual, I must say." Carrie would've been proud of my self-control.

"What can I say?" He shrugged. "I do things differently." His eyes narrowed, studying me. "I don't like fake people, and this town has too many of them already. I want one hundred percent honesty and trust from all my employees. In return, I don't bullshit them, either." He rested his hands on his desk. "Do you think you can do that? Be honest no matter what?"

That was an easy one for me to answer. "Absolutely. And I couldn't agree more. I hate liars."

He was silent for several minutes and I could feel his eyes boring into me, like he was trying to read something deep inside and determine if I was telling the truth. I tried very hard not to fidget. I'd never been very good at sitting still, and his heavy gaze wasn't making it any easier.

Finally, he spoke. "I'm not so sure you can be completely honest." He leaned back in his chair and set his elbows on the armrests. He pressed his fingertips together and peered at me over them. "How do I know you're not just saying that to get the job?"

I tried not to take offense at the question. He had a right to be suspicious. Some people would've had a problem promising honesty and actually delivering. For me, I actually liked that he required it. In fact, his statement about liars was probably the first thing I actually liked about him.

"I would say to trust me, but if you don't believe I'm telling the truth, it doesn't matter what I say."

He inclined his head, leading me to believe he approved of my answer. "I could conduct the interview in an...unusual way to determine if you will provide me with answers you believe I will want to hear or if you will answer honestly, no matter what you think my opinion will be."

That sounded like a very bad idea.

"I have found," he continued, "that if I ask questions of a personal nature – a very personal nature – I can determine if they are lying or not."

Yeah, agreeing to this 'unusual' interview was definitely not a good idea.

"A benefit of this will be that I will be able to provide you with a yes or no regarding the job once we are finished."

He was tempting my impatience, but that wasn't the main reason I wanted to agree. He'd caught me off guard yesterday,

316 M. S. PARKER

and while I'd managed to recover nicely, he'd still shocked me. I had a feeling whatever he was going to ask would be sexually loaded and he wanted to see if I'd crack. It wasn't just about honesty. It was about seeing if I could handle the pressure of working in a place like this. Whether I got the job or not, I was determined to let him know that he couldn't break me.

"All right," I agreed.

I could see a pleased light in his eyes for a brief second before it was gone again.

"My questions will deal with things that you may not feel are appropriate for a work situation, and I will not take kindly should you decide to complain after having agreed to this interview." His tone was sharp as he gave me the warning.

"I'm waiting for the first question," I said mildly. No way was I backing down.

He chuckled. "Then we begin." He crossed one long leg over the other. "Are you a virgin?"

I almost rolled my eyes, but remembered that I needed to keep it professional, no matter how unprofessional the questions were. "No."

"What were the circumstances surrounding your first sexual encounter?"

One side of my mouth quirked up. "I was fifteen, and my boyfriend and I did it in the back of his car." I raised an eyebrow as if to ask him if that was all he had.

"And your most recent sexual encounter?" He didn't react to either my answer or my change in facial expression.

"I hooked up with a guy at my friend's burlesque club. I think his name was Frank." If that didn't tell him I had no problem being honest, I didn't know what would.

"Do you make a habit of fucking strangers?"

Okay, so that's how we were going to play it.

"I do it sometimes, but I wouldn't consider it a habit," I

admitted. I'd never been ashamed of my sex life and I wasn't about to begin now.

"But you refused to join me yesterday."

"That's not a question," I retorted.

This time, his lips definitely twitched. "You're right. My question then: what was the reason for declining my invitation?"

I almost cringed. He wanted me to be honest, but I knew he wasn't going to like my answer. "Two reasons. One, I don't fuck my boss, or potential boss. Two, you were being an asshole."

He did smile this time, and it was all I could do not to smile in response.

"Have you ever slept with someone you worked with?"

I nodded. "Co-workers, yes, but never someone in a position above or below me." I bit back a laugh at the obvious joke there.

"Have you ever had sex with someone in exchange for a favor?"

I frowned. "Does sleeping with my college tutor count?" When DeVon didn't answer, I clarified, "That wasn't how I paid him. It was more like a bonus...for both of us. But, no, I don't ask for things in return for sex."

He nodded, but I couldn't tell what he thought about my answer. "Have you ever dated a client?"

I noticed the change in verb but didn't ask about it. "It depends on your definition of client."

"Spoken like a true lawyer," he said.

"I haven't slept with or dated anyone who was my direct client," I answered. "But I have had relationships with men who were clients of other lawyers in the firm where I worked."

"You understand that this is not acceptable at Mirage," he said, his tone almost scolding.

My temper flared. How dare he talk to me like he was on some high moral ground? I didn't snap at him, though. Instead, I said, "Completely. I would never consider propositioning anyone involved with the company, or accepting a proposition from someone Mirage represents. It would be unprofessional."

A flash of amusement crossed his features, and I knew he'd understood my dig at his behavior yesterday. "Do you consider yourself sexually adventurous?"

I couldn't quite stop myself from being a bit saucy in return. "I'm always open to new experiences."

"Good to know."

I shifted in my seat as I felt a sudden zing of arousal. Dammit. I didn't care how sexy his voice sounded when he'd said that. He was going to be my boss. And he was an asshole. Both reasons why I hadn't slept with him yesterday were still applicable today.

"Do you have any problems taking orders?"

That question made me blink because I wasn't entirely sure if he was still asking sexual questions or if he'd switched to more job relevant inquiries since he was satisfied I was telling the truth. Something in his dark eyes told me that his question wasn't entirely innocent.

Two could play at that game.

"It depends on who gives them," I answered coolly. "I'm no pushover, but I also don't have a problem obeying someone in charge. If he's...worthy."

This time, DeVon was the one shifting in his chair. He made it look like he was just switching legs, but I had a feeling it was actually something else. The air had a thickness to it that hadn't been there a moment ago.

"Are you willing to accept...consequences for wrong behavior?"

"As long as the required behavior, and all possible consequences, are spelled out beforehand." I was now very sure that he was lacing his questions with double meaning and I fed my answers out the same way. "I don't think it's right to expect behavior that isn't explained."

He nodded, and I could see that he agreed. He leaned forward and rested his hands on his desk again. "It seems to me that you were indeed telling the truth. I have to consult with Mr. Duncan, but we will have answer for you tomorrow before you fly home."

Once again, my mouth decided to act before my brain could intervene. "Who's being dishonest now? You told me if I went along with your interview, you'd tell me yes or no at the end of it."

He smiled, and I wondered if that had been another test, one to see if I was willing to hold others to the same standard to which I was being held. "I did promise that," he said. "Perhaps I was too hasty. What I can tell you is that your answers mean you're still in the running. Had I not been pleased with what you said, I would've just told you no and sent you home."

He picked up his paper again and I knew the interview was over. I stood. I would just have to be satisfied with what he gave me. My stomach gave a little twist as my brain automatically translated my innocent statement into an innuendo. Shit. His questioning had got me thinking that way and now it was going to take forever to stop.

I really disliked that man.

NINE

KRISSY

I was considering heading back down to Sunset Plaza for lunch again but as soon as I stepped into the hotel lobby, I knew I was going to have to go somewhere else, just to avoid the awkward moment I was currently experiencing as Taylor beamed at me from where he was leaning against the front desk.

"Krissy." He took a step forward. "I just got an invite to this fancy party in the Hills tonight and was wondering if you wanted to come with me."

I was shaking my head before he'd even finished speaking. "No."

He held up his hands in a gesture of surrender. "It's not a date. I was just thinking that you might want to come because there are going to be a lot of actors and potential clients. It'll be a great chance to mingle." He added, "Think of how good it'll look when you get the job if you already know the names of clients as they come in."

He had a point. I crossed my arms and gave him a stern look.

"All right," I said. "I'll go." He opened his mouth to speak and I held up a finger. "Only if you stop flirting."

He grinned. "I can't promise anything one hundred percent, especially if I get some alcohol in my system, but I'll do my best."

A try was probably the best I could hope for. I nodded. "Okay."

"Great!" He turned and did that thing where he was walking backwards and talking to me at the same time. I'd seen it on movies but didn't think anyone actually did it. "I'll pick you up a little before eight. We want to make an entrance, after all."

I couldn't believe I was going to my first Hollywood party! I smiled so widely that it hurt my mouth. This was going to be amazing! I took two steps towards the elevator and realized that I didn't have anything to wear. I'd brought a business outfit for a second interview, comfortable clothes for the flight home tomorrow and two cute dresses for sight-seeing. None of those were going to be right for a party in the Hills. I should've brought my green dress, the one Carrie referred to as Christmas ribbon.

I looked at the concierge. "Is the car available?"

He nodded. "Any specific destination in mind, Miss Jensen?"

I smiled again. I was going to fulfill another of my fantasies. A Beverly Hills shopping trip.

When I told the driver where I wanted to go, my day got even better. His sister worked at Barneys. That was exactly what I needed. Someone in the know of what was hot in Hollywood right now. On the ride over, the driver told me all about Jamie and how she was working towards becoming a fashion designer. Like I'd said before. Hollywood was where everyone wanted to be something else.

The moment I stepped into the store, I felt like I was in heaven. I'd gone to one of the most elite boutiques in New York with Carrie, but that had been different. Even though Gavin had bought me something, we'd been shopping for her. Today was all about me.

"Miss Jensen?" A cute little thing with strawberry blond curls came bounding up to me. I could tell she was one of those people who always had too much energy and never walked anywhere. She also looked like she was twelve, even though I'd been told she was nineteen.

"Jamie." I smiled at her.

"My brother said you were going to a party in the Hills?"

I nodded.

"I have just the thing." She motioned for me to follow her. "We just got this in today. In fact, we're not even technically done putting them on the floor yet."

I was starting to have my doubts about the young woman's ability to pick a dress as we passed gorgeous dress after gorgeous dress. Then she stopped in front of the most beautiful dress I'd ever seen.

"I had a couple in mind since I didn't know what your coloring was, but as soon as I saw you, I knew this would be perfect."

I had to agree. If it looked as good on me as I thought it was going to, Jamie had just outdone herself. She handed it to me and pointed me to the dressing rooms. I maneuvered into the slinky garment and zipped up the side. It fit like a glove.

I turned so I could see my reflection. The hem hit me at a little above mid-thigh, high enough that I knew I was going to have to be careful how I moved or I'd flash someone. The neckline plunged down between my breasts, revealing quite a bit of flesh without being tacky. The color was a rich purple that brought out the blue-black highlights in my hair. I'd never been so in love with a dress in my life.

I stepped out and Jamie voiced her approval. Then I saw the

price tag and my stomach sank. Four hundred dollars. I couldn't afford that.

"I'll give you my discount," Jamie said, correctly interpreting my expression. "It's thirty percent off."

I made a face. That was still a lot of money.

"You look amazing in that dress," Jamie said. "I can show you other ones that will look good on you, but nothing like that one."

She was right. I looked at the number again. I had spent more than that on shoes before. I made up my mind. "I'll take it."

Jamie let out a squeal of delight, and I couldn't help but laugh. She was adorable.

We chatted as she rang me up and continued to talk on my way out to the car. She talked to him then for several minutes before he was able to remind her that they were both still working. She took his gentle reminder in good stride and waved at us as we drove away.

"Back to the hotel," I said. I would order room service so I could take my time getting ready. I was going to make sure that I was nothing short of breath-taking tonight. It would be my first impression on some of Hollywood and I wanted it to be a good one.

TEN

KRISSY

I had to admit that I was a little nervous. New York was big and busy, full of interesting and exciting people, but LA was different. I knew I was hot. I'd had men and women telling me that since I hit puberty, but this was the place where all of the beautiful people gathered. But, when I saw the expression on Taylor's face when I met him outside the hotel, my confidence was bolstered. Jamie had definitely picked the right dress.

Now I just had to focus on not looking like the wide-eyed newcomer, completely mesmerized by the glam and glitter. When we pulled up in front of a pair of massive iron gates, it was more difficult than I'd expected not to gawk. I'd grown up with money, but there was a huge difference between the elegant old money of Chicago high society and Hollywood money. I mean, my family had a couple maids and groundskeepers, and we had a driver because my mom hated driving herself, but the way high society showed their wealth was in art and with charity. This was definitely flashier. First of all, there was a valet waiting.

Taylor grinned. "It's typical for parties in the Hills to have valet service, especially the ones on these windy, narrow roads."

I nodded. That actually made sense. It didn't make it less impressive, but at least I knew it wasn't just some sort of pretentious thing. Taylor and I walked up to the large, muscular man who stood in front of the gates. Bar or mansion, there was no mistaking a bouncer. Taylor gave the man his name and introduced me as his plus one. I bristled, but didn't contradict him. Now that I was here, I wanted to go inside.

The bouncer nodded and the lock on the gates clicked. He pushed them open and we started up the driveway. It wasn't a long one, but it had a curve that kept the house from sight until we went around it. As soon as I saw it, I corrected my mental labeling of the place as a house. This was a mansion.

In New York, the rich lived in expensive lofts and had homes in the Hamptons. In Chicago, it was very similar. My family owned a house in the city and three vacation homes that included a cottage in Maine, a beach house in North Carolina and a villa in Italy. Our main house was one of the bigger ones in our affluent neighborhood, but it couldn't truly be called a mansion. In fact, it was half the size of this one. All columns and arches, some impressive architecture that I had no name for, and landscaping that had to cost more than my entire firm made in a year. As Taylor and I stepped inside the mansion, we were treated to a breathtaking view of the city lights through a panoramic glass wall, and waiters carrying finger food weaving between all of the beautiful people.

I was so busy staring at everything that I didn't see the waitress heading my way until her arm hit mine. I side-stepped, narrowly avoiding getting something that looked like caviar all over my dress. The tray crashed to the ground, spraying food across the floor.

"I am so sorry!" The waitress was a cute little blonde who looked a little younger than me. Her face was red, and her eyes were wide, one of those 'deer-in-headlights' expressions on her face. "Damnit! So stupid!"

"It's okay," I tried saying.

"No, no it's not." She was shaking her head and I could see tears forming in her dark eyes. She looked up at me. "Please don't tell my boss. I'm so sorry. Please don't tell him. He'll fire me."

"Hey, it's okay." I put my hand on her shoulder, hoping the contact would break through. "No harm done."

A look of relief washed over her face and I started to smile.

"Elise!"

Her face fell, and I turned towards the voice. A man was striding towards us, his face red with anger. He got in the girl's face, his eyes narrowed.

"Go get your things, you're done!" He didn't even bother trying to keep his voice down.

"It was my fault." The words popped out of my mouth and I went with it. "I wasn't watching where I was going and I bumped into her." I gave the man what I hoped was a sheepish-looking smile. "Sorry."

The man looked at me for a moment, as if trying to decide if he wanted to believe me, then he shook his head and turned back to Elise. He scowled at her, but his voice was back at a normal level when he spoke again. "Clean up the mess and get back to work. There are plenty more trays to be handed out."

Elise waited until the man was out of earshot, then said, "Thank you for covering for me."

I shrugged. "Anytime." I shot a glance at the man's back as he disappeared back through the door he'd come through. "What an asshole."

Elise gave me a brief smile. "Good luck."

Before I could ask what she meant, she hurried away, presumably to find something to clean up with. Did she think the guy was going to come back and call me a liar?

I didn't have time to think about it anymore, though, because the music had changed and Taylor grabbed my hand and pulled me towards the dance floor. If there was one place I felt comfortable around a bunch of gorgeous strangers, it was on the dance floor. Some of the women here might've been prettier than me, but I knew I could dance, and not just well, but good enough to have all of the straight men and more than a few women thinking about what it would be like to get me in bed.

For an hour, I forgot about everything else but the club music pounding around me. I danced with Taylor, but let myself move around as well, turning around to move with one stranger, then another. Never touching, always just out of reach. The air was electric and I'd never felt so alive.

"I need some air," Taylor practically shouted in my ear.

I nodded and let him lead me outside. For people who lived in rural areas, the one-acre backyard might not have seemed that big, but for someone who'd lived in Chicago and then New York, it was huge, and absolutely gorgeous.

Taylor started down the stairs and I fell in step next to him. We walked along a stone path that curved through the grass, heading for the fence at the far end.

"What do you think?" he asked.

"It's beautiful," I answered, craning my neck to see the stars. It was too bright to see them all, but I could still see them better than I could back home.

"You're beautiful."

I looked over at him, opening my mouth to tell him that he couldn't say things like that.

"I can't explain it," he said before I could speak. "I'm drawn to you."

He reached out and grabbed my hand, his fingers warm as they curled around mine. I knew I should pull away, but I was frozen to the spot. Then he was leaning towards me and, for a brief moment, I was tempted. He was so hot and his lips looked so soft. I wanted to know if he was as good a kisser as I thought he would be. What harm would there be in one kiss?

I sighed and took a step back, taking my hand from his. "You promised," I said. I had to look away so he couldn't see how close I'd been to letting him kiss me.

"Come on, Krissy," he coaxed. "Why are you doing this? I know you want it, too."

Apparently, I hadn't looked away fast enough. I turned back towards him. "Maybe I do," I admitted. "But I can't. You're Mirage's client and there's a strict policy about not dating clients. You know that."

I didn't add that if I didn't get the job, I just might call him up and take him for a ride or two. At least then I'd get something good out of this trip. I looked over towards the pool just as a couple guests stripped off their tops and jumped in.

"I should get back," I said. "I have a final interview tomorrow and I don't want to screw anything up."

Taylor sighed and I could hear the disappointment. "Come on, I'll take you back."

The ride back to my hotel was quiet and a little awkward, but at least Taylor didn't try anything. If I got the job, I'd be able to get past the flirtations and the almost-kiss, but if he tried again, we might have a problem if I had to work with him in the future.

He pulled up in front of the hotel and put the car in park so he could turn to face me. I really hoped he wasn't going to make a pass after having come all this way without one. I wasn't sure how many rejections he could take before he'd get mad.

"I hope you get the job," he said sincerely.

"Thank you," I replied, startled. That had been nice of him. I got out of the car.

As I moved to shut the door, he spoke again, "I'd like it if you stuck around."

He waited until I reached the hotel doors before he drove

away. Maybe he was more than a gentleman than I'd given him credit for. I smiled as I rode the elevator up to my room. After my encounter with Mr. Ricci, I hadn't been sure those existed anymore.

End of preview
The Club Prive series continues in Krissy's story,
Chasing Perfection (Club Privé Book 3), available
now.

ABOUT THE AUTHOR

M. S. Parker is a USA Today Bestselling author and the author of the Erotic Romance series, Club Privè and Chasing Perfection.

Living in Las Vegas, she enjoys sitting by the pool with her laptop writing on her next spicy romance.

Growing up all she wanted to be was a dancer, actor or author. So far only the latter has come true but M. S. Parker hasn't retired her dancing shoes just yet. She is still waiting for the call for her to appear on Dancing With The Stars.

When M. S. isn't writing, she can usually be found reading–oops, scratch that! She is always writing.

For more information:
www.msparker.com
msparkerbooks@gmail.com

 facebook.com/msparkerauthor

ACKNOWLEDGMENTS

First, I would like to thank all of my readers. Without you, my books would not exist. I truly appreciate each and every one of you.

A big "thanks" goes out to all the Facebook fans, street team, beta readers, and advanced reviewers. You are a HUGE part of the success of all my series.

I have to thank my PA, Shannon Hunt. Without you my life would be a complete and utter mess. Also a big thank you goes out to my editor Lynette and my wonderful cover designer, Sinisa. You make my ideas and writing look so good.

Made in the USA
Las Vegas, NV
17 April 2024

88790778R10187